A FLAW IN THE BLOOD

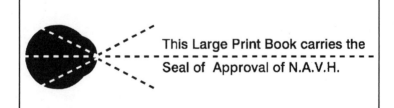

This Large Print Book carries the
Seal of Approval of N.A.V.H.

A FLAW IN THE BLOOD

STEPHANIE BARRON

THORNDIKE PRESS

A part of Gale, Cengage Learning

GALE
CENGAGE Learning

Detroit • New York • San Francisco • New Haven, Conn • Waterville, Maine • London

LIBRARY OF CONGRESS CATALOGING-IN-PUBLICATION DATA

Barron, Stephanie.
  A flaw in the blood / by Stephanie Barron.
    p. cm. — (Thorndike Press large print historical fiction)
    ISBN-13: 978-1-4104-0919-5 (hardcover : alk. paper)
    ISBN-10: 1-4104-0919-8 (hardcover : alk. paper)
    1. Windsor Castle — Fiction. 2. Victoria, Queen of Great Britain, 1819–1901 — Fiction. 3. Large type books. I. Title.
  PS3563.A8357F63 2008b
  813'.54—dc22   2008017633

Published in 2008 by arrangement with The Bantam Dell Publishing Group, a division of Random House, Inc.

Dedicated to the strongest women
I know —
Jo, Pat, Liz, and Cathy.

Love you.

ACKNOWLEDGMENTS

I have long been seduced by the possibilities of the past: the secrets buried there, the personalities lost to time. The support of an editor equally bewitched by these things is of immeasurable importance, and I am grateful for the keen mind and exacting standards of Kate Miciak, Executive Editor, Bantam Books. Kate is the sort of person who will devour an entire library of reference works merely to edit a manuscript, and our conversations about Victoria's life and world shaped this book.

Thanks are also due to my copyeditor at Bantam, Lorie Young, whose thoroughness and patience are endless; and to Molly Boyle, assistant editor, who ensured that every *i* was dotted and every *t* crossed. Sharon Propson shepherds my work through the slings and arrows of publicity's fortune, and I am grateful for her unquenchable enthusiasm.

7

Rafe Sagalyn, of the Sagalyn Literary Agency, has borne with me for more than fourteen years. Rafe and his dedicated team make it possible for me to write — and for that, I owe them the world.

My family endured endless lectures on sewer systems, nineteenth-century prostitution, medical ignorance, and the state of the Irish in Victorian England — without committing periodic acts of violence or moving out. Thanks, Mark, for putting up with the madwoman in the attic; and to Sam and Steve, for loving words as much as I do.

Prince Albert's Descent

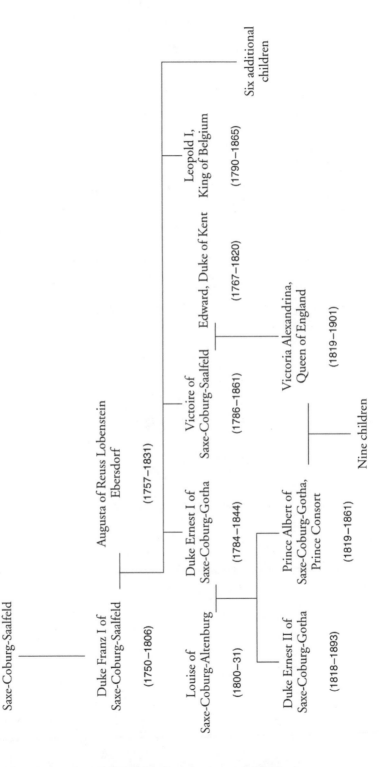

PROLOGUE

Coburg, 1 October 1860

When the agony of the state dinner was over and his wife was preoccupied with the other women, he ceased to talk quite so feverishly before the crowd of people who'd come to the Rosenau to see them. He knew his bright chatter had fooled nobody. They were all frightened by his brush with death. The telegrams had been pouring in all day, from Paris and London and North America. He'd fallen when he'd jumped from the runaway carriage and his nose and chin were bruised. The others ignored his bandages, just as they ignored his near-hysteria, his desperate grasping at normalcy.

He abandoned his brother and the others as soon as he decently could and avoided the noise of the grand saloon altogether, taking a side passage away from the public rooms toward the rear of the palace. He had grown up in the Rosenau and he loved it

11

better than any place on earth; it was here he'd been happiest, despite his father's rages and his brother's reckless pursuit of pleasure, the serving maids thrust up against the ancient walls, their skirts fanning around Ernest's thighs. Ernest was the duke now, and the old people were buried with their secrets; he, Albert, was forty-one and king of England in all but name.

He mounted a back staircase and without hesitation made for the nursery wing. The noise of the chosen world receding behind him.

As he hurried along the corridor, a phrase recurred in his jangling brain: *Mein letztes Stündlein gekommen wäre. My last hour had come.* He would write it to his daughter, Vicky, who'd already gone back to Berlin and thus would have been spared the horror of his death; it was what he'd felt overwhelmingly as the carriage swayed toward the railroad crossing, the horses maddened by his whip. Death waited beyond the crossing bar.

At the schoolroom door he hesitated. There was no fire in the grate, but a single candle burned in a sconce on the far wall. Too late to step back or move on; too late to pretend, as he had for most of his life, to be someone else. A dim silhouette in candle-

12

light; the man turned.

"My dear boy. I thought you might come."

Stockmar; of course it was Stockmar. Of all the teachers in Albert's life, he was the least official and the most trusted. The baron was seventy, now, and refused to travel to England even for Albert; but if any man was responsible for the Consort's fate, it was he.

Albert slumped down in one of the hard schoolroom chairs and waited.

"You've had a narrow escape."

"Yes."

The old man shuffled to the door, closed it with a palsied hand. "You know what they're saying? Not to your face, of course — but in the back rooms and alleyways of Coburg? *How could as fine a whip as the Consort lose control of his horses?*"

"Perhaps I'm less of a whip than they thought."

"That's what we'll tell them, of course." Stockmar nodded. "We'll put it down to too many years in England, where nobody at all understands horseflesh. Even a lie as implausible as that is preferable to admitting suicide."

Albert said nothing. He gingerly touched the bandages on his nose. Stockmar sank heavily into another chair. The two of them

13

faced each other as they had thirty years ago, when the subjects at issue were also duty and character.

"Well? Are you going to tell me about it? Or do you want the old man to go away and leave you alone with your demons?"

Albert shrugged. "What is there to tell? I had a stupid accident. I'm thankful to be alive."

"I've never known you to drive four-in-hand without so much as a groom up behind you. That's another thing people will talk about. *Why did he go out alone?*"

"Precisely to *be* alone! And I don't give a damn what people say!"

The outburst was uncharacteristic; Albert was never uncontrolled. He cultivated self-restraint the way other men pursued God. Stockmar raised one eyebrow and sat stiffly, arms folded.

"There was . . . a waggon at the crossing bar," the younger man relented. "A farmer, waiting for the train to go by. I couldn't avoid hitting him, so —"

"— So you jumped, rather than kill the man outright. That's like your kindness. Even in the depths of despair you'd think of the poor fool you might take with you. Jump, and the horses would be bound to veer off. But it must have been disappoint-

14

ing, all the same. You were so close, weren't you? The train. The impact. The blessed release."

He was right; as always, Stockmar was right — and Albert felt himself sway with sudden dizziness and relief, as he had when some childhood peccadillo was discovered and all that remained was atonement. He had wanted death. He had gone out that morning hunting for it. And the bitterness as he plummeted through the air, the impact of the ground, had been as brutal as a public flogging. *Disappointment* didn't even begin to describe it.

He rose and paced before the cold hearth. "Christian, what am I to do?"

"Consider the farmer and his waggon to be signs from Providence," Stockmar suggested. "— Who, in Its infinite wisdom, prefers you alive to burning in Hell."

"And if I already burn, here on earth?"

"Endure it for your wife's sake. And that of England. They both need you."

"My wife!" Albert barked with sudden laughter. "Victoria!"

"You've always loved her." Stockmar stared at him, the beginning of a frown creasing his brow. "My dear boy — what has broken your heart so completely?"

Albert turned. "That Hell you spoke of,

15

old friend. It comes to men like me in the form of a paradox: the lie you cannot accept, versus the truth you cannot utter. In that kind of world, Death is the only honourable choice."

"I was wrong," Stockmar said. "You *have* been in England too long."

Albert drew his chair close to the baron's ear. He began to talk. And late into the Coburg night, Stockmar listened.

■ ■ ■ ■

PART ONE
LONDON

■ ■ ■ ■

CHAPTER ONE

14 December, 1861

The carriage made little sound as it rolled beneath the iron portcullis of Windsor; the harness and wheels were wrapped in flannel, the paving stones three inches deep in sawdust. But its arrival fell upon the place like an armed attack, shaking the ostlers out of their torpor. They sprang to the horses' heads before the equipage had even pulled to a halt, as though Patrick Fitzgerald brought tidings of war.

Fitzgerald made no move to step down into the sawdust. His hands were thrust in his coat pockets for warmth, his eyes fixed on the flaming torches and silent men beyond the carriage window. Once before, he had been to the great stone pile west of London — summoned, as tonight, by the woman who ruled there. But he was thinking less of the Queen now than of the man who lay in her private apartments, shuddering with fever.

"Let me come with you." Georgiana's gloved hand — that supple hand, so deft with the knife blade — reached for him. "I want to come with you."

"No."

Darkness filled the carriage. Only the gleam of her eyes suggested a presence; she had drawn the hood of her cloak close about her face, like a thief.

"It may have nothing to do with you, Georgiana. You cannot always presume —"

"And what if *I* have something to do with *it?*" she interrupted. "With *him?*"

"Georgie —"

But she'd turned her head away, her profile outlined against the squabs. She was biting down hard on her anger, as though it were a haft of iron between her teeth.

"And she'd never let you near him," he attempted. "You must know that."

"Then she's a fool!"

The coachman stumbled as he jumped from the box; the noise reverberated against the chilled stone like a gunshot, and the ostlers stared in outrage. *Silence in the Old Quadrangle, in respect of the dying.* Fitzgerald caught the coachman's indrawn hiss of breath, ripe with fear, as he pulled open the door.

"Wait," he told Georgiana. "I shan't be long."

She didn't attempt to argue. She would be freezing soon, he thought, despite her layers of petticoats. But Georgie would never ask for a hot brick, a brazier of coals. Her pride would kill her one day.

A footman led him into Windsor by the lower entrance, and there, too, the stone floor was blanketed with sawdust. The castle was known for its menacing silence — the vast, carpeted halls absorbed every footfall, and its people trafficked in whispers. Fitzgerald neither spoke nor offered his hand to the man who awaited him — William Jenner, court physician and eminent man of science.

"You took your time," the doctor snapped.

Fitzgerald handed his gloves and hat to the footman before replying. "I was in Dublin but two days since."

"And you stink to high heaven of strong spirits."

"Would you have had me miss my dinner, then? I only received your summons at five o'clock."

"It is nearly ten! As I say — you took your time." Jenner's eyes were small and close-set, his jowls turned down in perpetual disappointment. He surveyed the Irishman's

21

careless dress, his unkempt hair, with disfavour. "It may be that she will not receive you, now."

"I didn't ask for the audience." Fitzgerald shrugged indifferently. "Is it so necessary?"

"I would not thwart her smallest wish at such an hour! I fear too much for her reason."

"And your patient? How is he?"

"Typhoid."

Jenner had made his reputation, years ago, by distinguishing typhoid fever from its close relative, typhus. The physician was the acknowledged expert in the thing that was now killing Prince Albert.

"The Prince will rally," Jenner said.

From the vehemence of the doctor's words, Fitzgerald concluded that there was no hope.

He followed Jenner up a broad staircase. Through shadowy passages and paneled doors. The final hallway was remarkable for its dimness; oil lamps burned low. A pair of footmen stood immobile by one chamber. He was led beyond, to the Red Room.

"Wait," Jenner ordered, and stalked away.

To sit would be forbidden. Indeed, it was a testament to the chaos of this night that Fitzgerald was left alone at all, in such a place — that he should have the freedom of Windsor — and for a wild instant he was tempted to fly back into the passage, to trust in the footmen's trained invisibility, to roam at will over the seat of British power and take from it such tokens as he chose. But Patrick Fitzgerald was not quite the savage young man he'd been on his first visit more than twenty years ago. He was six-and-forty years now and had earned a dubious reputation at the Bar. His views were Liberal and his opinions on the Irish Question — the eternal Irish Question — sometimes surfaced in the London papers. For an instant, Georgie's eyes rose before his mind and he wished with all his heart and soul that he was still raw, still young, still braced with hope. Then the rustle of silk proclaimed her coming.

"Your Majesty." He went down on one knee.

"Mr. Fitzgerald."

She had taken up a position behind the sopha. The plump white hands grasped the wooden frame; had her grip been less fierce, the fingers might have trembled. She was a short woman of forty-two, with sagging cheeks and a mass of dark hair dragging at her temples; but once she had been a dab of a girl — a joyous girl, tricked out in silver net and flashing diamonds, her hand co-quettish on her husband's arm as he led her into the opera. A bruising rider on her gallops through the park — a passionate performer on the pianoforte. The unkind and malicious said she ate like a glutton. That she was given to odd fits of temper and caprice, like her mad old grandfather. They said a woman was too weak to rule. Fitzgerald knew better. Weakness had never been Victoria's failing.

"I am here at your command." He chose his words carefully. "Pray inform me how I may serve Your Majesty."

With a gesture, she bade him rise. "You know of our great trouble? Of the Prince's . . . illness?"

"You have my deepest sympathy."

A blank expression of terror in her blue eyes; contempt as she looked at him. "We do not *want* your sympathy, Mr. Fitzgerald! Our doctors assure us there is every cause for hope."

"There must be, while Prince Albert breathes."

Her gaze slid away from his face. "He *will not* fight it as he ought. He has no tenacity for life. If it were *I* —"

"Your Majesty should have rallied days since."

Perhaps she had been speaking only to herself. She flashed a look of pure hatred in his direction, as though he had overstepped some boundary.

"Good God, that we should waste our precious moments in *this!* Mr. Fitzgerald, some two decades ago you inserted yourself in our affairs, on the occasion of an attempt on our life in Green Park. You undertook, during the summer of 1840, to insinuate yourself among those who were not our friends — to purchase scurrilous information — in short, to besmirch the reputation of the Royal Family — with a view to vindicating the wretched creature who would have murdered his Queen."

She had torn him to shreds in just this way, all those years ago. Then he was an ill-dressed solicitor's clerk, cap crushed in his hands and heart pounding in his chest. And the dupe, Oxford, had waited to be hanged in Newgate Gaol.

"I was a servant of justice, Your Majesty!"

"You were an uncouth lackey of the Irish rabble," she retorted. "And your late success has not improved you one whit. I know what you are, Patrick Fitzgerald. I know that you have chosen to insert yourself *again* in my affairs — that you will not rest until you have toppled this monarchy!"

Angry heat mounted in his cheeks. "That is a lie! *Yes* — though the Queen herself says it!"

"I would not spare a blackguard such as you one second of notice," she continued, "were it not for the Angelic Being who lies wasting in the next room! Were it not for the ravings he has uttered —"

She broke off. She closed her eyes, swaying slightly.

"Ravings," Fitzgerald repeated. "The Prince has . . . wandered, in his fever?"

"Oh, God," she murmured brokenly. "My reason — *my reason* . . . Do you care nothing that I shall go *mad?*"

She sank heavily against the back of the sopha, her nails raking the silk.

"Majesty . . ." He crossed toward her, afraid she would collapse at his feet — but one upraised arm checked his steps.

"Do not even *think* of touching me." She said it venomously. "Get Jenner. He will tell you what to do."

She pulled herself upright. Drew a shuddering breath. And, without glancing again in his direction, left him.

"What is it?" Georgie asked the moment he slid into the forward seat of the coach and the muffled wheels began to turn. "What did she want? What did she ask of you?"

"It doesn't matter."

"Tell me! I've waited nearly an hour —" Georgie bit her lip. "*Please,* Patrick."

"I was ordered to sign a bit of paper," he answered. "Affirming that every fact I discovered, every witness I deposed, every rumour I substantiated in the summer of 1840, was nothing more than a fabrication of my own treacherous Irish mind. And that, having repented of my calumnies, I hereby swear to lead a better life in allegiance to my Crown, so help me God —"

"No!" Georgie gasped. "But that is . . . that is *wicked!* You did not sign it?"

"I threw it on the fire, lass."

"Why does it matter? Why should she care about that old business? With the Prince so ill?"

"Lord alone knows. Poor thing was half out of her mind, I think." He glanced at Georgiana — her luminous skin, her eyes filled with intelligence and fatal truth. "She talked of conspiracy. Accused me of trying *again* to topple the monarchy. As though I ever have!"

"There must be some mistake. A misapprehension —"

"The Prince is raving, seemingly. In his fever."

"And when you refused to recant?"

"Jenner threatened me. Informed me my life has no more purchase than a sparrow's." Fitzgerald smiled faintly. "If I'd signed, of course, he'd have made me an honourary Englishman."

Humour for Georgie's sake, but she knew Jenner, and she seized on his significance at once.

"He was there — attending to the Prince? Then it *is* typhoid." She reached impulsively for the carriage door. "We must go back, Patrick. You know I could prevent the spread of contagion —"

Fitzgerald's heart twisted. All her passion in her beautiful eyes.

"Georgie love," he said gently as the bells of Windsor began to toll, "the Prince is dead."

CHAPTER TWO

It is true that I was a dab of a girl at twenty, a coquettish young thing on Albert's arm. I loved the attention of men, the interest and conversation of brilliant blades like William Lamb, Viscount Melbourne, who taught me when I first came to the throne how to think on every subject of importance. I loved Melbourne like a *father* — the father torn from me too early — and but for the impertinent who dared call me *Mrs. Melbourne,* might have lived entirely in his pocket, as the saying goes. He was such a droll character, despite a tendency to talk to himself or snore in church — and so clearly handsome at sixty, that I must have been quite overpowered to have met him in his prime. I was, however, not even thought of *then* — and he was his wife's devoted slave. Lady Caroline Lamb trampled Melbourne's character and name in the dirt, offered every possible exhibition of indecency to the wondering eyes of the *ton,* and destroyed all hope of future happiness by producing an imbecile son almost as recklessly as she seduced Byron — but Melbourne stood by her until her death.

In this, too, Melbourne *most truly* taught me the meaning of the word *gentleman:* one who backs his wife to the limit, however grievous the peccadillo or infraction; one who, having loved, can never recant or betray.

I may declare that Melbourne loved *me,* in his fashion — and had the tides of politics not utterly divided us, might have continued to haunt my Windsor walks until his death. As a woman's first Prime Minister, he was all that could be desired. And though in later years he resented Albert's monopoly of my interest, and a coolness fell between us, indeed I am *very fortunate* to have known him —

But I was speaking of myself, not dear William Lamb, who has been dead now these thirteen years.

I am capable of the most profound and intense love, but must confess that I am capable of loving only *one person* at a time. As a child, I adored dear Lehzen, my governess, and *quite hated* Mama; when Albert came, Melbourne was forced to quit my heart. So it has always been. And that is how it happens that I am lying here, with my cheek on Albert's breast, my hands clenched in the bedclothes Jenner drew, at the last, over his *dear face* — I must endeavour to explain how love, the *purest love,* for that Angelic Being, has brought me to this parting.

Perhaps I was a little drunk early in my reign, with my first sips of independence and power — I had banished Mama from my household and thought the credit of a queen equal to even the most *daring behaviour.* I played favourites; snubbed those I ought to have embraced for political reasons; circulated scandal; laughed at the scoundrels of the press. I loved to dress, too — dearly loved the feel of silks and satins next to my skin, loved jewels and the way they took on the warmth of my full breasts, swelling above the line of my gowns. I was *never* beautiful, not even at twenty, my features too lumpen and bourgeois for beauty; but Albert was extraordinary — tall and graceful and muscled — and when he looked at me I felt as bewitching as the most celebrated courtesan in London.

My mother was sister to his father. Albert and I were delivered by the same midwife, a continent and a few months apart. We watched each other grow with the disinterest of children. For years, my cousin thought I was a spoiled little frump; for years, I considered him fat and stupid. His elder brother Ernest was far more *dashing* — Albert preferred books to flirtation. Until that day in October, more than twenty years ago, when he traveled from Germany straight to his doom, knowing he must accept my hand in marriage whether he wanted it or not. The Family — the Saxe-Coburgs, our Uncle Leopold most of all — said it was his *Duty*. The idea of Duty fascinated Albert as flagellation haunts an ascetic; it meant Sacrifice. Otherwise, Duty would have been called *Pleasure* — and Albert would have had nothing to do with it.

He came reluctantly to London in 1839. He hated the English damp, missed his friends and his hunting grounds *acutely.* He despised women on principle and was keenly aware that I was graceless — too short in the neck, too full in the cheeks, my chin receding. He had only just completed his studies at the University of Bonn, and was so serious and melancholy he looked like a martyr of old. I could not drink in his beauty enough as I stood at the head of the stairs, *stunned,* to receive him. I was of an age when I *craved* the touch and passion of a man — and here was a god, handed to me on a silver salver! I may honestly say I fell in love at first sight.

During the month of his visit, *everything* about our lives was perfect. We two seemed lost in a rosy world of our own, which nothing — not the hatefulness of Parliament, the ridicule of the press, the jealousy of my relations — could influence or mar.

Mama, of course, loved him from the first. He called her his *Dear Aunt,* as was most proper. We sang duets, we rode together, Albert sat by my side as I wrote my tedious letters — asking only for the privilege of licking the stamps. And when we were left alone at last, he would take down the pins in my hair and let it tumble across my shoulders, *wanton* as he loved to see it. Clasp my face between his palms to kiss me.

In body and soul ever your slave, he wrote the night of our betrothal. No mention, then, of the *abandonment* of Death. And I did not apprehend, as I cried over his passionate note, that it was the slave I was marrying: Albert's Master always — Duty.

In the morning, I would be barred from this room; Albert would be given over to Löhlein and MacDonald, his valets; to the hideous men of the undertaking firm. Now, as the bells continued to toll, negating the individual hours, I could lie with my face pressed into his groin. Drinking in the last warmth of his soul as it fled through the darkness of Windsor.

I sobbed aloud. I reproached him bitterly for leaving me helpless — and of course he was unreachable, as he always was when passion deranged me. How many times in the past had he shut himself up in his private study? How many times had he locked the door and taken meals on a tray, while I *screamed* into my pillow? He wrote me long lectures, like a remote Papa; and I reproached him for that — for growing *old* without me. He even called me *Dear Child, Dear Little One* — I, the most powerful monarch in the world — and thought the condescension charming!

But I am no longer, and never will be again, a dab of a girl.

Children came between us so early. I was pregnant with Vicky when Oxford tried to murder me, a mere four months after my wedding, on Constitution Hill.

We were driving to Mama's. I remember the softness of the June air. I had retched three times that day and already hated the change in my body — I felt betrayed by Albert, by the *intensity* of the pleasure I took from his sex, the way animal need had produced such misery. That day he almost carried me to the carriage, determined to get me out-of-doors — and, indeed, the air improved me. My head felt clearer. I could look about and nod to the people in the Park who stopped to watch us pass.

And then without warning Albert seized my head, forcing it down, as the lead ball whistled viciously over us.

He would have protected me if he could. That was his nature. But I fought his hands, staring without fear at Edward Oxford, a half-mad son of a mad mulatto labourer. I defied him to shoot as he raised his second pistol. The coachman did not drive on. Albert cried out in German. The second ball sang wide.

It was Providence, I suppose, that preserved me. And I read in that preservation a *sign:* that I am ordained to rule. That it is God's will for me to endure as Queen of England.

The lunatic Oxford was seized by passersby, and the whole episode devolved into the sordid business of *courts* and *newspapers* — of men like Patrick Fitzgerald. Men who owe no one loyalty. Who *profit* from conspiracy. Who believe a killer may be innocent, simply because he is mad.

Would death then, in the full flower of my youth and love, have been preferable to this abandonment? This grief cutting a trench through my heart?

All those years of pregnancy — child after child after child, nine in all; the deep abiding depression that rode me like a curse; the weight I could not shed; Albert more remote with every birth; the demands of Royalty I refused to face; the way he became King without ever needing the crown.

Only once in recent memory did I recognise the ardent lover of 1839 — the youth who took my face in his hands and drank from my lips. It was the day he nearly perished in the wreck of his carriage, and the mistress he pursued was Death.

Did Albert feel that same clarity, as his horses raced toward the crossing bar last autumn? Did he stare down the train as I had Edward Oxford? Neither of us lacked courage. It was for Death to decide whether to take us.

And now I have given Her my Albert. No one will shield me any longer. No one will treat me like a child. It is for me to suppress his ravings, the mad words that drowned him at the end — for me to protect what he was, at last — from such *villains* as Patrick Fitzgerald.

CHAPTER THREE

"How *did* you attempt to topple the monarchy?" Georgiana asked. "All those years ago?"

They had not yet achieved London, inching painfully through the dense fog that swamped the dells of Hampstead Heath. By the time Fitzgerald had descended from his audience in the Red Room, the last evening trains had departed Windsor. There was no choice but to be driven home, by a man indifferent to their comfort now that the Queen had no further use for them. It was cold enough that Georgie's words hung in the air, opaque as the fog.

"Faith, and I told the truth — in court," Fitzgerald answered satirically. "You must know Truth's a curse to monarchs everywhere."

"You're the worst of unrepentant radicals." She smiled, her eyes on the clouded coach window. "I was barely five years old

38

and living in Calcutta, when it happened. Tell me, Patrick."

It was clear Georgiana was suffering. Fitzgerald could not say what she felt for Prince Albert, how deep her grief went; he lacked the courage to ask. Even his jealousy was a presumption. So, like all good fathers with wounded children, he told her a story.

"There are two versions, Georgie. The one Oxford told and the one put down as history."

"— That the fellow was mad?"

"Delusions of grandeur, most said. A craving for the world's notice. Oxford put himself on Constitution Hill at a time when Victoria was known to pass. She'd made a habit of driving out to her mother's place in Belgrave Square every afternoon. He fired two balls, both of which went wide. He was overpowered, then, and confined. The prosecution would have it he acted alone — out of hatred for his betters. And it certainly could be made to *look* that way."

"But you disagreed?"

"My employers did. I was then Head Clerk to Mr. Charles Pelham — Edward Oxford's solicitor. Lord Normanby, the Home Secretary, retained Pelham in Oxford's defence — and Pelham brought in Septimus Taylor as barrister."

39

"Sep!"

"The very same. I was dispatched to Newgate, where Oxford was jailed, to pump the fellow. His wild charges led me on all sorts of adventures — and the intelligence I gathered provided Sep with his case."

"Which was?"

"Conspiracy, as the Queen would have it. Oxford claimed he'd been hired by Victoria's uncle, the Duke of Cumberland, who thought she'd diddled him out of a throne and wanted it back. The Queen was pregnant, y'see, so the Duke had to act fast if he meant to kill her. Two birds with one stone."

The carriage jolted through the rutted roads of the Heath, the silence beyond broken only by the muffled hoofs of the horses.

"I see why Oxford was judged insane," Georgie said. "To blame a royal duke for the assassination —"

"It wasn't the easiest defence to argue. Septimus did his best. The pistols Oxford used had the Duke's initials engraved on them. And a packet of letters posted in Hanover was found at Oxford's lodgings."

"But Cumberland?"

"— Denied everything, of course. As did Victoria. Lord, she was a fury! That was the occasion of my *first* summons to Windsor."

He could recall the scene vividly: a scorching afternoon in August, the twenty-year-old Queen already great with child. Ringlets of hair plastered against her temples. Her protuberant eyes blazing.

"What did she say to you?"

Fitzgerald sighed. "It all came down to my Irishness, love. A *real* gentleman would never have published such a scandalous story! That I had presumed to attack the Royal Family — and chose to do so in the criminal courts — was the height of vulgarity. Or radical sentiment. I'm not sure which she thought was worse."

"But it was Sep who argued the case, not you —"

"Aye. And me who gave it to him. The idea that a man could be innocent, if he was out of his mind, was quite new in legal circles."

"Oxford was sent to Bedlam?"

"He's still there, I believe."

"And you became a barrister?"

"Sep took me on."

Georgiana studied him doubtfully in the poor light of the carriage lamps. "But, Patrick — why bring all this up *tonight?* When the Prince —"

Whatever else she might have said was cut off by the shrill, whistling scream of a horse

41

in terror, the sudden, overwhelming force of a team impaled on a bristling wall — rearing and jibbing in the traces, falling back upon themselves, the equipage jackknifing viciously and the whole box of a world kiting over and over, the curses of coachman, the glass shattering under Fitzgerald's shoulder as he was thrust brutally against it, Georgie yelling less in fear than in shock — and then, abruptly, stillness.

His ragged breath was the only sound in the shattered cage, his hands slippery with blood.

"Georgie," he said. And again, *"Georgie!"*

She did not answer.

Fog rolled into the broken body of the carriage. There was blood in his eyes and a frantic warning in his brain that urged, *Run, run, they will be upon you in an instant.* He tore at the splintered wood, part of the carriage roof that still stood between him and the Heath. Forced his shaking arms to break a passage.

He was out. Stumbling. Uneven ground, brambles clutching at his trousers, a horse whickering like a whipped child.

The carriage lamps had shattered in the crash. But through the darkness and mist he could make out a palisade — a lashed fence of spikes, tossed in the road like some medieval war engine. The horses had impaled themselves on it, blind in the pitch black. The animals were caught now in the tangle of their own traces. Night and fog and the trapped beasts trampling the coachman's body —

He reached back inside for Georgie.

The hood of her cape was soaked in blood.

Muttering hurried Papist prayers under his breath, *O Holy Virgin we implore thee for the benediction of thy healing Grace,* he fumbled for a pulse, he screamed for a pulse, he kissed her sweet mouth, forcing air into her lungs. Then he lifted her and staggered off, a middle-aged man clawing his way up the hillside, heedless of the broken nags behind him or the hideous angle of the coachman's neck, as the corpse lay sightlessly staring at the Queen's cypher, *VR, Victoria Regina,* on the shattered coach's door.

CHAPTER FOUR

He carried her to a public house in Hampstead, where he cried up the tavern keeper with what remained of his breath. He refused to set down his burden on the damp paving stones, and she remained insensible — perhaps dead, he could not tell — but at last the innkeeper unbolted the door and peered out at the lunatic, the weaving drunkard with an armful of woman. Fitzgerald did not wait for an invitation but thrust his way in. Calling for brandy, and a doctor.

It was two o'clock by his pocket watch when he reached Hampstead. At three, Georgiana was still insensible, though he'd bathed the gash in her scalp, forced a dram of spirits through her clenched teeth, and tucked her up warmly in an available bed. The local doctor, a man by the name of Smythe, held Georgie's wrist a good long while without offering an opinion. From that much, at least, Fitzgerald understood she still breathed.

"An overturned carriage." Smythe's fingers were delicate as a bit of jewelry on her arm. "A *Royal* carriage? That would be the fog, no doubt."

"Not only fog, I'm thinking. A thicket of spikes, set down to maim the horses. I saw them, look you."

In Fitzgerald's trouble and despair, his Irish was back in force, obliterating three decades of life in London; it did not win him any friends in Hampstead.

"Spikes? To maim your horses? Is it possible, Mr. Fitzgerald, that you also received a knock on the head?"

Smythe did not turn from his patient, but the doctor's mild disbelief sparked Fitzgerald's fury. He had already said too much. Anxiety had made him foolish. He reached for the bottle of brandy and took a long draught. His hands were shaking.

"Happily I did not, sir. Or this lady would still be lying in a ditch with a broken-necked coachman."

"As you say," Smythe replied mildly, "Torning will have looked to the matter of the coachman, I expect."

Torning was the innkeeper. Fitzgerald's jabbered tale had sent a party of men and boys out onto the Heath in the bleary night, searching for the wreckage. Fitzgerald was an event in Hampstead, a throwback to the bad old days of highwaymen, a Paddy in the guise of Quality. The fact that he had survived the attack only added to the sensation.

"You are not this lady's father, I understand?"

Fitzgerald winced. "No."

"Does she have one?"

"Miss Armistead is alone in the world," he retorted. "I am a family friend of long standing — an acquaintance of her uncle's. Being a medical man yourself, you may have heard of him — Dr. John Snow."

"Ah." Smythe released Georgie's arm and looked at him at last. "What a loss to the world when that genius was taken! Such a man would wish to be with this lady now — and would send *me* speedily about my business!"

The name had done what Fitzgerald's could not: blotted out in an instant all questions and doubt. John Snow, child of a lowly Yorkshire carter, who had revolutionized medicine in his day; Snow, who had declared that the great London cholera epidemic of '54 was a disease born of fouled water, and proved it with a map; Snow, who had advocated the use of chloroform in la-

46

bour, despite the outcry of the clergy —
who insisted that Woman must bring forth
her babes in suffering and pain. Snow, who
administered that twilight sleep to no less a
personage than Queen Victoria herself, at
the birth of her eighth child, Leopold. . . .

"Her Majesty must sorely miss Dr. Snow,"
Smythe observed casually, "with the Prince
so ill."

Fitzgerald might have replied that yes, in
her trouble the Queen had summoned
Snow's niece, for the comfort of former as-
sociation; or he might have told Smythe the
Prince Consort was dead. But the bells were
tolling throughout the boroughs of London
now and Smythe did not require Fitzgerald's information. He took another drink of
whiskey and let the doctor pack up his bag
in silence.

John Snow would not have thanked his
old friend for taking Georgie anywhere near
Windsor. He'd hated his ward's unwomanly
skill with the scalpel, her passion for science
— though he had taught her most of what
she knew.

"Summon me if she wakes," Smythe said.
If.
He showed himself out.
Fitzgerald settled down to pray for life.

■ ■ ■ ■

What in God's name were you thinking, man, to tangle her with the Queen?

She won't sit quiet at home, John, when there's a sick man at the end of the road.

Bollocks.

Snow had a right to be angry. He had commended Georgie to Fitzgerald's care on his deathbed some three years ago — gone at forty-five, all his brilliance snuffed out like a candle. She was not really his niece and Fitzgerald was the last man to stand as guardian, being already enslaved to Georgiana Armistead and dangerous with it. Perhaps Snow expected him to carry the lass off somewhere. Perhaps he ought to have moved heaven and earth to snatch her from London, his careful years of ambition gone over the bridge and into the river, the past tossed like dirt in John Snow's grave. Fitzgerald did not know. He knew only that never, on the day of Snow's death or any day thereafter, did Georgie give the least hint of desiring a conventional life. She had lived a singular one for too long.

The daughter of Charles Armistead, a military doctor attached to an Indian regiment, she was fretting herself in a finishing school when Snow rescued her — Armistead dead of a fever in Calcutta. Snow took Georgie back to Sackville Street and put his housekeeper in charge of the girl. But Georgiana demanded a different kind of education.

From the very first, she haunted Snow's surgery. When he set out on his wanderings through the back slums of London, she had insisted on riding in the coach. He refused to teach her medicine, but when the cook complained of dissections of poultry and the odd hoarding of beef organs — a heart, a liver carefully saved — he began to lend Georgie books from his own library. A satisfaction of curiosity, he thought, however improper for a woman. The girl talked so intelligently that before long she was observing his anatomizations at the College of Surgeons — suitably veiled, of course, and always accompanied by her maid. After the first maid swooned, she went alone.

Snow blamed himself. He knew he had ruined her — for what gentleman would marry such a girl? Georgiana was Eve, all apples and dangerous knowledge. No London medical board would certify a woman, so Snow sent her to school in Edinburgh. He shared his guilt with Patrick Fitzgerald — whose peculiar loneliness and unfortunate circumstances made him an eligible confidant, an expert at sorrow. Fitzgerald absolved John Snow of all sin.

Georgiana was singular among females, to be sure; the lass was what the fearful and the envious termed a bluestocking. But she was also magnificent. The full bloom of her mind animated her every word. If this was the terror of the Garden, Fitzgerald was already seduced, a worshipper of apples.

Then take her away. Take her anywhere. You did not keep her safe, Patrick.

She didn't want me to, John.

It was John Snow who made the acquaintance of the Prince Consort.

That would have been in connexion with the Great Exhibition, ten years ago now. Albert, with his German love of science, had seized on this rising man, this ambitious doctor who kept meticulous records, who believed that statistics held the key to the spread of disease. Snow's orderly method, his emphasis on fact rather than God or superstition, appealed to Albert's clockwork mind. The Prince had never been a great one for Society; where an English peer might cultivate the Ancients, or turn a compliment for a lady, Albert preferred to analyze machines. He loved steam and turbines, factories and shipping; he worshipped gasworks and railways and guns. John Snow was one of the few who might be said to have understood him. It was probably Albert who urged the Queen to try Snow's chloroform at the birth of Prince Leopold. The year was 1853. What Snow witnessed at Windsor then was to change all their lives.

Georgie's head turned on the pillow; she gasped in pain. Fitzgerald had not prayed much — but perhaps he had gotten Snow's attention, wherever he was.

"I'm going to be sick," she said. And reached for the washbasin.

They brought in the dead coachman at twenty minutes past four.

"Neck's broke," the innkeeper said with satisfaction. "Wrung clean as a chicken's. You were lucky to crawl away from that smash — but then, the Irish are born with the Devil's own luck."

Fitzgerald was leaning over the corpse, laid out on a scrubbed oak table in the public room — a man younger than himself, hatless but clothed in the scarlet livery of Windsor. The brown eyes were still staring; he closed them gently. "You found the spikes?"

"What spikes?"

The voice came from a tall figure looming behind the innkeeper, a deeper shadow in the darkness beyond the candle flame.

"A palisade of lashed poles, set out in the road to snare the horses." Fitzgerald straightened. "And you, sir, would be . . . ?"

"Wolfgang, Graf von Stühlen." He stepped into the light.

He was dressed for riding, in the polished boots and hacking jacket of a gentleman, a cloak flung carelessly over one shoulder. Gloves and a top hat under his arm, a luxuriant moustache and side-whiskers on an otherwise clean-shaven face. Had Fitzgerald never heard the name, he still would have known von Stühlen instantly: Wolfgang von Stühlen was one of the Prince Consort's cronies, famous for the black canvas patch that covered his right eye. A duelist had winged him there, before dying. He was roughly Fitzgerald's age — but looked younger, fitter. And far better bred. So much elegance at four o'clock in the morning made Fitzgerald feel like a peasant.

"I set off immediately when news was received of this . . . accident." Coburg in his tone; a faint Oxonian drawl. "The Queen will be most displeased. Two horses dead.

And a coachman."

"Not to mention the shock to her guests," Fitzgerald retorted. "You astonish me, Count. Such an errand's beneath you, surely?"

A flash of white teeth, with no mirth behind it. "Nothing the Queen desires is beneath her loyal subjects. Particularly at *such* a time. You will have heard of the Consort's passing?"

"Aye, that we have."

Von Stühlen bowed; the Count's gesture had the force of an insult. He said to the innkeeper: "You will see that the body is kept in order until the inquest. It must be held here. Send word when the panel is done."

"Yes, yer honour."

"But I saw the palisade myself," Fitzgerald persisted, "when I quitted the wreckage. You'll find the wounds from the spikes on the dead horses."

"I found nothing," the German returned, "but the evidence of my nose. The corpse reeks of whiskey. As, I must say, do *you*. If you will excuse me, Mr. . . . ?"

"Fitzgerald."

"Ah. An Irish name, I collect?"

Fitzgerald's fist clenched. "And what is that to the purpose?"

Von Stühlen's lips pursed in amusement. "The Irish are a race known for wild imagination. No doubt you conjured up this . . . palisade. A phantasm of shock. Or deep drinking."

He reached in his purse and tossed Fitzgerald a shilling. "Buy yourself another, by all means. And then may I suggest you leave Hampstead?"

"Von Stühlen! What are you doing here?"

Georgiana's voice. She was poised on the stairs, swaying as though she might faint, a bandage tied round her head.

The German Count's face flushed red, then drained white. "Miss Armistead," he said with a sweeping bow, nothing of insult in it this time; "I might ask the same of *you*."

CHAPTER FIVE

I formed the habit of keeping a diary from a very little child. Or rather, *two* such volumes. Like most solitary children who are forced to protect themselves, I lived one life for public view and another entirely inside my head. The first journal was delivered up to my dear governess, Lehzen, at the close of every day — a compilation of doings, pallid emotions, pious sentiments on the subject of Family and Duty. Lehzen corrected my expressions in English or German or French, guided my conduct with a thorough review of my motives, reproved me when necessary — and supported me during times of trial.

The other journal I kept hidden under a loose floorboard beneath my high four-poster bed, in my apartment at Kensington Palace; the space was never dusted, so nobody liked to venture there. Precious were the stolen hours when I tucked my skirts under my legs and sat with a candle stub in that subterranean world, writing for all I was worth; such periods of unattended leisure were rare, so the secret volume is by no means as encyclopedic as the official one. Its contents are far more compelling, however. Mama insisted upon sleeping in an adjoining room with the connecting door propped wide; I was left to my own devices only when she had gone out, on the arm of the Demon Incarnate — or when I was in disgrace, and not even Lehzen was allowed to come near me. Raw necessity drove me to the secret journal's pages; indignation and fury and a desire for revenge are what it principally records. It is a compilation of screed — and loneliness. Even now, as I write to myself in the solitude of this Windsor apartment, the necessity remains the same.

I do not think I exaggerate when I say that I witnessed a surfeit of unpleasant episodes when I was young. Only a courage native to my breeding stood between me and a despairing death. When I recounted for dear Melbourne the sort of perfidy to which I was subjected, and all at the hands of those I ought to have been able to trust, he could barely credit the tale! But the truth of it is set down, day by day, in my private journal

— the one dear Lehzen never saw. Indeed, she did not even *suspect* its existence.

When I removed to Buckingham Palace some three weeks after my accession to the throne, the builders still in residence, the rooms not even done up, I saw my private volumes safely stowed where nobody should find them. I shall instruct the undertakers to place the entire collection in my coffin before it is nailed down. I would not have these words exposed to another human being — not even *He Whom I Loved with All My Heart* — for all the empires on the globe. It is *essential* to the peace of mind of a monarch that some part of her soul remain hidden.

It was near dawn when I emerged from the painful doze to which Albert's death consigned me, and drawing back the heavy green velvet hangings at my window, recollected his private cabinet. How feeble was the light of this Sunday morn, my first without my Beloved! The hour must be barely past six, and if my private attendants were as yet abroad, none had seen fit to disturb the sacred quiet of my bedchamber — which must, today and every day henceforth, be as *devoid* of *animation* as the tomb. No fire burned in the grate, no tea was waiting on a tray, and it was with the weakness of a very old woman that I attempted to draw back the seven layers of draperies that shrouded the outer world from my own. *Albert's cabinet,* I thought; it was *his* term for the private study where he spent so many happy hours. And so many painful ones, too — the room to which he retreated when our relations were unsettled, so that he might write to me in the quiet so vital to his studious, inward-looking mind. There he kept his essential correspondence — of a kind never permitted to fall under the view of his secretaries. It was as though he had spoken to me as the draperies parted, and the feeble December morning graced my brow with benediction; it was as though a whisper of the Hereafter instructed me: *Go, my little one, and burn them.*

I tarried only to don one of the sad black gowns I have worn ever since Mama's passing last spring — how dreadful to find oneself a belated survivor of those one has cherished, *utterly unloved* by another human soul! — and moved in rustling agitation through the hallways. Below me and at every side, Windsor slept — as though that Perfect Being had never suffered, and struggled, and breathed his last in the Blue Room but a few hours before! I *shuddered* to consider of the coming day — the counsels that must be held, over the Departed's body; the morbid attentions of Bunting's, the undertakers; the officious pieties of the Master of Household. Bertie should be left to manage the business; it should be his *penance,* for having broken his father's heart and soul so completely, that the Grave was the last comfort remaining in the world!

A turning in the corridor brought me to Albert's room — quite dark, and chill, and desolate. A very brief search revealed to my grateful eyes the letters I sought: bound up with ribbon and secured in a japanned box. He had left it, quite carelessly, among his books. Some of the letters were from *that woman* — and the rest from Baron Stockmar, a man whom once I had believed my friend. I did not pause to read them. I had a fair idea already of what they contained — the seeds of my Beloved's destruction. The horrid fodder of his final madness.

I flew back along the corridor and lit the match with my own hands. It was necessary to unfold the letters, in order to crumple them. One only I saved — from Stockmar, written in the first weeks after our return from Coburg last autumn. Of the woman's, I kept nothing. Her handwriting, sloping across the cream-coloured laid; her extraordinary confidence, as she shattered my Darling's world — I felt much better for watching them go up in flames.

By the time von Stühlen rode in from Hampstead, I was having my breakfast on a tray.

He told me what he could of the ruin of poor Fyfe, our coachman, and of Fitzgerald's escape. It will be best to avoid all scandal for the present — the Metropolitan Police are not to be informed — dear von Stühlen is to manage everything. I endeavoured to convey to the Count the depth of my gratitude, tears standing in my eyes. How fortunate I am that Albert's beloved friend has not deserted me in Death! Indeed, I feel even *his* Divine Presence hovering near, just beyond the range of sight, gone the very instant I turn to look for him. I move, now, in an extraordinary kind of peace — *his guidance* consoles me.

Not even the intelligence von Stühlen could supply — that Miss Georgiana Armistead was injured last night in Fitzgerald's company — could overset that peace. Clearly, Providence has ordered events according to Its will — I am but an instrument.

If only dear Albert had accepted as much, while he yet lived —

CHAPTER SIX

The German count had spoken the truth, as far as it went, Fitzgerald thought: no evidence of the deadly palisade was to be found on Hampstead Heath.

He had seen Georgiana safely into a carriage bound for Russell Square, then set out on foot to view the wreckage himself. It was easy enough to find — perhaps a half mile back along the rutted carriageway meandering toward the village from the north. In the darkness of the previous hours his breathless struggle to carry an insensible woman had felt endless; in daylight, he'd managed the short distance in a few minutes.

A welter of churned mud announced the place. The carriage still lay where it had overturned, down the side of a ditch half-buried in the Heath; its shafts were shattered like straws. Fragments of wood and glass littered the bracken, and two of the four-horse team lay dead on the slope, legs splayed and eyes staring. The remaining pair, presumably, had broken free of the traces and run off into the night fog, suffering God knew what fate.

Torning's party of men — three labourers from the village — were busy collecting rubbish; one of them was securing canvas tackle to the chest of a dead horse, preparatory to dragging it away.

"Poor beast," Fitzgerald said.

The man glanced up. Sandy hair, a face indeterminately middle-aged, the nose blunt and veined. A drinker in Torning's pub; a man of solid substance, with the neatly-mended clothes of a family prop. "Terrible accident, it was. Coachman was drunk as a lord — broke his neck. And the *Queen's* coachman, at that. As if they hadn't enough of death, last night, at Windsor."

"How did it happen?"

"Ran up against summat in the fog." The fellow looked back to his straps, securing a buckle with thickened fingers.

"That's quite a wound in the horse's chest," Fitzgerald observed, crouching down to stare at a deep and ugly puncture. A vision of the spiked stockade rose in his mind. "Bled to death. I suppose this was one of the leaders?"

"Reckon. Took the impact full-on, and spared the others. They'll be trotting down Islington High Street by this time, I wouldn't wonder."

"But what did it?"

"Sorry, sir?"

"What killed these horses? Overturned this carriage?"

The man glanced around vaguely. "There's all kinds of rubbish out here in the dark, sir. It don't pay to cross the Heath on a night without a moon."

Fitzgerald pursed his lips. "I shouldn't relish this job of work. How long have you been at it?"

"A good while now. Helped old Torning bring the corpus back to Well Walk, then the foreign gentleman paid us all to tidy up the mess, like."

"The foreign gentleman?"

"German toff. From Windsor, Torning said he was."

Fitzgerald abandoned the slope and walked back up to the carriageway, studying the trampled earth. A light rain had begun to fall, but it was still possible to discern the marks of a heavy object, dragged across the packed stone surface. While he'd beseeched the shade of John Snow at Georgiana's bedside, the engine of their destruction had been carted away. That was natural; murder had been done, and murder must at all costs be concealed. But the swiftness of its execution suggested an efficiency — and the command of resources — far beyond a simple highwayman. The Queen's carriage had not been attacked by a random thief. It had been the target of a conspiracy. Because Fitzgerald rode in it? — Or for reasons having nothing to do with him?

Like the barrister he was, he considered the evidence. They'd followed no predictable path last night, and they'd traveled at anything but a routine hour. Whoever overturned the carriage and tidied up the mess had done so with foreknowledge and a clear purpose. It was Fitzgerald who groped in the dark. He felt suddenly chilled. The unknown hand had taken such care — surely it would strike again. . . .

"Are you a stranger here yourself, sir?"

He looked at the labourer. "From London. I was in that carriage last night."

The man's eyes widened.

Bedford Square sat in the heart of Bloomsbury: staid, respectable, and so anxious lest it be thought less fashionable than Mayfair, that shops and taverns were discouraged and the square itself pompously gated.

65

Fitzgerald kept a set of lodgings on the north side, in one of the sedate row houses dating to the last century; his man, Gibbon, opened the door before he'd found his latchkey.

"Good morning, Mr. Fitz. Bath's waiting and breakfast's in twenty minutes."

"The Lord knows I could do with both." The rain had increased in force, and the world outside was wet and raw. He stepped into the narrow passage, pulling his hat from his head and leaving a trail of water all over the floorboards.

Gibbon surveyed him with dismay: mud-spattered coat and boots, collar wilted and cravat untied. "Aren't you a sorry sight. Long night?"

Fitzgerald closed the door behind him. "Very. Have the morning papers arrived?"

"Already ironed and set out by the bath. Sad news about the Consort, in't it? And him only forty-two. I don't suppose the Queen had anything particular to say? Strange, you being called to Windsor at just the moment the Consort should be passing — you wouldn't have happened to *see* anything, Mr. Fitz?"

Gibbon had little in common with the usual breed of superior servant. He had never learned the art of concealing all

66

independent thought behind a correct façade. He was twenty-eight, with a curly mop of hair and a snub nose; he'd been in Fitzgerald's service nearly seven years. They had met before a magistrate — Gibbon, a footman at the time, having been dismissed by his previous employer with an accusation of thievery. A valuable necklace had disappeared from the noble household. In the usual way, a servant would never merit representation; he would have little recourse but to protest his innocence, suffer the unequal course of justice, and be transported to Botany Bay. But Gibbon's mother knew Septimus Taylor, Fitzgerald's partner — and Sep thought the lad was owed a defence.

Fitzgerald was too little accustomed to the ways of gentlemen himself to mind the footman's outbursts, his unbridled curiosity, his inadequate respect for station. He had taken an immediate liking to Gibbon. The footman's despair at the ruin of his prospects had been little allayed by the discovery of the true culprit, the noble household's fifteen-year-old son. Exposed as a thief, the young gentleman hanged himself in the gardener's shed. When Fitzgerald told him the news, Gibbon had wept.

He'd proved a loyal man: coping with Fitzgerald's temper, his sudden plunges into despair, his bouts of stunned drunkenness. Gibbon had fought off armies of duns when Fitzgerald was short of cash, and silently tightened his belt when Fitzgerald forgot to pay him. He never gossiped. He kept the lodgings tidy and food on the table.

"Gibbon, I have no anecdotes to share, no glimpses of Royalty to offer you. Have any messages come while I was gone?"

"No, sir. Excepting Mr. Taylor — his compliments, and would you step round to chambers when it's convenient; but I reckon he didn't intend for you to do it of a Sunday, and not when the whole world's in mourning for Prince Albert."

Fitzgerald stopped at the foot of the stairs. "Did Septimus call? Or send round a messenger?"

"Came himself, after you'd gone to King's Cross last night. I told him you'd been summoned to Windsor. You'd have thought I'd said you'd gone to your hanging. But then, we all know Mr. Sep's politics."

Taylor liked to call himself a Radical, and publicly urged the end of the monarchy; he'd joined the Reform Club on the strength of his views, though Fitzgerald suspected the barrister's allegiance was really to Alexis

68

Soyer, the Reform's celebrated chef.

He glanced at his watch as he mounted the stairs: half-past eight. "Thank you, Gibbon. I'll be wanting a cab in an hour."

"But you haven't slept! Nor eaten!"

"Send up some coffee. I'll breakfast with Mr. Taylor."

He closed the bathroom door on his man's protests, and slid into the water. With all the conversation, it was already cooling.

He did not find Taylor at the Reform Club, and a brief cab ride to his partner's home in Great Ormond Street failed equally to produce him. Perplexed, Fitzgerald debated whether Taylor was likely to be at church, in respect of the universal mourning that had swept the City — or to have visited chambers on this dark and stormy Sunday, when any sane man would be established before the fire. He decided against church, and directed his cabbie to Temple Bar.

The Outer Temple was deserted; his footsteps resounded in the desertion of Middle Temple Lane; and when he reached the entry of his chambers at the Inner Temple, Fitzgerald felt a sharp upsurge of unease: No light shone through the mullioned windows, but the outer door was unlatched, and swinging gently in the gusty rain.

He entered as quietly as he knew, even his breathing suspended, and paused on the inner threshold.

The clerks' room, empty of life, was a chaos of paper, strewn over floors and desks; smashed bottles of ink trailed black smears on the floorboards; an entire ledger had been tossed in the cold grate. "Sweet Mary and Jesus," he muttered, and crossed to Taylor's room.

He was lying on his stomach, one arm trapped beneath him, the other flung over his head; he had been struck a hideous blow from behind, probably as he rose from his chair. The ooze of blood through Sep's sparse grey hair testified to a cracked skull. Fitzgerald's stomach lurched with sick despair as he probed the wound; the bone beneath his fingers was fragile as eggshells, the scalp spongy with blood. He bit off a curse and rolled Sep carefully on his side. His friend gave no sign of consciousness; not even pain could recall him to the world.

Fear, sharp and jagged, knifed through Fitzgerald. Had Sep surprised the searchers when he entered the chambers? Or had *they* surprised *him?* Probably the latter, given that he'd never gotten farther than a yard from his own desk.

"Sep," Fitzgerald called urgently, searching for a pulse in the neck, "for the love of Christ, who did this to you?"

His friend did not reply. But he was still warm, and there was a flutter of life in his veins. For the second time in the space of eight hours, Fitzgerald ran in search of aid.

CHAPTER SEVEN

My darling did not enjoy an easy night's sleep for weeks before he died. He was haunted, I believe, by a conviction of unworthiness — which must always be Duty's sneak thief, robbing us of the pleasure we ought to derive from sacrifice. It was Albert's habit to answer every call, no matter how humble: he directed Boards, governed Universities, patronised Science; effected economies in the household accounts, set limits on the use of candles, decided the servants' quarrels; drafted architectural plans for each of our homes, and oversaw the design of gardens; averted war, or made it, throughout Europe, and brokered entire Cabinets here at home; mended dolls and shoveled the moats of toy fortifications — in short, he made himself indispensable to me, to his children, to the English nation — only to discover, in middle-age, that *there was no one in the world who could replace him.*

If he lay sleepless of nights, it was in agony at his inevitable failure: *He would die,* and the son that must follow him was not one-hundredth of Albert's quality.

You will think me harsh, and utterly lacking in the sentiment proper to a mother — but I am a monarch *first,* and mother as well to all the Kingdom.

"Dashed bad luck," Bertie stammered, as he stood before me in that dreadful room, with his father's body cooling beside me. "Never thought the Governor would take off — the most *trifling* cold! All the betting in the clubs was odds-on for the Old Man's rallying! *Assure* you!"

Even in the face of death, my son and heir was incapable of frankness. No word of the tortures his father suffered at the knowledge of Bertie's *affaire* with that sordid Irish trollop. No remorse at the disgusting headlines that have surfaced throughout the Continent, or the damage to his reputation. Bertie is incorrigible. He cultivates excuses. Although the entire world knows that Albert contracted typhoid through walking in the rain with his son at Cambridge a month ago — anxiety having driven him to confront Bertie about the debauchery with Miss

Clifden, the dire consequences that must result, the possibility of a disease or bastardy, etcetra, etcetra, *all* of which was to have been kept from me, and all of which Albert shared — Bertie insists his father died of a *trifling cold.*

He was mortified, I suppose, at his father giving him a trimming before his schoolfellows, and suggested a walk through country lanes in an attempt to snatch at privacy. It is a scene so entirely typical of Bertie: a November storm coming on, his utter confusion in the landscape, Albert steadily more morose, the silence and misery growing between them. Bertie never learned his way around Cambridge, it would seem, never having spent much time at his studies — and the betrayal of his ignorance could only sink him further in Albert's estimation. It was ever thus. When Albert sent him to Curragh to be trained as an officer, Bertie could hardly meet his superiors' requirements, and failed miserably to attain his expected rank. His tutors, from the time he was a little child, despaired of his mastering *anything.* In one field alone does Bertie excel: He dresses to admiration. His style and appearance are the envy of his set. In such frivolous distinction he takes inordinate pride, and will suffer any expense to meet it. I need not observe how little Albert found to approve in his son's dissipation — or the fondness for Society, and gambling, and low entertainments, that inevitably followed on its heels. Even as my Darling's death-hour approached last night, Bertie was summoned from a *party* at Natty Rothschild's. He arrived at Windsor in evening dress, the odour of cigar smoke clinging to his hair.

When Albert's last breath was drawn, and I lay upon the sopha in the Red Room in the most bitter agony, incapable of tears or speech, Bertie simply stood like a stone with the other children, mute and unmoved as they sobbed. Perhaps at that moment he felt how much he was to blame. I cannot say. His failure to betray the slightest suffering has utterly closed my heart to him. I do not think I can bear to be in the same room with my son.

The betting in the clubs was odds-on for the Old Man's rallying. Dear God — and the Old Man was all of forty-two. . . .

CHAPTER EIGHT

"Assaulted? In your chambers?"

He had run Georgiana to earth at last, after a fruitless interval at her home in Russell Square, spent pacing before the drawing room fire and fingering the calling cards he found there. None of the servants could tell him where she had gone; in rising anxiety, he resorted to the cab stand.

The fifth man in the queue admitted he'd driven Miss Armistead to Covent Garden that morning. Twenty minutes later, he deposited Fitzgerald before a tenement dwelling in the rookery known as St. Giles.

It being winter and early in the day, the females of the district were within doors; but Fitzgerald had known them to stand in front of their dwellings, naked to the waist, with a bottle of gin in their hands. Most of them were Irish. What could Georgie possibly find to occupy her in this wretched place?

He entered a narrow hall stinking of urine and cooked pork. There was no light, and he cursed as a cat twined itself sinuously between his legs. A blasted staircase led upwards, past a group of children disposed on the treads, playing at skittles with bleached bones. They told him where to find the lady.

A cramped set of rooms, notable for a smoking coal fire and four young faces that turned to him expectantly as he hesitated in the doorway. A boy he judged to be no more than ten was toasting a hunk of bread on a poker thrust near the coals; the others huddled at his knees. The straw pallets on which they had slept lay tousled by the fire.

"Is Sep conscious?" Georgie asked now as she closed the door behind him. "Patrick? Have you summoned a doctor?"

"He was insensible when I left — a severe concussion of the brain, so the sawbones says. I asked that I be sent word, when he wakes. But I've not been home since —"

She took his hand, squeezed it briefly. "You believe the attack not unconnected to our adventure of last night?"

"How could it be else?" he burst out, pacing across the dirty floor. "— Though as God is my witness, Georgie, I've no idea why. It must be papers they wanted — and

Sep got in their way. Our chambers were turned topsy-turvy. I'd no time to learn which documents were taken — though I'd wager a guess —"

"You need a drink," Georgie interrupted quietly. "You're all to pieces."

He broke off, his eyes following the progress of a filthy child, possibly a girl, who stole up to Georgie's skirts and hid her face in the French twilled silk. Georgie swayed slightly, and touched the child's head; he noticed then how dreadful her pallor was, how the exhaustion of last night, and her own accident, had never left her. She still wore a bandage about her head, disguising the ugly bruise at her temple.

"Did you sleep at all?" he demanded.

"Perhaps an hour."

"You shouldn't be here. You should be tucked up on a sopha with a novel and a pot of tea."

"I have a patient within."

"A patient!"

"The poor have as much need of doctors as the rich, Patrick," she flashed.

"I'm the last man to argue that, Georgie — but need the doctor be *you?*"

"I'm fortunate to win the custom! The rich prefer their doctors male — these women have no choice but to accept my services. In return they give me experience — and so we each barter what we can."

He glanced around the slovenly room. "Snow would hate to see you here, lass."

"It was Uncle John who introduced me to the neighbourhood," she retorted. "Do you think his cholera researches were conducted in Mayfair? He was often in far worse places than this — Whitechapel and Spitalfields. Although these women die of syphilis far more than cholera, of course."

Syphilis. Her casual use of the word rocked him. To another man — a true English gentleman, reared with all the prejudices and ignorance of his willful class — Georgiana's worldliness must ruin her. Fitzgerald suspected she betrayed it less to the circles she usually frequented; but to him she always spoke her mind. They argued constantly and Fitzgerald invariably lost.

"Why have you come, Patrick?"

"I want you to leave London. Immediately."

"Whatever for?"

"You're in danger."

"Nonsense!"

"Georgie, my chambers have been ransacked, my partner nearly killed, and my carriage overturned — for what do you wait, a pistol to the head?"

"I have *nothing* to do with your affairs!" she cried. "Even if we accept that these events are linked — and that they are animated by some power at Windsor — no one there could possibly know that I rode in your carriage last night!"

"Your friend von Stühlen does."

"Von Stühlen is *not* my friend, Patrick," she said sharply.

"I found his card on the mantel at Russell Square. Did he call this morning to inquire after your health?" He grasped her wrist, his persistent jealousy flaring. "*Tell me* how you come to be acquainted with that man — and why he hated to see you at Torning's inn."

She stared at him as though he'd run mad. "I don't have time for this! There is a girl on the brink of *death* in that room, and it is my duty — my *calling,* Patrick — to do what I can to save her." She shook off his hold.

"What's wrong with her, then?"

"Ignorance and desperation." Georgie threw the words over her shoulder, already leaving him. "Lizzie is but fourteen — on the Game, like her mother — found herself in the family way, and consulted an abortionist. Whatever the butcher did has infected her blood. Her mother, half wild with fear, sent round a note to Russell Square at

80

midnight. I blame myself that I did not find it until this morning."

At midnight, Georgie was rolling toward Hampstead Heath in the hands of the Queen's coachman. Fitzgerald's fault, again.

"What will you do?"

"I shall have to remove the uterus."

"Surgery! In this place?"

She stopped short in the doorway. "I can hardly transport her to the College. As you're here, you might boil water on that hob and scrub the table. We shall have to operate by the fire — and send the little ones out into the hall while we do it."

He wanted to tell her that no common prostitute, however young and desperate, was worth the sacrifice of her safety. He wanted to tell her that the girl would die, no matter what she did.

"Georgie —"

"Not another word, until I am at leisure to hear you. Mr. Fitzgerald requires some water, Davey," she ordered the boy. "Be so good as to fetch it for him."

CHAPTER NINE

Whatever brutal words he might have thrown at Georgie were stopped in his mouth when he saw the girl.

She was not a pretty thing, being too thin and already gapping in her teeth. Her faded blond hair was a mass of tangles, her face grey and drenched with sweat. But there was in her slight frame and fragile wrists, in the delicacy of her fingers as they plucked at the rags that covered her, all the possibility of a different life — one of expression and feeling, a world glimpsed but never grasped. The sight of her shamed Fitzgerald. As he bent to lift her in his arms, to carry her to that scrubbed old table where Georgie would slice into her flesh, he thought of all the other men, breaking the twig of her body in half. How many? For how many years?

Her mother, who was called Button Nance, swore beneath her breath in a continuous stream of vituperation half-realised, half-heard, a diatribe against the world and God and doctors of every description, against men in general and men who paid and men who didn't, men who demanded little girls instead of women like herself who could stand the nonsense; against little girls, too, and Lizzie in particular — more fool her for not bearing the brat and then pitching it in the Thames — and finally, against Fitzgerald for causing her daughter to cry out in pain as he lifted her. Nancy drank deep from a pitcher of gin, and though it was only noon by the time they laid Lizzie before the fire, her mother was dead drunk.

He had never seen Georgiana administer the chloroform that John Snow made famous.

It was a ticklish business, and in the hands of Snow's imitators, occasionally a fatal one. Impossible to predict how a weakened frame might react to the drug-induced night — whether the constitution, already brought low by illness or accident, might not be extinguished altogether. There were stories indignantly circulated of patients dead at the extraction of a tooth, because chloroform was used; of labouring women whose ease of delivery was swiftly followed by the

83

grave. But John Snow, to Fitzgerald's knowledge, had never lost a patient. And the possibility of enduring surgery without pain had made his discovery wildly popular, so that for the first time patients went under the knife without terror. Chloroform had revolutionized the practice of medicine in the past decade; all of Europe was ready to take its risk.

"Patients die because their doctors, terrified of waking them with the knife, continue to drug them long after they are unconscious," Georgiana said placidly as she placed a drop of chloroform on a square of linen and held it to Lizzie's nose. "Then the heart rate is depressed and the lungs collapse. Sheer stupidity on the surgeon's part — but so many of them are untrained, and besieged with requests for anaesthesia. It's no wonder they kill with kindness."

The girl reached out and grasped Georgie's hand. "Don't cut me," she pleaded. "The last one cut me and I've not been right since — men don't like a girl what's cut."

"Hush," Georgiana said, smoothing the rough hair. "You shall feel a world of difference soon."

The steady application of drops to handkerchief continued; Lizzie's eyelids fluttered, her breath fell slowly into the oblivion of sleep.

The surgery required almost an hour. Fitzgerald stayed at Georgiana's side and did as he was instructed, though he'd never been one to love the smell of blood. In Lizzie's case the rich animal scent was overpowered by the stronger one of decay: Her body stank as he remembered the wounds of soldiers stinking, with the foetid pus of inflammation. Georgiana's face was grave as she opened the girl and removed the perforated uterus, which lay like the liver of a butchered cow on the scrubbed table.

"A knitting needle, I think," she murmured as she carefully sewed her incisions closed with catgut. "The abortionist's oldest trick. The man should be hanged."

Fitzgerald stepped to the room's sole window and opened it a crack, greedily breathing in the cold air. Freezing rain still fell steadily, mingling with the coal smoke and pale northern light of December; it was as though all of London had drawn a cloak of mourning about its shoulders. His hands were shaking again and he craved a drink: He took great draughts of polluted air instead. The stench of the rooms — sweat and stale alcohol and semen — had conjured a march of demons through his brain.

Unwashed female bodies, torn shifts, a tangle of arms on a single mattress, hair spread like matted fur across the worn boards of the floor — a public house in Cork City. The sweet rot of bodily fluids and spilled ale. *His mother.*

His gorge rose; he closed his eyes. The vision was so powerful that for an instant it eradicated the present and he could feel the earth crumble beneath his knees, as he knelt at the edge of her grave.

He'd been thirteen, the eldest of five, when she died. Fitzgerald was *her* name, none of them claiming a father to speak of. Cork City was one of Ireland's finer seaports, and Ma enjoyed the custom of sailors from all over the world — though it never brought her riches. What she made, she spent on drink and her children's bellies, in that order. When she died, the three girls were sent to an orphanage and the two boys cast out into the world. The innkeeper — whom the Fitzgeralds called Uncle Jack, though he was no relation of theirs — offered to keep young Liam, an open-hearted, grinning lad obsessed with the workings of the brewery. Patrick was good for nothing, being shy and bookish. Uncle Jack bluntly called him a penniless bastard not grand enough for making a priest, and suggested he join a mendicant order. Instead, Patrick stole the pub's earnings one moonlit night and walked to Cobh, where the great ships left for the English coast.

He had lived in London for thirty-three years; he'd turned a trick of pure luck and made a life from absolutely nothing — but that grim spectre of the past, the want and the stink and the desperate cruelty of living, could still bring him to his knees.

The curtain of sleet thickened and lowered. He studied the narrow courtyard below — the buildings leaning on one another's shoulders like drunkards, the stray mongrel carrying a rat between its teeth — and felt his breath catch in his throat. A man had appeared around the crumbling edge of the tenement opposite; a complete stranger in Fitzgerald's eyes, but too well-dressed to belong to the rookery. Barrel-chested, heavy-limbed, with luxuriant muttonchop whiskers, he carried a heavy club known as a cosh. As Fitzgerald watched, he stopped in the centre of the courtyard, his eyes roving among the derelict entries. Was this one of Nancy's regulars?

A regular would know where she lived.

Three other men materialised at the first's back, obviously in support, and stood silently waiting. Then, in the space of a heartbeat, two more approached from a narrow passage at the courtyard's far end.

Six men. Converging.

Fitzgerald could hear Georgie murmuring to her patient, who was waking now with wracking sobs. She would ask him to carry the girl back to her pallet, soon.

He opened the door to the hall. "Davey."

The boy was minding the younger children on the stairs.

"Is there a back door out of the building?"

"Yessir."

Fitzgerald tossed him a shilling. "Run down and see whether it's all clear. Don't talk to anybody — there's a good lad."

The child vanished with stealth and swiftness, the coin clenched between his teeth; Fitzgerald turned back inside, and lifted Lizzie in his arms.

"I might send to Covent Garden for some fresh linen," Georgiana worried, as he set the girl down on her straw, "but all the shops are closed. I shall simply have to bring some things tomorrow from Russell Square —"

"You won't be in Russell Square tomorrow."

"Nonsense," she retorted crisply. "This child must be examined daily. Would you

88

consign her to her mother's care? She might as well be left for dead."

Fitzgerald glanced at Lizzie; she'd lost consciousness from the pain. "There's a party of killers in the courtyard below. If they've found you here, Georgie, they've already been to Russell Square."

Her face was suddenly, sharply, white. *"What?"*

He grasped her shoulder, pulled her from the inner room to the window. *"Look.* There. On the paving. A man with a cosh. Probably still stained with Sep's blood."

She shook her head wildly. "I see nobody!"

Fitzgerald cursed. Heavy boots resounded through the lower entry; the men were already inside.

"Get your cloak and satchel. Quickly!"

She asked him nothing this time, though he could read the disbelief in her face. He seized her hand and pulled her after him, through the hallway.

CHAPTER TEN

There is nothing more trying to the affections of a mother than the caprice of a daughter. I say this with a rueful appreciation of Fate — having been daughter myself to Victoire, Princess of Leiningen and Duchess of Kent, and mother in turn to five girls of my own. I do not believe there is a woman now living who possesses a finer sense of the emotions that tremble between two such females: one in full-blown rebellion against the maternal efforts of the other to guide, to rear, to direct. I considered of this as I studied my second daughter around the hour of ten o'clock, as she sat with bowed head in St. George's Chapel of a Sunday morning — the holiest place in Windsor. She was weeping for her Papa. The sight of such misery wrung my grieving heart.

"Alice."

The name floated beneath the Gothic

architraves, the leaded windows transmuting the wretched December day to a light more infinite and sublime.

Her head was cradled in her hands, her slight frame already swathed in black — a summer mourning gown she'd last worn for my mother. Alice looked crushed and frail, as though she had been whipped to submission by an overpowering master; it was brutal to disturb such suffering, even by whispering her name.

Alice is eighteen — a good and affectionate soul, although perhaps a little spoilt by dear Albert. She is engaged to marry Louis of Hesse-Darmstadt, and will too soon escape my influence forever. In the short time that is left to me I must endeavour to correct those little flaws that might naturally result from a too-careless indulgence, lest her husband be appalled at her headstrong nature. Albert was undoubtedly appealing to the child, particularly after Vicky went off to her Prussian marriage — but I may say her father delighted perhaps *too much* in their conversations. Alice is clever, you see; and Albert encouraged her to put herself forward to an unbecoming degree.

"Alice!"

She straightened — her head lifted from her black-gloved hands — her crinoline swung, bell-like, as she rose from her knees — eyes trained on the altar. Albert was not yet there, although it seemed as though he ought to be — arranged on a pyre like a barbaric lord of old. *My burnt offering.* My Beloved's body still lay in the Blue Room, where the Royal Valets — MacDonald and Löhlein — were bathing and dressing him like a doll. I would *not think* of the undertakers. Nor of funerals in general. I would make no arrangements. Bertie would, of course, handle everything.

Alice walked slowly by me, her expression blank, her arms stiff at her sides, to the chapel door. She hesitated at the threshold, but did not turn or glance back; she merely quitted the place without a word. Wonderingly, I followed.

"Alice!"

The black figure halted. "You wished to speak to me, Mama?"

"Indeed."

I longed to take the dear child in my arms, to mourn with her over the loss of her Sainted Papa — but Alice looked as approachable as marble. Impossible to caress. Her fortitude was all that was admirable during the last days of Albert's illness. She haunted his rooms, followed in his steps as he moved sleepless through the Castle at night — played beloved German airs upon the piano to ease his fevered brain. But for all her goodness, I sense in Alice an unfortunate tendency to *obstinacy*. When she might have served as prop and comfort to her Mama, she prefers to ally herself with the younger children — Leopold, for example, upon whom she foolishly dotes. *And* Louise. *And* Helena. They refer to me as "Eliza" behind my back; Alice is the prime mover in all my children's conspiracies.

"Pity your poor Mama, my child," I began, "and do your utmost to console her — though none *can,* considering the *All-in-All* I have lost."

"You have my pity, Mama," she returned dutifully. "Of that you may be certain."

"Pray sit down, dear child."

Near at hand was a settee, placed in an alcove of the wall; after an instant's hesitation, Alice bowed her head. She sat.

"I am so very tired," she murmured.

"Naturally." The word had more asperity than I intended. "You have sacrificed yourself perhaps too much for poor Papa — waiting upon him tirelessly, as though there were not a household of servants and doctors at Windsor, possessed of far greater experience and wisdom! But your vigilance could not keep Death from the door, my unfortunate Alice."

"No," she agreed. "Quite useless. All my love and anxiety for him —"

"I notice that your brother is now resident in the Castle. Who summoned him from Cambridge, pray?"

She raised her head. "I did, Mama. I could not allow Bertie to remain ignorant of Papa's crisis."

"*You* could not allow!" Overwhelmed by a sick feeling of despair and helplessness — uncertain what *could,* or *ought,* to be revealed to such an innocent of her brother's moral lapse — I was, for an instant, deprived of speech. "Are you unaware, Alice, that it is because of *Bertie* — his transgressions, the severe anxiety his weak character has caused — that your Papa lost all will to live? You did very wrong in summoning him. But for Bertie's presence in the Blue Room —"

"— Papa might have rallied?" Her lip trembled. "Good God, Mama, when will you see the truth? Papa has been ill for weeks — months, perhaps!"

"Your father was well enough before the Prince of Wales broke his heart," I cried. "And then *you* must dig his grave for him!"

Alice's hands twisted convulsively in her lap, but her eyes remained fixed; she did not break down.

"I hope you will behave with greater modesty, in future," I said lamely. "There is a degree of self-consequence in all your actions, Alice, that cannot be considered either proper or becoming. I shudder to think how your future husband may remark upon it."

"Yes, Mama."

I hesitated; there was much I yearned to know. And yet Alice is such a difficult creature — so aloof, so acute in her understanding . . .

"You were almost the last to attend him," I observed. "You were by his side from morning until night. Never, from this day until the hour of your death, my dear, shall you have the slightest call to reproach yourself. You may be happy in the knowledge that you did your Duty."

"Yes. I have that comfort."

"He was so cold at the end," I murmured. "His hands, his face, almost blue. As though the midnight of Heaven had wrapped itself already around him."

Alice looked at me finally. I sank down beside her, clasped her hands in mine.

"And he whispered in your ear. German, of course. A few words, I think?"

Abruptly, she rose.

"Dear child, what did he tell you? Did he

say anything of . . . the family? Anything, perhaps, of . . . *me?*"

Alice's eyelids flickered. "There are other people in the world, Mama, besides yourself. Though you can never be brought to see it."

Such cruelty, at an hour when too much has already been torn from me! I rose and faced her.

"Pray consider, Alice. Do you think it is *quite* what Beloved Papa would wish — that you should *refuse to confide* in your suffering parent?"

She sighed, and closed her eyes. "Papa's words were utterly unintelligible. The merest ravings. Question me as you choose, Mama, you shall never divine his meaning."

She stepped deliberately around me and moved off without haste, unrepentant and unassailable, in the direction of her private apartments.

CHAPTER ELEVEN

The tenement stairs led up to the garrets, and Fitzgerald took them two at a time, Georgie's medical bag in his right hand. She followed, her skirts bunched in her fists, her breathing audible and rapid. She would, of course, be fighting the iron grip of stays around her rib cage; it was a small mercy, Fitzgerald reflected, that she hadn't worn a crinoline that morning. She kept a kind of work uniform — of which the French twilled silk was one — of neat walking dresses designed to be worn over petticoats rather than the swaying bell of whalebone and stiffening; but all those layers were a treacherous impediment to haste. How would she navigate the roof? And was she in slippers or boots?

The staircase ended abruptly in a landing. Three doors gave off the hallway beyond — and the farthest one was ajar.

Somewhere below them, a shout went up

— a curse of pure rage. The man with the cosh had found Button Nance — and from the squeal that followed, he hadn't liked how the whore answered his questions.

"Patrick —"

"You're not to go back." He gripped Georgie's hand, ignored her frown of protest, and pulled her through the doorway.

There were at least a dozen people in the shadowy room. A few women, a clutch of children, an elderly couple huddled by a smoking fire. Barely a stick of furniture, and the single dormer window had rags stuffed where glass should be. These were sodden with sleet and the air was cold enough to see your breath.

"Oi!" a woman shrieked. "Whaddya think yer about, then? This ain't a flophouse; you can't bring yer fancy-piece 'ere!"

The idea of Georgiana Armistead as prostitute would normally have fired Fitzgerald's tongue, but he merely brushed his way past the woman's upraised fist, and made for the dormer window. He threw wide the casement.

"Can we get out?" Georgie asked.

"It's good and steep, but we've no choice. We'll have to slide." He scanned the tiles; they were slick with slush and treacherously cracked. Where the downslope of the garret

98

met the upslope of the neighbouring hovel, a guttered roof joint ran between. Georgie would find safer footing there; he just hoped it did not lead to a sheer drop — he had no way of knowing, and no time to reconnoiter.

"Didn' you hear me? *Get out!*" the woman shrieked in his ear.

"Aye, and we're just going." He reached for his purse and found her a shilling — enough to cover her share of the rent for a month. "Take this for your trouble. Now, up you get, Georgie!"

He put his hands together and she stepped into them, hoisting herself onto the sill. Then she swung her heavy skirt through the window, while all the children in the place ran up to Fitzgerald to tug on his arm and beg for coppers. He scattered coins at his feet and told the largest boy, "Close the door and bolt it, there's a good lad." Then he followed Georgie out onto the tiles, sliding toward the roof joint.

She was already at the bottom, picking herself up and brushing at the back of her fine dress with a quarrelsome expression. The silk was in a fair way to being ruined. She glared at his heels as they slid into the gutter, spraying her boots with filth.

"Was this *really* necessary, Patrick?"

Before he could answer, a cosh shattered

the frame of the window above their heads and fragments of wood rained down on the icy tiles. Georgie turned without another word and began to inch along the gutter, toward the edge of the roof and whatever lay below it.

Fitzgerald thrust himself to his feet. He stumbled after her, waiting for the impact of another body behind him — when it came, he looked back and saw the ruffian with the cosh.

The garret room was at the very end of the hallway; there were no more windows giving out onto this section of roof. The gutter ran toward St. Giles Street in one direction, and in the other, toward the warren of alleys behind it. Georgie was headed away from the street, deeper into the rookery maze. But when Fitzgerald looked ahead, he saw she had come to a complete halt — poised on the edge of nothing.

A rough hand snatched at his shoulder. He lost his balance, feet flying out from under him, and fell backwards. Georgie's medical bag sailed out of his grasp — and it was probably this sound, of the bag bursting open and the instruments clattering across the tiles, that brought her head around in search of him. Fitzgerald heard her yell — not a high-pitched woman's scream, but a guttural, savage sound wholly unlike the Georgie he knew. He wanted to tell her to save herself — to get away while the tough was on top of him — but the man's hand was at his throat. And then the cosh rose wildly above him —

Fitzgerald pulled his knees up, hard, into his attacker's groin and dodged sideways, the cosh smashing into the tiles where his head had been moments before. The man toppled. Fitzgerald rolled upright and leaned on his enemy's spine, taking great gasps of air through his grateful throat. The torso beneath him was broad, heavily muscled — the frame of a man who moved stone for a living, or hauled ropes, or placed a value on punishing strength in his line of work. There was the hand that held the cosh — Fitzgerald grasped the weapon and pulled back hard, as though it were a lever, shouting *Georgie, go!* while his enemy grunted and cursed his hatred of Fitzgerald and heaved himself upright so that Fitzgerald was straddling him now, the man corkscrewing like a maddened horse, the powerful wrist snapping in Fitzgerald's grasp and the cosh sailing free of the nerveless fingers —

"Patrick!" Georgie cried in warning. "Behind you!"

Of course there would be more men; he'd counted six. A few had probably posted themselves at the building's front and back doors, but the rest would be coming through the shattered window right behind their leader, and probably armed. He tossed the cosh in Georgie's direction, then lunged from the man's back toward the glint of metal in the gutter — one of Georgie's knives, from her scattered bag. The creature beside him doubled up in pain, clutching his broken wrist. The scalpel slid into Fitzgerald's palm, cold and wet.

He seized his attacker's head, pulled it back, and thrust the edge of the scalpel against his throat.

"You soddin' little Paddy," the man gasped, his fingers clawing at Fitzgerald's arm.

The second tough was almost upon them, but he stopped short when he heard his mate's bubbling gasp.

"If you come any closer, he dies," Fitzgerald warned, fingers clenched in the man's dirty black hair. "And then *you* die. Understand?"

The second man glanced sideways, no doubt calculating the distance from one roof to another, or searching for a broken tile he could hurl at Fitzgerald's head; over his shoulder, Fitzgerald saw a third figure easing across the garret windowsill. His grasp on his prey tightened, and the hum of violence sang in his ears, a familiar hymn as carnal as sex. The knife edge nicked the throat beneath his fingers and the throat whimpered faintly.

Georgie advanced, the cosh raised high, and said in that same guttural snarl, "We'll cut his neck and call you murderer. A gentleman's word against a labourer's. Are you prepared to hang, my friend?"

The man inched backwards, his eyes widening; then he turned and stumbled toward the garret window, kicking and clawing his way back up the tiles.

"Who sent you?" Fitzgerald demanded, in his enemy's ear. "Who pays your wage?"

An oath spat through his clenched fingers; nothing more.

"Patrick, they'll be back," Georgie said.

He released the black hair and forced the man beneath him, onto the tiles. Then he tore the cosh from Georgie's grasp and delivered a punishing blow to the back of the skull. The solid bulk went limp.

"Pray God you didn't kill him," Georgie said faintly.

"Why? He'd have killed *me*. He'd have killed *both* of us and left our bodies on the roof. Just as he left Sep to die in chambers."

She did not reply, her face as white as paper.

At the edge of the icy gutter, Fitzgerald knelt carefully and peered over the edge, senses swimming. He was unaccustomed to the eerie pitch, the irregular angles of this view of the world; he drew back, and waited for his head to steady.

"It's a sheer drop."

Georgie's teeth were chattering with cold and tension, but she had retrieved her bag of surgical tools. "I refuse to retrace my steps. I will not walk past that man. I'm a *doctor,* Patrick — to leave him in that condition, in this weather, *knowing* what the result might be —"

"Your scruples do you credit," Fitzgerald said dryly. "His men would be waiting for us inside, in any case. Georgie, that fellow called me a *Paddy.*"

"It's hardly the first time someone has."

"That's not what I mean. I hadn't spoken yet — he had no thought for my accent — and it's faint enough after all these years. He came *looking* for an Irishman. He was sent here. By whom?"

"He probably followed *you* from Great Ormond Street." She brushed the sleet from her cheek impatiently. "No doubt these people are watching Septimus's house — to learn whether he dies."

It was possible, Fitzgerald owned. And yet —

He glanced back, afraid of what he might see coming through the broken window, and said suddenly, "Would it cheer you to know, Georgiana, that our friends from the garret are already picking your man's pockets?"

She turned swiftly, saw the clutch of women and children hunkered around the body. "Without even pausing to know if he's dead or alive?"

"You might check his pulse yourself." Fitzgerald rose and brushed fragments of ice and slate from his trousers. "That lot would never be out here unless the gang had fled. Which means we can go home in peace."

CHAPTER TWELVE

"You think von Stühlen is behind these attacks," Georgiana said. "That's why you inquired about him."

They had retraced their steps through the tenement building without a further glimpse of the murderous pack. A swift walk up St. Giles to the hackney stand in Covent Garden, both of them unsteady from relief and fatigue. The early dusk of December fell swiftly, and the temperature had dropped as the afternoon waned. Georgiana shivered uncontrollably in her soaked gown, and Fitzgerald thought it imperative to get her home as soon as he could. Her gloves were torn and her hair sliding out of the bandage; they had not stopped to inquire of Button Nance where her bonnet had gone. She looked, in short, uncharacteristically slatternly. Fitzgerald looked as careless as always — but he'd lost his topper.

The sole cabbie lingering at the stand was

more interested in the sight of their money, however, than the state of their clothes. Fitzgerald did not respond to Georgiana's remark until the lap robe was tucked over her knees and the reins snapped over the horse's back.

Bells still rang throughout London for Albert's passing, a dull monotony after all these hours; lengths of black crepe had appeared on door knockers and window fronts. Shops in Henrietta Street, Fitzgerald noticed, already sported black mourning shutters — which were closed, like the premises. There would be a considerable loss of custom in the weeks running up to Christmas, except among the linendraper firms — everyone, even the children of the lowliest clerk, would go into blacks for at least a month.

"I asked about von Stühlen because I hated the way he looked at you," he told Georgiana.

"Like a wolf with a cornered sheep?"

"You saw it, too?"

"Well, he *has* earned a dreadful reputation."

"— For shearing sheep?"

"No. For raping the unwilling."

There it was again — Georgie's appalling worldliness. "How do you think he lost his eye?" she continued.

"In a duel — or so it's said. Was that over a woman?"

"A fifteen-year-old girl of excellent birth — kidnapped, raped, and returned like a piece of soiled goods to her family several weeks later, when von Stühlen tired of her. The child's brother tried to kill the Count — but in the event, only added to his air of dash, by giving him the eye patch."

"How do you know all this?"

She shrugged. "I may still claim a good part of the acquaintance I formed at school, you know — and am everywhere received. Do you really think ladies talk only of fashion?"

"I'll warrant the word *rape* never crosses the lips of your select friends."

"No. They use gentler terms — a kind of code for men of that stamp. They call von Stühlen dangerous, or the very worst of rakes, or *unreliable.* By which they mean he hasn't a feather to fly with, is a gazetted fortune hunter, and has any number of women in keeping." Georgiana's eyes were trained on the horse's head as it trotted toward Russell Square. "He even offered to keep me, if it comes to that."

"He *what?*"

"— Was so obliging as to suggest I should

be his mistress. In the enclosure at Ascot, last June. He gave me his card on the strength of it." Her smile was twisted. "Women such as myself, he assured me, were excessively diverting because of our intelligence; we added a certain spice to *amour;* but we could never hope to receive an offer of marriage in the general way. I believe he considered his notice an exceptionally great honour."

"I'd like to whip him the length of Pall Mall," Fitzgerald said through his teeth.

"I'm afraid I did something much worse. I *laughed* at him. And tossed his card back in his face. He was furious — publicly humiliated. If I'd been a man, I daresay he'd have demanded satisfaction."

"How could he think you'd listen to such a dishonourable proposal?"

"He first made my acquaintance in the company of the Prince — and no doubt assumed I was Albert's mistress. Although the Consort was the least likely of men to have a lady in keeping, I daresay any number of gentlemen have made a similar error. How else to account for my intimacy with the Prince?" She worried the torn leather of one glove, her face averted. "But tell me, Patrick — why should von Stühlen be concerned with these attacks? That pack of ruffians may be bent upon killing Septimus Taylor for reasons wholly unrelated to us. Perhaps they merely followed you because you'd discovered their handiwork."

"Sep was at the Inner Temple, nowhere near Hampstead last night," Fitzgerald said flatly. "Somebody cleared away that palisade on the Heath — and your dangerous Count was on the scene within hours of the wreck. That much we know. I go further, Georgie — I say von Stühlen saw murder done in the wee hours of the morning, then ordered the destruction of all evidence."

"Why?"

"What other business could bring him to Hampstead? He came direct from Windsor!"

"He admitted as much," she retorted impatiently. "But you've nothing to tie him to the attack at the Inner Temple, much less that pack of hounds in St. Giles."

"Sweet Jesus, woman — would you *defend* such a man? This madness began last night, with my summons to Windsor. I was probably called there *in order* to be killed on my return."

"But *why*, Patrick? Why is it necessary to silence you? What do these people fear?"

"I don't know," he admitted bleakly as the hackney pulled to a halt before Georgiana's door. "But I won't risk dying before I find

110

out. I leave London tonight — and you're to come with me, Georgie lass."

Her smile wavered. "Another *carte blanche?*"

It was the polite term for von Stühlen's type of sexual arrangement. Fitzgerald's heart stuttered, and a wave of heat surged through his body. Before he could speak, however, she pressed her fingers against his lips.

"I should be so fortunate. No, Patrick — I won't come with you. I have poor Lizzie to think of, and others —"

But her words died in her mouth. Fitzgerald looked toward the doorway. Georgie's housekeeper was racing to meet them, a stricken expression on her face.

Georgiana's rooms were like the woman herself, Fitzgerald thought — elegantly spare; intelligently arranged. Not for Georgie the excess of velvet hangings or the wave of bric-a-brac crowding every surface, the plant stands overflowing with ferns; Georgie's walls were cream, picked out with gold, the simplest of hangings at the tall windows. Light poured into the rooms even in the darkest months of winter. To sit there with Georgie was to stem the turbulent beat of his days, the wild disorder of his thoughts and passions. Georgie was the voice of reason. The air of decision. The order of science. Caught in a form as breathtaking as Venus.

Now, however, the house was a scene of devastation.

The Aubusson carpet was rucked up over the floorboards; a gilt picture frame lay smashed in the fireplace, its canvas torn; a piece of the marble mantel had been broken off and tossed at yet another picture, which hung askew and ravaged above the settee. Chair upholstery was slit down the middle and feathers strewn everywhere.

"I just stepped round to St. George's, Hanover Square, to pray for the repose of the dear Consort's soul," the housekeeper said as Georgie stopped dead in the middle of her drawing room, her medical bag slipping to chaos on the floor, "and you always give the staff their afternoon out, of a Sunday. So the place was empty, do you see? And when I returned — just *look* at it! We've had thieves, miss, and what I can't make out is what they thought to come for! All the silver's in the pantry, and your jewels never touched in the boudoir . . . but my word, your *desk!*"

"My desk?" Georgiana repeated faintly — and then swept through the drawing room

112

to the library beyond. "Oh, Patrick!"

Papers scattered everywhere, as they had been in Fitzgerald's chambers.

He took one step forward into the room and stopped short. He had never seen Georgie cry before — not even when John Snow died.

"My darling," he said, and went to her.

"It's just that it's so cruel," she muttered against his shoulder. "These aren't my things, Patrick — they're Uncle John's. All his case notes. Documents he kept for *decades* — statistics of populations, meticulous research. It will take me days to reorder them all. And for what?"

He held her away from him, studied the swimming eyes.

"You'll have to find out," he said. "Now, not later — because whatever you may think, Georgie, you're leaving London with me tonight. I *will not* allow you to remain in this house."

"But —"

"Those men came *here.* They tracked you to St. Giles. They wanted something *you* had. They didn't come because of Sep or even because of me — they came because von Stühlen glimpsed you in Hampstead at dawn. Do you understand? *You're in danger, love.* Now start picking up these papers and

113

tell me what the men found. They didn't want your candlesticks — they wanted something in this room, in your desk. What was it?"

"My letters." Her voice was colourless. "All my private correspondence is gone."

CHAPTER THIRTEEN

I know exactly what age I was, when I learned that Mama was a whore.

Well-bred and exceedingly high in the instep, to be sure — demanding the respect and consideration of the Polite World, as must be only natural in one of *Royal blood* — but a whore regardless.

It was in the midst of one of our incessant Progresses, when Mama and Sir John Conroy — her Master of Household, the Demon Incarnate — put the Heiress Presumptive on display, among the great houses of England.

I was eleven. My uncle, George IV, had died at last and I was exceedingly angry at being forbidden to attend Uncle William's coronation — Mama ascribing this calculated rudeness on our part to her *delicacy of feeling.* As Uncle William claimed ten bastards by the lovely Dolly Jordan, he could not be deemed fit company for the Heiress

Presumptive — although he *was* King of England.

And so I snubbed the new monarch, whose throne I must eventually fill, and was carried off to Holymount, in the Malvern Hills — by way of Blenheim, and Kenilworth, and Warwick Castle. The year was 1830, and the weather close and hot.

We had halted perhaps an hour short of Blenheim, so that the horses might be baited and the entire party refreshed. I stood in the private parlour of the inn and stared through the half-open casement, the panes clouded with summer dust. The footman was lording it over the humble ostlers in the stable yard, bragging of his intimacy with the Great; I watched him hawk and spit, and drag his sleeve across the back of his mouth.

And then a ripple of laughter floated through the open window. *My mother's laugh.* It was of a timbre I knew well — low and suggestive — followed by John Conroy's lilting Irish brogue. My cheeks flushed without warning and I felt an angry heat burn behind my eyes, an impotent fury clenching my fists. *How could they?* Mama had insisted on lying down for a while before nuncheon; she had complained of the heat, she had threatened to swoon. And

Conroy had found her there, in the bedroom upstairs. His hand, as I had seen it once before in a chance moment at Kensington, sliding beneath the hem of her thin summer gown and rising along her leg, bare in her sandals at this season, his sensuous lips curling with lust —

Mama's laughter rippled again.

Dear Lehzen hurried to the casement and pulled it closed.

I suppose I ought to have been more understanding. My mother had, after all, buried two husbands — both older than she, both more powerful, both men she was ordered to marry and for whom she cared not a jot. She had borne children as demanded, without the slightest reward of affection or income. My father's death when I was yet a babe at the breast had deprived her of the rank she was owed — something on the order of: *Princess Dowager of Wales,* or, *Queen Mother,* when once I took the throne — titles she made up, in her idle hours, along with lists of stipends, honours for herself and Conroy, peerages and imaginary posts —

It was Lehzen who instructed and supported me, Lehzen who revealed to me, quite young, what Fate intended I should be. My cherished governess placed my

117

genealogy as if by chance before me, during our long schoolroom hours; and it was only then, examining the family tree, that I comprehended my nearness to the throne. I burst into tears, overwhelmed by the horror of it. That was the moment I suddenly understood exactly *why* Sir John Conroy ruled my weak and silly mother — why his charmed caresses formed a noose round my neck. He meant to *own* the next Queen of England.

He nearly succeeded. It is in the nature of men to strive for supremacy. All my life I have fought men for power, for the right to claim what is by birthright *mine.* But on the occasion I would mention, I was but sixteen, and ill with fever, and quite deserted by my friends; and Conroy thought to seize his opportunity.

A squalid bed in a Ramsgate inn, the Demon towering over me in my fever, a pen in one hand and a riding crop in the other. . . . *You will sign, Princess. You will sign this document your mother and I have drawn up, or you will not see a doctor again this side of the grave.*

Mama whipped my thighs herself with the crop that day; she bound my wrists and plunged my head into water until I despaired I would drown.

Silly girl. Do you not understand what you owe your mother? What you owe the nation? So many sacrifices as Sir John has made for you . . .

Later I learned that John Conroy believed himself descended from some bastard Royal, that he regarded it as his Destiny to rule England. His madness was animated by the grandest of private delusions.

That endless day, I refused to sign his scrawl — I sweated, I vomited, I cried out for Lehzen when the pain in my throat grew unendurable — and still they would not relent.

No doctors, my mother hissed. *No doctors until you sign.*

It was weeks before the bruises on my thighs faded. Months before I could tolerate the sight of my mother. From that day forward, I never looked Mama directly in the eye; I spoke always with the royal *we.* And two years later, when I ascended the throne of England, Sir John Conroy was banished utterly from my world.

The Irish are born gamblers. When forthright dealing fails them, they resort to guile and subterfuge; violence and charm are their left and right hands. That day in Ramsgate the Demon Incarnate threw his cup of dice and lost; but I have not been able to abide his race from that day to this.

CHAPTER FOURTEEN

Like every other establishment the length and breadth of England, The Bear was closed in respect of the Sabbath — as well as the Consort's death. But the publican was willing to let von Stühlen conduct his private business in a parlour upstairs of a Sunday — for a consideration.

The Bear dominated a corner of Milk Street, in the very heart of the unfashionable part of London known as the City. The bankers and merchants who made money there were officially beyond the jurisdiction of the Metropolitan Police. They disdained the protection of mere Bobbies. They maintained instead a private constabulary of toughs. The City's watchmen answered only to money, and they were ruthless in earning their wage.

Such men had no interest in justice or enforcing the law; they could be bought and used, and this was why von Stühlen cultivated them.

He had hired a few in the past — when a courtesan proved too demanding; when a friend failed to honour a debt. This was the largest undertaking he had ever attempted, however. His orders were clear: Find Patrick Fitzgerald and Georgiana Armistead quietly and quickly. Make certain they never posed a threat to Her Majesty again.

If he had a secondary motive, he kept it firmly to himself. That was von Stühlen's way. He made friends easily and widely, he was spoilt and sought after as a darling of Society — but nobody in England knew him at all. Not now that Albert was dead. He wore his fundamental loneliness like a well-cut coat, and the world mistook it for elegance.

By four o'clock that Sabbath, he was engaged in the final interview of the day.

Jasper Horan was stooped and simian; his teeth had rotted in his head, but his fists were as blunt as a blacksmith's. Most days he worked as a warehouse foreman for a reputable firm of tea importers, but in his hours of leisure he earned far more against his old age. Already that Sunday Horan and his toughs had found Patrick Fitzgerald's chambers, ransacked Miss Armistead's home in Russell Square, and hunted her down in St. Giles. Now he was back in Milk Street to tender his report.

"You lost them in Covent Garden?"

"I wouldn't go so far as to say *lost*," Horan countered. "The Paddy put up a devil of a fight, he did. My blokes call him a murderin' savage, like what all them Irish are. Left one man fer dead on the rookery roof, and the rest scarpered."

"Then I suggest you hire some Irish, capable of killing him," von Stühlen said evenly.

"I've got them papers as you wanted from the Temple." Horan tossed an oilskin packet on the table, nearly oversetting von Stühlen's claret. "And look what I pinched from the bird's 'ouse."

The Count's eyes flicked up. "I believe I *told* you what to take. You were not to steal anything else."

"Nor have I." Horan reached into his vest and withdrew a packet of letters, tied with a narrow black ribbon. "These 'ere have the Royal crest, they do — fetch a pretty penny from the newspapers, I reckon. What'll you give me for 'em, then?"

With his good eye, von Stühlen studied the foreman. "Do you read the newspapers, Horan?"

"Sometimes."

"Then you must be aware of the tragic end of the Queen's coachman?"

"Aye. Broke his neck on 'ampstead 'eath."

"There are so many ways to die in the dark." Von Stühlen extended one white hand for the stolen letters. "Don't haggle with me, Horan. I might consider too deeply how you failed me today — losing Patrick Fitzgerald in St. Giles."

It was Alice who drafted the telegram to the consulate in Nice. She had sent one the previous night, at eight o'clock, when Papa was still alive.

Pray break to Prince Leopold that the Prince is very ill and we are in great anxiety about him.

During the past week she had sent letters and telegrams to brothers and sisters far from Windsor: to Affie at sea in the North Atlantic, and to Vicky in Berlin. Vicky was the most desperate for news, being Papa's firstborn and special pet. When Papa asked what she'd written, Alice said calmly: *I told her you were very ill.*

He had looked at her with his heartrending smile. *You did wrong. You should have told her that I am dying.*

Which made her press her hand to her mouth in agony and walk swiftly from the room.

He had known what was coming. He had looked over the black edge of the abyss, and hurled himself in.

Alice wished she had held his hand, and gone, too.

Her father had never been a man to cling to false comfort. He spoke the absolute truth, no matter how brutal. Which made the words he'd muttered into her ear, in his final hour, all the more disturbing.

There is no one I can talk to, she thought. Not Vicky, far away in Prussia. Not Bertie, already burdened with guilt. Never Mama.

She looked up from her paper and pen, overwhelmed with the sharpness of loss, with the terror of being alone. She missed Leopold acutely; despite the ten-year difference in their ages, they were fond of each other. What would Papa have said to her eight-year-old brother? What should she write to a child, so utterly alone?

Stay away from this place, my darling. There is no home here anymore.

But she could not send such a telegram over the wire. They would think her mad, at the consulate in Nice.

Please break to Prince Leopold that the

125

Prince Consort passed away at ten minutes before eleven last evening. . . .

Mad.

Alice closed her eyes. She would have to tell someone. But who?

CHAPTER FIFTEEN

These are the symptoms of typhoid fever, as I have observed them in the wasting frame of my Beloved: stomach pains, a general weakness, persistent aching of the head, loss of appetite. And fever, naturally — although Albert's was not so high as is often seen, Jenner tells me. My Dearest was sleepless, and spent much of the last week of his life in roaming about the halls of Windsor, murmuring under his breath, which Jenner also declares is not generally associated with the malady. Albert failed altogether to throw out the characteristic typhoid rash of flat, rose-coloured spots. I asked Löhlein whether he had observed such a thing in his washing and dressing of the Prince, when I met the valet in the Blue Room this evening; he replied in the negative, his dear face quite contorted with emotion. Albert suspected Löhlein was his natural half brother — the old Duke his father being a dissipated and corrupt man, much inclined to exercising his *droits du seigneur* among the household servants, of which Löhlein's mother was one. The intimacy of blood would perhaps explain the valet's devotion.

I had gone to the Blue Room just before dinner to strew flowers about the bed on which Albert expired. His remains have been moved to the neighbouring one, and he looks very fine in his uniform — although rather like a wax figure out of Madame Tussaud's. Jenner would not allow me to touch the corpse or kiss it for fear of infection, which I know to be sheer nonsense — no one else in all of Windsor has contracted typhoid — but I submitted to his strictures, as being the best course of conduct for the Kingdom.

It was only a few weeks ago that our dear nephew, the King of Portugal, was carried off by typhoid, along with his brother; it is this, I must suppose, that has given Jenner the idea of it. Stomach pains, weakness, persistent aching of the head — it might have been any kind of disorder that killed that Angelic Being. But Jenner is an acknowledged expert in typhoid; he sees it everywhere. For my own part, I will maintain Albert died because he preferred it to

128

living.

"Do you feel at all indisposed, Mama?" my daughter inquired as we met before the door of my rooms. "You look decidedly unwell."

"That is to be expected, dear child, is it not?" I attempted. "I have lost the *All-in-All* of my existence. I cannot long endure on this earth without the support of my Beloved. You will understand a little better, Alice, when once you have been married."

She took a step closer, and searched my countenance keenly. "Perhaps you should take dinner on a tray, Mama."

"I have no appetite. My head aches acutely. But if you would be so good, dear child, as to order a pot of tea, and perhaps some gruel — and a few of the Scotch oat cakes — to be sent up to my rooms, I should wish for nothing more."

"Very well." She turned away, then hesitated a moment. "Violet informs me, Mama, that some of my silk flowers — for the dressing of my hats — have gone missing. She found them absent from the wardrobe when she turned out my gowns."

I stared all my bewilderment. "I must suppose that such things are often gone missing! In a household so large as this — And who is Violet, pray?"

"My dresser, Mama," Alice faltered. "We were to meet with the seamstress, to prepare my mourning clothes — and it was then Violet noticed. She thought perhaps my little sisters had taken the flowers for playthings."

"I know nothing of trumpery trimmings," I returned, with a commendable hold on my patience, "— other than that you cannot expect to require them for the next twelvemonth. I do not suppose the flowers were *black?*"

"No, indeed," Alice said. She curtseyed dutifully, and quitted my presence without another word.

I studied her the length of the hall, until she turned at the landing and disappeared from view.

I shall have to speak to the Master of Household about Violet.

Once in the privacy of my own bedchamber, I withdrew Albert's nightgown from his wardrobe and pressed my face into its dear folds, drinking in the scent even as it vanished — that ineffable, unforgettable odor of a distinct and irreplaceable human being. It was then, at long last, that the dreadful sobs were torn from me — the stricken grief of one who has lost the core of strength from the very centre of her being. I did not bother to undress; I did not admit my personal maid; I lay in a paroxysm of weeping in the centre of the great bed, my husband's linen entwined in my arms, until all light had failed and a discreet knock at the door informed me my tea and gruel were arrived.

I have written frankly, in these secret pages, of the intensity of my passion for Albert; how I craved the touch of his hands, the alabaster smoothness of his body — the muscles of his legs, firm and etched like a stallion's. I cannot entirely comprehend that no hand will ever touch me in an intimate way again — that no one will call me *Victoria* any more. Once our marriage vows sanctioned physical love, I abandoned myself to the enjoyment of his body — little dreaming that Albert regarded my passion as unseemly. *Liebchen,* he would mutter, face flushed with embarrassment, his erection surging despite his distaste, *a little conduct, if you please. Remember who we are.*

It became a habit between us: Albert aloof and cold, fastidious as a cat, until my appetites whipped him to heat.

All my life, I have been cursed by fits of despondency — a habit exacerbated by the excesses, so my doctors hint, of childbearing I have endured. When my fits of temper frayed Albert's patience, he would retreat to his study and write long lectures in German. Remote as Zeus upon Olympus, he denied me his sex — and I would fall sobbing on our bed and sulk behind locked doors. Albert treated me as he might an unruly child, sick from greed and sweets.

Your passions will kill you, Albert wrote. *They are unbridled. Sinful. Beneath the dignity of a woman, much less a queen.*

And worse — Bertie inherited every one of them.

Gradually, I understood that I was wanton, a whore like Mama — that I possessed a flaw in the blood I could not fight. *A whore like Mama.* The Demon Incarnate in the upstairs room, the low suggestion of Mama's laughter, the coarse Irish hand sliding along the leg and the stink of the semened bed — With the intensity of my love came a jealousy of all Albert touched, all those to whom he spoke. To give to *them* the attention denied to *me* was insupportable.

When I learned, perhaps a month before our final visit to Coburg, that he had gone so far as to cultivate *that woman* — Miss Georgiana Armistead — who could boast of no marriage vow; who threw every outrage

132

in the face of public decency, through her way of life; who had the impertinence to write his *Adored Name* on a piece of common writing paper — oh, my darling, how could you desert me so?

He is beyond the reach of my sobs now. But Miss Armistead — she might be exposed, she might be made to answer for her crimes before the public view, and know what it is to deprive the frailest of women of that peace and security found only in the arms of her Beloved.

Chapter Sixteen

The boy Davey was exhausted that night as he entered the rookery in St. Giles. It had been a fruitless and dispiriting day — first Lizzie so ill, and the lady doctor butchering her like a side of beef; then the gentleman sending him down to stand watch at the back door, where he'd been cuffed in the head by one of the coves who'd torn through the tenement. Davey had slipped outside, not wanting to be kicked like a ball of India rubber among the lot of them. He realised the fight had moved to the roof only when the gentleman's topper came spinning over the tiles to the street below. Scooping it up, he'd run off immediately to sell it in the Garden.

Three shillings richer, courtesy of a bank clerk with an eye for quality, he spent his largess on a pork pie and a tankard of ale in Bow Street — then wasted several hours in such jobs as boys of his ilk were fitted for:

walking horses or sweeping crossings. When customers proved scarce on the ground, he tried cadging pennies in St. Paul's churchyard — with the Consort dead, the nobs' hearts might've softened. But he ended the day only a few coppers richer, and just as hungry.

He was cursing his hard luck as he mounted the stairs of his tenement, fists thrust into his pockets and eyes on the filthy treads. So great was his self-absorption that he failed to see the hand before it snaked out at the landing, grabbing his neck.

"You dirty little frog-spawn," the man muttered, his black eyes boring into Davey's choking face. "Thought you could nobble Jasper Horan, did ye? Take yer prize villains up the roof and diddle an honest man? A mate o' mine 'as been coshed in the head, and ain't likely to wake this side of Judgment. Murder's a hangin' offence, I'm told. I think I just caught me a murderer." He swung Davey hard against the cracked plaster wall, stunning him, then released his punishing grip on his throat. "Where've they got to? Yer lady doctor and her fancy man?"

"Dunno." Davey staggered, gasping.

Horan hunkered down on the landing beside him. "Tell me where they've gone, boy, or by all that's holy, I'll see you swing for my mate."

"I was never on the roof!"

"Sing it to the magistrate! Yer old whore of a mother might not care if you dance on the nubbing-cheat, but yer sister will. If she lives, that is. Last I saw, she were right poorly. Comes of poking around where ye didn't oughter."

Davey hurled himself without warning at Horan, his thin fingers clawing at the man's face, and with a cry of pain the watchman teetered back against the banister. Quick as lightning the boy darted down the stairs and out into the foggy dark, making once more for Covent Garden.

Horan let him go. He'd already found Button Nance and her girl — and knew all he needed to.

"Evening, Mr. Fitz — and a pleasure to see you again, miss, if I may be so bold," Gibbon said as he drew off Georgiana's wraps in Bedford Square. In all the confusion of her ravaged home, she hadn't bothered to change her twilled silk gown. The valet preserved a serene countenance; perhaps he was accustomed to ladies sporting muddy and torn attire.

"Have you anything for us to eat?" Fitzgerald inquired. "We're famished."

"Couple of nice soles and a brace of partridges in half an hour, with leg o' mutton to follow."

Fitzgerald glanced about at the tidied rooms. "Well done, lad. A glass of sherry for Miss Armistead, when you have a moment. She's chilled to the bone."

Georgiana was already standing before the roaring fire in the sitting room, her hands extended to the warmth. It was probable, Fitzgerald thought, that she had not yet accepted the necessity of flight; although she had a satchel of hastily-packed clothes, she had refused to bring her maid. If they were to flee London together, he would have to take care her reputation wasn't ruined.

She's safe enough with you, John Snow barked in his head; *you're old enough to be her father. Don't flatter yourself she's fighting shy of your Irish charm.*

"I'll need you to run an errand for me, Gibbon, when you've carved the mutton — and tell me: Have any shady characters come nosing about?"

"Couple of coves holding vigil over a nice bit o' fire in an ashcan," the valet returned promptly, "but they're beyond the square. Happened to clap eyes on 'em when I returned from the butcher."

137

"Did ye now?" The gate that barred traffic in Bedford Square was manned by a private watchman, and only known tradesmen and residents were admitted — but such watchmen could be easily suborned, in Fitzgerald's experience. He would have to look to the pair of strangers.

"I won't lie to you, my Gibbon," he said. "Miss Armistead and I have been set upon. A nasty scrap of it we had, but gave as good as we got. I'm thinking it's possible the same devils attacked Mr. Taylor in chambers this morning."

Gibbon halted on his way to the pantry, brow furrowed. "Then the murderin' louts will be disappointed, sir, for they shan't be admitted here." He drew a letter from a silver salver. "Speaking of Mr. Taylor, this come round from Great Ormond Street about an hour ago. Private messenger."

Fitzgerald took the envelope; the direction was penned in an unfamiliar handwriting.

"What is it?" Georgie asked as he entered the sitting room.

"A note from Sep's doctor." His eyes flicked up to meet hers. "The skull is fractured. But the sawbones says he's not without hope of eventual recovery —"

He broke off, crumpled the note in his fist, and tossed it into the flames. "God, I'm in want of a drink."

"Had the blow been going to kill Sep, it should probably have done so well before you even found him," she said gently. "He's fortunate you did."

"If the man dies, Georgie, I swear —"

"He will not die."

"If he dies," he repeated with sudden savagery, "that's two lives we put down to your German princeling's account. And by all that's merciful —"

"He's not *my* German princeling."

"— yours won't be the third life he takes."

Gibbon appeared in the doorway with sherry. Fitzgerald tossed off a glass, though he'd have preferred good Irish whiskey. He knew this feeling, as though the slightest pressure might cause him to snap; it invariably preceded one of his momentous rages.

She waited until the valet quitted the room to say, "I have decided to trust you, Patrick."

"You'll leave London tonight?"

"I will go to a hotel, if Gibbon will be so good as to secure me a room — and thence to my cousin's home in Hertfordshire. It is nearly Christmas, after all — I might spend the interval among family . . ." She broke off. "You do not look as though you approve! I thought you would pay me vast compliments, Patrick, on my humility and good sense!"

Abruptly, he set down his glass; the crystal clanged like a bell. "*Georgie* — Forgive me, darlin', but I cannot let you out of my sight. The key to this coil is in your hands — and if I'm to unravel it, you must help me."

"What do I know of Windsor that you do not? It was *you* the Queen summoned last night, Patrick."

"Those letters. Why should the thieves take *them,* above all else?"

She did not reply. There was mutiny in her looks, as though Fitzgerald had trespassed on private ground.

"You did not summon the police," he persisted, "though your house was robbed and your things were destroyed."

"Of course I did not inform the police." She said it scornfully. "You have yet to report the coachman's murder, though you fear murder was done."

She was too protective, too combative, for a woman whose home had been plundered. Jealousy flared in Fitzgerald's gut. "Were they von Stühlen's letters? Bound up in pink ribbon? Are you in love with the rogue, Georgiana?"

"How *dare* you," she retorted, her fists clenching. Her fine grey eyes sparked with sudden contempt.

"I *will* know," Fitzgerald said through his teeth.

"By what right? You don't *own* me, Patrick. You're not even my guardian! You're a man I keep about me on sufferance — to honour the wish of one who is dead. But if you try to *rule* me, so help me *God,* Patrick Fitzgerald —"

Her words cut as cleanly and deeply as one of her lancets. He wanted to cry out that he loved her, that he'd ever loved only her, that from the time she was a wee lass he'd watched her grow in strength and intellect and beauty as though she were meant only for him, for his arms and his bed and his delight — and now she had scorned him. *A man I keep about me on sufferance.* Why stay at heel then, tugging on her leash? — So that she could use his blind, dog-like devotion to keep other hunters at bay? His passion for her clouding his senses, while she pursued bigger game? Was she holding out for that dandyish German count to *marry her?*

She saw that he was stunned. A ready flush suffused her delicate skin and for an instant, remorse flooded her eyes. But she did not run to him, as she might have done at seventeen. She merely bit her lip and clasped her arms under her breasts, as though suddenly chilled.

"I did not mean that. Patrick — I should not have said such ugly things. You have been my dearest friend, my dearest . . ."

"Slave."

Her lips compressed. "I am sorry. What I said was unforgivable. It is just that you *assume* a *right* —"

"— I have no right to assume," he finished. "Granted. It's become a habit in me to offer advice — though the Lord knows you never take it. But as a lawyer, my fine girl, I'd say those letters were stolen for one of two reasons. To be destroyed, by one who fears them — or used, by a canny blackmailer. Which are we to expect in the coming days?"

She studied his angry face, the self-control he was barely managing. Fitzgerald could see her striving for balance: so much weight of argument on this side, so much on that. *The scales of justice.*

"Very well," she said at last. "I will tell you. The stolen letters were written by the Prince Consort. You understand now my reticence. I would not expose His Royal Highness to the impertinence of strangers if he lived — and shall never do so, now that he is dead."

"I'm afraid," Fitzgerald returned with bitter irony, "the time for discretion is over. Your letters are gone. You can no more conceal their existence now than you can raise Albert from the grave."

They stood for a moment in utter silence, Georgie's hands defiantly on her hips, as though she intended to do battle. The enemy, however, was beyond her reach. Fitzgerald had no intention of serving as proxy.

"Is there scandal in the letters?" he demanded. "Is that why a body went the length of stealing them?"

"Scandal? They were almost entirely about the nature of the London poor!"

Fitzgerald made a sharp sound of annoyance, unable to believe her, and threw up his hands.

"Prince Albert honoured me," she said with difficulty, "by soliciting my opinions on a range of subjects. The condition of housing, for example — he had designed a model tenement himself, for the use of charitable organizations. Or reform of the waterworks, and the construction of Mr. Bazalgette's new system of sewers — you will have seen the works of the tunnels presently being undertaken . . . the Middle Levels near Piccadilly are actually complete. I toured them in the Consort's party only a few weeks ago —"

"Sewers," Fitzgerald repeated sardonically.

"They are *vitally important,* Patrick," she persisted. "Recollect that Uncle John established that the transmission of cholera is through tainted water; indeed, were it not for his researches, I am sure Bazalgette should never have been commissioned to embark on this massive reform — or at least, not in my lifetime. It requires an Englishman to fear for his life before he will consider of his drains. Prince Albert wished me to consult with Mr. Bazalgette regarding the sewers' outfall. They are far down the Thames, almost to the sea, where the chance of contamination with drinking water must be minimal. The various London waterworks are also undertaking programs of filtration, which should go far in improving public health."

"Your Prince cared about public health?"

"He was intelligent enough to know the Crown would pay for trouble, soon or late," she returned crisply. "Better sewers now, than an epidemic later. And water hit home — Buckingham Palace, to my knowledge, has some of the very worst in the city. And Windsor's drains are not to be spoken of. It is no wonder that he died of typhoid fever — it, too, is a disease of fouled water. Poor man."

"Did the Prince seem ill, when you toured the Middle Levels?"

She considered an instant. "I didn't notice. Not that afternoon — there was too much to be viewed and decided. And I am never entirely at my ease, you know, in such a company of gentlemen — all of them distinguished in some field or another, and drawn to the Consort because of his power. Only *he* accorded me the kindness of listening to my observations — and because he did so, Bazalgette was forced to attend. I wonder how many of them believed me to be Albert's paramour?" she added on a note of bitterness.

"And were you?"

He had not been able to stop himself; he needed to know the answer too badly.

She turned and stared at him. "I should strike you for such a question, Patrick."

"You should strike me for any number of reasons, Georgie — but not my frankness. Look you, there's never been a breath of scandal about Albert and the ladies, but you'll admit it's dodgy business to be adding a girl like yourself to a company of engineers! I never met the man. I want to know how deeply he went with you. How much pain his death has caused."

She drew a shaky breath. "One need not have . . . intimate relations with a gentleman . . . to mourn his loss."

"No." Fitzgerald rubbed his hand over his eyes. Why hate a dead man so much? It was he, Fitzgerald, who was dining with her, after all. But Georgie's voice, whenever she spoke of Albert, was taut with respect. And something else. Was it *yearning?*

"So he looked well," Fitzgerald said with effort. "And yet, a few weeks later —"

"I did not say he looked well," she broke in quickly. "Indeed, I do not think he has been in health for some months. That particular afternoon I should describe him as preoccupied. He listened to Bazalgette — he asked all the appropriate questions — but there was no Albert in his eyes."

Fitzgerald snorted.

"It was an art he perfected, Patrick — a sort of inward flight. How do you think the man endured twenty years in this country else? A foreigner — and from that Germany which so many English despise — a person compelled by social reform and the advancement of science, rather than his own gain. He was inexplicable to most of those he met."

"But not to you," he countered. "That was a bond between you, wasn't it — being out of step with your peculiar worlds? You have your own form of inner flight, love."

"Perhaps. I may say that the Prince was never truly at ease with women."

"No?" Too much hope in his voice.

"Females made him acutely uncomfortable. He had a horror of impropriety; and he seemed to consider it a woman's disease. I suspect he regarded me as he did his daughters — intelligent, and safe."

Fitzgerald flushed; he'd caught the echo of regret in her voice. She'd have preferred to be dangerous.

"Patrick — if I thought the correspondence between us should be publicly exposed — and by some mischance *diminish* the Prince's reputation in the eyes of the world — I should . . . I should . . ." Her fists were clenched again, and a storm of futile anger swept over her face.

"It may not be the Prince those thieves thought to strike at, love," he said wearily. "*You* may be the one they intend to harm."

She frowned. "What can you mean?"

"Revenge."

She was very still for a moment. "Von Stühlen. You believe he paid for the ransacking of my house? He *does* hate me. I humili-

147

ated him too publicly."

"You'd have done better to slap him, that morning at Ascot."

"But to laugh was irresistible." She began to pace before the fire, her lips working. "My God, Patrick — if von Stühlen should presume to attack Albert publicly — one of the Consort's oldest friends — and at *such* a time —"

He noticed that she cared nothing, in that instant, for her own reputation.

"What else did Albert write, in his bit letters?"

There was a pause; in the silence he caught the soft thud of coals dropping from the grate, and the discreet clink of cutlery from the dining room.

"What was written, was written in confidence —"

"Aye! And now the letters have been stolen, the whole world may soon read them!"

She met his eyes frankly. "He consulted me about his son. Prince Leopold."

Fitzgerald was about to speak when the front bell rang through the rooms. Both of them froze.

"News of Septimus?"

There was a murmur of conversation from the front passage; then Gibbon appeared at

148

the parlour door.

"A letter for miss," he said. "Sent round from Russell Square. I've told the man to wait."

She tore open the flap and read the brief message.

Fitzgerald watched her colour drain. "Georgie?"

She looked up. "It's that girl in St. Giles. *Lizzie.* She died an hour ago."

CHAPTER SEVENTEEN

"I've decided the funeral shall be on the twenty-third of December," Bertie said diffidently, "so as to salvage something of Christmas. Mama does not attend — she goes to Osborne in four days."

"And I shall have to go with her." Alice kept her head bent over her needlework, aware of a creeping sense of oppression. "*Christmas!* I have not the heart for it. Mama will shut herself in her rooms, and stare at the sea. There is nothing so wretched as Osborne in winter. You'll return to Cambridge, of course?"

"On Christmas Eve. The funeral party shall be entirely gentlemen. The service here in the Chapel Royal. No public parades, no scenes about the cortege to remind one of Wellington —"

"No. Mama would not have it. She abhors such display."

"Mama hasn't said a word about the arrangements," Bertie mused. "She left everything to me — though she refuses to speak directly, or remain in any room I enter. It's almost more than one can bear, her stony looks. Her contempt for one."

Alice measured her brother obliquely, her needle moving in and out of the square of canvas. His gaze was fixed on the coal fire that warmed her private apartments, and one elegant boot rested on the fender. At age twenty — indulged, protected, heir to the greatest Kingdom on earth — Bertie should be the picture of ease. But Alice felt his agitation like a powerful draught sweeping through the room. His pallor was dreadful. Deep shadows welled at his eyes. He hadn't slept since well before Papa's death last night.

"If Eliza treats you thus," she said, using their private name for Mama, "you owe her nothing now. To be *free*, Bertie!"

"I shall never be free." He fidgeted with his watch chain. "Never again. I thought, when I was in Curragh — and on my tour of North America — but all that is at an end. We cannot expect her to long survive our father. I must prepare for a higher duty."

"Mama always defies expectation. Indeed, I believe she *prefers* to dash all one's hopes."

"Hopes! I did not mean to say I *wished*

her in the grave —"

"Of course not. To wish such a thing would be fatal. She would endure another forty years."

"I think Eliza is terrified of death," Bertie said unexpectedly, "with a fear that is quite pagan. The Lord Chamberlain took a mask of Papa this morning and Mama refuses to look at it. Of course, she can't bear to have it destroyed — that would do violence to Papa, or perhaps to his memory. So I suppose she'll end by shelving it in a storeroom somewhere, for future Windsorites to discover amidst the rest of the cast-off lumber. Rather pathetic, really."

"Eliza confused the mask for the man."

"What do you mean?" His slightly protuberant eyes — so like Mama's — studied her acutely.

"She deals with the surface of things. As though the world went no deeper than her mirror. Papa has been ill for months, Bertie. She would not see it."

"Months! Surely not! Clark told me he suffered from a low fever — a severe chill, taken when he . . . when *we* walked out together in Cambridge a few weeks ago."

"And Jenner calls it typhoid. But typhoid is contagious and nobody else in Windsor has contracted it. I nursed Papa myself for much of the past fortnight — and I am perfectly well."

"Perhaps you're stronger than we guessed. Or he was weaker than I knew."

Alice raised her head from her needlework and regarded her brother. "You didn't kill him, Bertie."

He started, as though she'd read his mind. "Of course not. How absurd! I've a few years to go yet, Alice, before I regard myself as God."

"They blame you for Papa's death — Dr. Clark, that unspeakable Jenner, Eliza. I'm well aware how they've made you suffer. It's nonsense. Papa did not die because you lost your way for hours in the rain, that day in Cambridge. And he did not die because you took an actress to bed and broke his heart."

The boot was pulled abruptly from the brass fender. "I didn't know you were aware of . . . Miss Clifden."

"I had the story from Vicky. In strictest confidence, of course. Apparently rumours reached the Berlin newspapers. She says you'll never get a German princess to marry you, now."

"Thank God for that." Bertie smiled faintly. "Papa assured me it was only a matter of time before I was notorious throughout Europe. The visions he painted! My

153

bastard children. My appearance in court, to answer the charge of paternity. The sensation in the press. The shame and infamy I would visit upon Mama. He could not speak enough about it, though I begged him to desist — though I assured him I had broken entirely with the lady . . ."

"Is Miss Clifden a lady, Bertie?"

"Not in the least," he retorted, "but she was very good fun all the same, and a delightful change from tedious old Bruce and my tutors."

General Bruce served rather ineffectually as Bertie's governor at Cambridge; but the Prince of Wales, deplored by both his parents for laziness, stupidity, frivolity, and a host of other crimes, had long since learned to outmaneuver his watchdogs.

"Say what you like, Alice — my indiscretion cut up the old man's peace quite dreadfully. I've never seen him in such a taking as he was that day in Cambridge." Bertie inserted a finger in his cravat, loosening the choking folds. "Papa actually said that no good could be expected of me, given the *bad blood* that ran through my veins. Conceive of it! The insult to himself — not to mention Mama!"

"Bad blood?" Alice half-rose from her chair, the needle pricking her thigh. "He

154

said that? *Bad blood?*"

"My death — no, my public *hanging* — would have been preferable to such a disgrace! You'd think nobody'd ever taken a tumble with a girl before! Why —"

"Bertie," Alice interrupted, "what exactly did Papa say to you? *Your* blood is *mine,* after all!"

Bertie blinked at her. "It was while we were lost in the rain, and I put it down to exhaustion. He didn't make a great deal of sense, actually. He muttered to himself, like a sick man raving. *Your bad blood to usurp the sacred throne of England.* I suspect he regarded poor Nelly as a kind of contamination."

"Raving," Alice repeated. "Yes, that's how he seemed — wandering in his reason. Shall I tell you what he said to *me,* Bertie, at the end?"

Her brother sank onto the arm of her chair and regarded her steadily.

"He murmured quite low in my ear. *You cannot marry Louis, Liebchen. You cannot deceive him so. The flaw in your blood —*"

"You?" Bertie repeated. "But that's absurd. You've never enjoyed the mildest *flirtation,* Alice, much less a tumble."

"I know." She stared down at her hands. "His words have haunted me, Bertie. To

155

know that he went to his death believing me *unworthy* . . ."

"Never." Her brother uttered the word with the force of a curse. "You misunderstood him, that's all."

"I didn't! I know what he said."

"You misunderstood him." The Prince of Wales rose abruptly, and strode to the door. "There's enough guilt in this poisonous place to drive us all mad, Alice. Don't invent more for yourself. Let Papa go. Marry Louis. For God's sake — *be happy.* I'd like to think that one of us is."

Chapter Eighteen

"She is an abortionist," von Stühlen said as he stood at his ease before the Red Room fire this evening.

I consented to receive him despite a general prohibition on visitors at Windsor. Dismissed my ladies and servants, so that we might be entirely frank. Such an intimate acquaintance of Albert's, a schoolfellow from Bonn and the dear days that are gone, could hardly be denied, regardless of how much I craved privacy in my grief. To see von Stühlen again is to recall a thousand painful moments to mind — his tall form beside my darling's as they carried in the evergreens, at Christmastime; his clear voice joined with Albert's in the singing of the German *Lieder,* of an evening at Balmoral or Osborne; his patient handling of Lenchen — my daughter Helena — as she schooled her first mount over a series of jumps. He is a beautiful figure of a man, of course — but beyond his personal charm, displays a steadiness of purpose, a degree of self-command, that must always win approbation. Albert regarded von Stühlen as almost another brother — so closely were they allied in temperament; and if I was a *little excluded* by the depth of their friendship, I do not regard it. I have an idea of the abyss of grief the unfortunate man must now suffer.

But he had introduced a subject I understood not at all.

"*Who* is an abortionist?" I asked him. "And what lapse of decency urged you to *mention* so unspeakable a horror? We have borne nine children, Count!"

I pressed a square of linen to my lips; von Stühlen bowed.

"I must beg Your Majesty's forgiveness. Necessity urged the disclosure; I speak of Miss Georgiana Armistead — the young woman who styles herself a doctor."

His words *must* lash my heart, though I cannot pretend to surprise — the basest of evils must be commonplace to Miss Armistead, who has so divorced herself from woman's nature. But I would not betray the degree of my interest to von Stühlen.

"And of what possible concern is Miss Armistead to us, Count?"

158

He affected an air of easy amusement. "I had thought that quite obvious, Your Majesty. Miss Armistead was with Fitzgerald last night on the Heath."

I lifted my shoulders a little in disdain, and made as if to turn the subject. "We hope that you signed Albert's Visitors Book when you entered the Castle."

He looked all his confusion. "I am afraid — that is, I did not presume . . ."

"But you *must!*" I cried. "We have said that *everything* is to be kept as usual — all his dear personal effects, his clothes and brushes, his hot water for shaving. The linens are to be changed every day, and his chamber pot scrubbed. The Blue Room — where that Angelic Being breathed his last — is not to be a *Sterbezimmer,* a death chamber; but a sacred place, with pictures, and his bust, and perhaps a display of china . . . We might work there, from time to time, and feel his dear presence."

"No doubt that is as he would wish." The Count looked a little troubled, as though by invoking my Beloved I had recalled his mind to sorrow. He inclined his head. "But I was speaking of Georgiana Armistead."

"Were you, indeed?" I adjusted a Dresden figure on the mantel; a dying stag, beautifully fashioned. Have I mentioned that Albert was an accomplished sportsman? He formed the habit, in his Coburg youth, of attending *grandes battues,* in which an extraordinary quantity of game are driven by beaters into an enclosure and there slaughtered at will by the gentlemen. It is a nauseating sight, and one I endured on few occasions, but I learned its essential lesson: Animals destined from birth to serve as prey for their masters are easily led, and led most often to their doom.

"She could be arrested on the strength of the word alone," von Stühlen persisted. "But the unfortunate girl Miss Armistead quacked this morning has died of her injuries, and that deepens the magnitude of the crime — to one of murder."

"*Double* murder," I corrected. "You are forgetting the innocent babe that woman cut from its mother."

"Of course."

I caressed the stag. So smooth, the porcelain, it might have been my darling's thigh. "We do not know what you are thinking of, Count," I said fretfully. "You used the word *arrest.* However great the enormities committed by this . . . creature . . . we cannot allow her to be subjected to the scrutiny of the courts. Much less the Metropolitan Police. Such eventualities would be *most* undesirable. She is, by all accounts, not unintelligent — and we cannot rely upon her *discretion*. No — it is in every regard *unthinkable* that she should be pursued by so public a force as the Law."

"She might indeed talk — and Your Majesty is afraid of what she might say. . . ."

There was a quality in his voice that surprised me — a quality I could not like.

"One of my people searched Miss Armistead's lodgings this morning," he persisted.

"They had better have been in church," I returned tartly, "to pray for the repose of Prince Albert's soul."

"They found a surprising quantity of papers in her study."

"A *lady* does not possess a study."

"— Letters of business, and correspondence with men of science. Apparently she even presumed to share her views with *Royalty.*"

A vise closed around my heart. That firm, sloping hand I had consigned to the flames — the false propriety of her address — the hideous things she had disclosed to my Beloved, and the irreparable damage she had done to his Reason . . . "Impossible! You forget yourself, Count."

My darling's oldest friend drew a folded sheet of paper from his coat, and commenced to recite.

"My esteemed Miss Armistead: Pray allow me to assure you how greatly I enjoyed our conversations regarding housing
for the poor, and how deeply I value your
approval of my own poor contributions to
that realm . . ."

"Give me that paper at once!" I cried.

He eyed me satirically, the letter firmly in
his grasp. Can I ever have committed the
mistake of believing him handsome? Of
believing him a paragon of our age?

"I am in possession of a number of such
billets-doux," he murmured gently. "A correspondence spanning years — on all manner of subjects. Most of them insufferably
dull. I shall not trifle with Your Majesty's
patience by reading them: water quality,
epidemic illness, the management of charitable relief . . . but I am hopeful of discover-
ing more *intimate* views. Only one doubt as-
sails me, and I must put it frankly to Your
Majesty. How is the public likely to regard
our dear departed Albert, if his . . . *interest*
in a lady not his wife . . . were to be generally known . . . ?"

"You can say this," I faltered, "knowing
how that Angelic Being *loved* you?"

162

The dying stag trembled under my hand, and fell to the floor. Quite smashed. The jagged fragments glittered like knives in the firelight. All the knives were drawn out, on every side and by every hand; I kicked them away with my boot.

"My loyalty to Albert was of a different order from yours," he told me quietly, his visage dreadfully white; "I will not speak of it here. The problem of the letters is otherwise. Let us call it Albert's legacy to his old friend . . . he certainly bequeathed me nothing else . . ."

"I wonder you *dare* to speak his name."

"Your Majesty ought to thank Providence that these letters came to *me*," he cut in, suddenly harsh. "Had they been left to unreliable hands — Miss Armistead's, or Fitzgerald's — every sort of scandal might be expected. The question remains, however: *What is to be done with them?*"

"A true friend would have burned them long since." I said it with contempt. "That you have failed to do so — that you prefer to tease and bait us — suggests that you are our *enemy*, Count."

"My devotion was to Albert," he retorted. "But unlike him, I did not abandon my birthright to grovel at the foot of a foreign power. Poor Albert expired, worn out by his

163

service; I owe Your Majesty *nothing.*"

His peculiar emphasis did not escape me. I had long suspected the jeering ridicule of Albert's German coterie — I knew the coarse nature of their remarks.

I strode in a rustle of bombazine to the Red Room door. The blackguard called after me.

"I take it, then, that I may sell these letters to the *Morning Post?*"

I was tempted to tell him, as Wellington once urged a slighted mistress, to *Publish and be damned* — but the potential harm to the Kingdom stopped the words in my mouth. "Stay — You know that I may better the papers' price."

He inclined his head.

He *nodded,* when any other man would have been on his knees before his widowed and sorrowing Queen.

"I shall offer them to the highest bidder for publication, solely as a last resort — and only then if I am convinced that Your Majesty has no regard for Albert's memory."

I pressed my back to the door and stared at him. "Very well. And how must I demonstrate my regard, Count?"

"You might reward *mine.*" He smiled. "An English peerage. An estate and a sinecure, with an adequate income — let us say, of ten thousand pounds per annum?"

My throat constricted with rage and grief. "So little!"

"I have never been an unreasonable man."

I laughed — and felt immediately overcome by a remorse so profound it almost undid me. That I should *laugh,* when that dear form lay, cold and unresponsive, in the Blue Room; that the sound of mirth, however bitter, should resound within these walls! Even *I* am capable, it seems, of the rankest betrayal . . .

My fingers remained frozen on the door handle. If only my darling were present to advise me! That this man he had loved like a brother should blackmail me in my grief —

Von Stühlen waited, as patient as Death.

CHAPTER NINETEEN

"I must go to St. Giles," Georgiana said frantically. "Where is my wrap?"

"But you haven't eaten!" Fitzgerald protested. "There's nothing more you can do for Lizzie — she's gone, Georgiana. She's *gone.*"

"I might examine her." She moved swiftly to the hall. "Certify the death. It's the least I can do — having failed to save her life."

The bitterness in the words chastened him. "You mustn't blame yourself, lass. She was *exceedingly ill.*"

Georgie stopped short, her bag in her hands. "Who else am I to blame? Do you seriously imagine that Uncle John ever lost a patient?"

"O'course he did!"

"Not within my knowledge! And I have so few patients as it is —" She swallowed convulsively. "Only the desperate are willing to trust a woman doctor. And when I fail, I am judged far more severely than a man should be."

"You judge *yourself* too harsh, surely?"

"Patrick — that girl was fourteen! She had her whole life before her."

"And what a life it was! She was on the brink of death when you went to her — and not because of anything you did."

"How *dare* you?" she flashed. "How dare you presume to suggest that Lizzie, being only a girl of the streets, is better off dead? Oh, God, when I see the mess men make of the world! — Pray make my excuses to Gibbon, Patrick."

"Wait," he ordered, as she grasped the doorknob. "I'll fetch a cab."

He hastened into the scullery.

"Gibbon, Miss Armistead has been called out to a patient. The hour grows late, and I must ask you to ready the *Dauntless.*"

"The *Dauntless,*" the valet repeated. "Where bound, on such a miserable night?"

"Sheppey. We'll meet you at Paul's Wharf no later than half ten. Bring a carpetbag with everything I'll need for Shurland, there's a good lad."

"You're never taking that lady to Shurland Hall, Mr. Fitz!" Gibbon burst out, shocked.

"I must. It's the very last place anyone will look. Eat the dinner yourself, like a

167

good chap."

"I wish I'd never followed you onto that roof," Georgiana muttered as he settled her in the hansom a quarter-hour later. "If I'd spent more time with Lizzie — If I'd made certain the sutures were properly set —"

"You did your best, Georgie; the girl didn't die at your hands."

"No. She died for lack of them."

He could feel her seething beside him as the horse put its head down into the sleet, and turned toward Seven Dials.

"Tell me about the Prince's boy," he commanded. "Must be full young; I've never seen so much as a picture of the lad."

"Yes . . ." She marshaled her thoughts, recalled from some distant place. "He is perhaps eight years old — the youngest but one of the Royal children."

"Very well. And the Consort consulted you because . . . ?"

"Uncle John was present at Leopold's birth."

Memory dawned. "The famous anaesthesia! John *did* set the cat among the pigeons when he exposed the Queen to mortal risk, and all for the sake of a trifling bout of labour."

"Yes. There were those who maintained

that an eighth lying-in could never be so troublesome as to warrant the attendance of even a *doctor,* let alone such extraordinary measures as Prince Albert employed. Anaesthesia! When the monarch might die under its influence! The Consort — and Uncle John — should have been accused of murder, if Victoria had slipped away. But she did not: and was indeed so bewitched by the effects of chloroform that she demanded its use in her final accouchement — with Princess Beatrice."

"And the Consort thought of you — ?"

"Perhaps a year since. More — eighteen months, I should guess. He wished to know whether Prince Leopold would ever outgrow his present indisposition."

"What's wrong with the child, then?"

"A frailty in the tissues of the skin, which causes them to fray and bleed, almost without ceasing. The poor little fellow is as delicate as a piece of china."

Fitzgerald frowned. "That's right ghastly. Why have I never heard word of it?"

"The boy's condition is not generally known."

"Then how were you expected to offer an opinion? You've not seen the lad?"

"Indeed I have. Prince Albert sent Leopold to Russell Square in the care of his governor, the day after I had his letter." Georgiana glanced sideways at Fitzgerald in the darkness; her words were visible as chilled smoke. "Highly singular behaviour on the Consort's part, I admit. The boy has been in the care of a stable's worth of doctors from the time he was born. I must impute the Prince's decision to the degree of anxiety concerning the boy's health."

"And what did you conclude?"

"Nothing very extraordinary. When I examined the child, his knees were swollen and discoloured from the blood that seeps into his joints. He cannot often walk without the aid of a cane — and the usual romping of an eight-year-old is entirely forbidden to him. The slightest bruise or fall may send him to bed for weeks. I gather that the pain at times is excruciating."

Fitzgerald pulled his hat from his head and rubbed ineffectually at his temples. "But why did the Prince consult *you,* Georgie? You've no authority on such stuff, surely?"

She hesitated, unwilling to admit incompetence. "Because of Uncle John. The Prince was a great believer in science — and you know that Uncle regarded statistics, the data associated with all manner of disease, as the key to its explication. The Prince assumed that I am blessed with a similar genius."

The hansom clattered over the paving stones of Tottenham Court Road, heading south. "And what did you tell His Royal Highness?"

"— That statistically speaking, such illnesses are quite often found among *multiple members* of families. There may be a record of the progression of disease through generations. I suggested the Consort might wish to consult the Royal genealogies, in order to apprehend the progression of Leopold's illness. I then informed him that Uncle John had taken certain notes — conducted private researches — after having witnessed the child's birth in '53 . . ."

That was Snow's habit. The man scribbled lectures to himself during the course of every day — essays on future endeavours, a lifetime of possible projects carefully collated in a series of notebooks. Until he ran out of time to live.

"Prince Albert asked to see Uncle's notes," Georgie said.

"He's a braver man than I. John's fist was impossible to read."

"I sent them by messenger to Buckingham Palace. They were not returned. A letter, excessive in its politeness, informed me that the Prince had thought it advisable the notes be burnt."

"The rogue! Infernal cheek!"

"He then departed with the Queen for an extended visit to the Princess Royal in Berlin, and his brother in Coburg. You will recall the period — he had an unfortunate accident there, much publicised in the newspapers."

September 1860, Fitzgerald remembered: an overturned carriage — the Royal Family abroad. "But, Georgie, love — to burn John's private notations? What right —"

"I have a copy of them, somewhere in the ruin of my library."

Fitzgerald gave a bark of laughter. "So you expected the Prince to destroy the originals?"

"No. Over the past several years I undertook to set in order all of Uncle's writings, with a view to eventual publication — I thought it only proper, for the future of science. But there is a great number of notebooks still to be got through, I'm afraid. I have not had sufficient time —"

"Never mind that, now. What did himself observe at Prince Leo's birth?"

She clasped her gloved hands together. "He wrote about the chloroform first. The Queen's spirits and health are profoundly deranged by pregnancy, Patrick, and the Consort wished to spare her as much distress as possible — that was why Uncle was called in. April 7, 1853. A year before the Great Cholera Epidemic; five years before Uncle's death."

"And the labour went well. But the child?"

"There were any number of doctors and personages in attendance — but Uncle John was the first to notice Leopold's peculiarity. When the umbilical cord was severed, *it would not stop bleeding.*"

"And that is unusual?"

"It is potentially fatal, Patrick! Perhaps two minutes should have sufficed for the flow to cease. The cord withers over a matter of days, and the stump falls off. But from Uncle's notes, it appears that Leopold oozed blood from the abdomen — that the wound refused to heal — for nearly a month. His christening was postponed. The registration of his birth was delayed. The Queen — who is always wretchedly despondent after her confinements — kept to her rooms. And the Royal Physician — Sir James Clark, who has served Victoria from the first day of her ascension — privately declared Uncle John's chloroform to be the cause."

"Men have committed suicide for less,"

he observed.

She laughed; they both knew John Snow would never have killed himself over a rival's rumour. "Uncle told Prince Albert that some flaw in the child's blood vessels, perhaps, produced the painful result. He embarked on research — but so little has been published in this country regarding the malady. He learned of *German* families where it recurs from generation to genera-tion — and solely, it seems, among *males.* Indeed, Leopold's disorder is sometimes called 'the German disease.' "

"Then the Consort's to blame for his son's illness? Poor wretch."

"There's no lack of German blood in the Royal line," Georgie said impatiently. "In-deed, there is little else. But Uncle John could not discover a disorder similar to Le-opold's in any of his Hanoverian ancestors — nor among the Saxe-Coburgs, either."

"But if Leopold has been ill from birth, why should his father demand John's notes *then* — and destroy them?"

"He must have regarded them as danger-ous," Georgie said simply. "To the child, or . . . others."

She did not need to say *Victoria.* Fitzger-ald was silent a moment. "What did you tell your Prince, once you knew he'd burned

John's papers?"

"That if Leopold could not be cured, the boy would certainly die. I said it was imperative that the Consort make inquiries in Germany, if need be — that he canvass his relations in Saxe-Coburg — that he move heaven and earth to learn more of his son's illness. That was a year ago. This September, the Prince hired a young German doctor by the name of Gunther — and sent him to the south of France, with Leopold, *for the boy's health.*"

"You think he'd heard of a cure there?"

"Perhaps. Patrick —" She reached for his hand and clasped it. "Having told you everything, I still understand nothing."

"Not to worry, me darlin'," he said, with a conviction he did not feel. "We'll work it out together."

They had arrived in St. Giles.

Button Nance's rooms were cold, and the little girls were curled together near the dead hearth. They stared at Georgiana when she opened the unlatched door, but did not speak a word, their great eyes shining faintly in the gaslight from the street below. The acrid odour of wet charcoal lingered in the closed air of the room, a gutter perfume.

There was no sign, Fitzgerald noticed, of Davey.

"It is all right," Georgie said carefully as she entered. "I've come to see Lizzie."

"A deal of folk've come to see Lizzie," one of the girls said in a paper-thin whisper. "But Lizzie's dead."

"Where is your mother?"

"Gone t'pub."

Georgie hesitated, then moved softly toward the inner room.

The cold in the bedroom was bitter as a tomb. One of the windows had been left open, and a sulfurous fog wafted about the head of the dead girl like an emissary from Hell, waiting to snatch what remained of her. The delicate hands were raised on either side of her head, fists clenched as though in agony; but Lizzie's face, Fitzgerald saw, was wiped clean of both pain and hope, and the eyes stared blankly at the grimy ceiling.

A pillow lay beside the bed, on the bare floor. Without thinking, he picked it up.

Georgiana examined the body, and finally, with a sigh, closed Lizzie's eyes.

"I don't understand it," she said. "There is no visible sign on the face or limbs of what killed her. But look at her hands! It is as though she died in a convulsive fit."

"Perhaps she did. You said she suffered from a poisoning of the blood."

"Yes — but you can see from the clarity of the tissues around the nose and mouth that the fever had subsided at the last. She did not die in delirium. Indeed, I should have said she was *improving* — but for the fact that her heart has stopped."

"I'm that sorry, Georgie." Fitzgerald's fingers kneaded the goosedown pillow uselessly. "Do you trust this Button Nance with a certificate? Or should we knock up the coroner and trust it to him?"

"Where did you find that?" she demanded suddenly.

"Find what?"

"That pillow!"

Fitzgerald glanced down. "Sure, and it was on the floor."

"Not this morning."

There was a quality to Georgie's voice that raised the hair on his neck. "What would you mean?"

"I mean," she replied deliberately, "that nothing clean or fine has ever been found in these rooms."

"So it was brought here by someone else? And what of that? The child said they've had a deal of folk in to see Lizzie."

"After she died — or while she was yet

177

living?" With an expression of distaste, Georgiana reached for the pillow. "Patrick — look at her hands."

As he watched, Georgie lowered the thing gently over Lizzie's head. It rested perfectly on her balled fists.

"She fought him as he smothered her," she whispered, "but he was too strong —"

"Do you accept, finally, that you're as much at risk as I am?" he asked as they climbed back into the waiting cab.

"What of that?" she demanded contemptuously. "It is Lizzie, poor child, who has paid for my sins — whatever they might be. Can you explain, Patrick, why it is invariably the innocent poor who suffer in this world of ours?"

"Because they've nobody to protect them. Will you leave London with me now, Georgie?"

"I must."

Fitzgerald rapped on the hansom's roof. "Paul's Wharf. And quickly."

"A boat, Patrick? At this hour of the night?"

"We shan't go far. Just down the Thames, past Sheerness."

"Sheerness!"

He glanced at her, his expression curiously

closed. "I'm taking you to the Isle of Sheppey. It's a lonely place, but safe with it. You did *promise* to trust me."

"But we shan't reach it until midnight! Who will receive us at such an hour?"

"My wife," he said.

CHAPTER TWENTY

After Bertie left her, Alice spent an hour in the nursery reading to her little sisters. Louise, who was thirteen and considered artistic, looked drawn and frightened; she held her sketch book in her lap, staring at the blank pages. Helena, two years older, could not stop crying. But Beatrice was unquenchable — at four, the utter absolutes of loss escaped her. She was unlikely to miss Papa for long; there had been periods in her brief life when their paths crossed only once in three months. The Consort's duties had been that consuming.

Now Alice was undressing before bed. She had spent a dreary evening perusing one of Mama's volumes of sacred sermons, her usual duty on Sunday, and sought her bedchamber early, from a deep desire to end the hideous day. Violet, her maid, was respectfully silent as she removed the pins from Alice's hair — a girl who chattered thoughtlessly at most times, on every subject appropriate or scandalous. The maid's eyes were red from sympathetic weeping.

Alice studied her own reflection in the mirror. Black clothes brought out the sallowness of her skin. They deepened the charcoal shadows beneath her eyes; deep lines ran from her nose to the corners of her mouth, as though she had endured starvation or terror. Bertie had probably ascribed her dreadful looks to the sleepless nights she'd devoted to Papa's final illness. She hoped Mama would do the same. She did not want anyone to suspect she harboured a guilty secret. She was unequal to the forms of torture that might be applied to win the truth.

"Violet," she said slowly. "May I trust you with a particular service? One that is *quite private* — that you must not breathe to *anyone?*"

The maid's warm brown eyes widened avidly. "Of course, Your Highness! I shan't breathe a word — cross my heart and hope to be struck dead if I'm a liar!"

"See that this letter is collected with tomorrow's post." She slipped a common white envelope into Violet's hand. "I do not wish it to be known as *mine.* If anyone chances to observe you — destroy it."

■ ■ ■ ■

They made landfall south of Eastchurch, on the Isle of Sheppey, at twenty minutes past eleven o'clock by Gibbon's watch.

It was a tedious journey down the Thames, in a trim little steamer Fitzgerald kept moored at Paul's Wharf: past the looming ships of Her Majesty's fleet anchored off Greenwich, past Gravesend and through the mouth of the Thames Estuary, Fitzgerald shoveling coal into the raging gullet of the boiler while Gibbon steered and Georgiana shivered and dozed.

"Why a steamer, Patrick?" she murmured.

"Because the trains'll be watched."

"You regard von Stühlen as clairvoyant, then?"

"I regard him, love, as deadly."

From the estuary they might have turned north, toward Sheerness, the great naval port that sat at the northwestern end of Sheppey; but Gibbon knew his master's mind, and pulled the *Dauntless*'s wheel hard to starboard, sending the little boat into the Swale, a brackish channel that ran between the island and the northern coast of Kent. A slight chop, and sand banks numerous — Sheppey being famous for its wrecks — so that Fitzgerald sent Gibbon aft and took the wheel himself. He had known the Swale well in happier times.

Five miles along the winding coast they turned to port. They entered a creek that cut through the marshes, moving so slowly now they might as well have cut the engine entirely. Georgiana woke and took up a position on the starboard side, alert to snagging weeds and the narrowing of the creek bed.

"Black as Satan's bottom," Gibbon snorted, "and miasmic as only the sheep marshes can be. You'll have to walk a bit, miss, and the ground's boggy underfoot. But there will be a fire at the end of it, and hot soup if we're blessed."

"I must look dreadful," she said wearily. "To think that I should be presented to Mrs. Fitzgerald in such a case! And how will I explain — ?"

Gibbon glanced at her, then at the governor's back. Unlikely that Fitzgerald could hear them over the throb of the engine, and his attention was claimed entirely by the black water in front of him. "It's not likely she'll be awake at this hour," he answered, "so don't give it no mind. The companion as lives with her is French — with no cause to look askance at any lady's dress or manner, if you take my meaning."

Hard to judge from Georgiana's expression whether she was comforted or not. Gibbon was uneasy. He disliked the Isle of Sheppey and everyone on it. He would have shielded Miss if he could — urged Mr. Fitz to seek an inn at Queenborough, or turn toward Margate and avoid the island altogether. But worse trials than Shurland Hall lay before them in the coming days, and Lady Maude would hardly betray them. Shurland was the one place on the Channel coast they could be certain of refuge.

Except for young Theo, Gibbon thought grimly. He wondered if Mr. Fitz had considered that sprig of fashion when he made his plans. Then the boat squelched on the marshy bottom and the chug of the engine died. Fitzgerald drew a shuddering sigh — whether from relief or dread of the coming encounter, Gibbon could not say. In either case, it was time to abandon the *Dauntless.*

More ruts had settled in the gravel drive in the past six months, Fitzgerald noted, and the dilapidation of the Hall — which could be charming in high summer, raffish and open-handed — was rudely apparent in mid-December. Broken, sightless windows in the unused wing where Anne Boleyn

184

once slept; and the encircling walls in such poor repair that Gibbon stumbled over a chunk of granite. It was Maude who leased Shurland, not Fitzgerald; but he determined now that he must find a way to shift funds to her agent — undertake to order repairs, though she would fight his meddling if she learned of it.

It was then he remembered that the usual world was cut off as completely as this island. He could not consult his London bankers or send letters of instruction to anyone. Only Shurland stood between himself and all the hounds of Hell.

The great house rose from its pastures like a time-scarred monolith, unsoftened by trees; the profound island darkness could not diminish the severity of its haphazard outline. Fluid shapes blundered across the drive — sheep, always sheep. The animals milled through the darkened courtyard like mourners before a tomb.

And yet Fitzgerald had loved Shurland once.

"Hallo the house," he called out, as though he still commanded there, and trotted up the broken pavers of the stairs. "Madame duFief! Coultrip!"

He lifted the heavy iron knocker and let it fall. The thud echoed through a vastness beyond.

"Twelfth-century," Gibbon whispered to Georgiana, "and not much been done to it in the past seven hundert years. I wonder if even Mrs. Fitz has given up, and gone back to England?"

But a light, faint and wavering, was growing in one of the leaded front windows. As they watched, it steadied and was set down, as the massive front door swung open.

"Brandy, sir? Or a glass of wine for the lady?"

Coultrip was a local name on Sheppey, and the family could be found in all the towns that dotted the island — sailors, most of them, dedicated to the Royal Navy. Samuel Coultrip had chosen merchant ships, and lost a leg during a fracas with Barbary pirates off the coast of Malay in 1836. Fitzgerald had hired him as a rough butler and footman twelve years ago, when he still spent several months a year at Shurland; now the old man ran the household.

"Mrs. Coultrip will shift to set a light supper before the company," he offered. "Bread and cheese and some cold ham — her la'ship having dined at five, and long since retired."

"Sure, and that'd be welcome," Fitzgerald

186

said. "My compliments to Mrs. Coultrip, and beg her to prepare a room for Miss Armistead. Gibbon will shift with me — on the cot in my dressing room."

"Mr. Theo has taken your old apartment," Coultrip said steadily, "so as to be closer to my lady — but I will have the Yellow Bedchamber prepared for you, sir."

"Thank you." Fitzgerald betrayed no emotion — how could he expect his rooms to be kept in readiness, against a chance arrival? — yet the knowledge of his inconsequence stung. He reached for the brandy decanter. "Mr. Theo is here, then?"

"He arrived on Friday, sir." Coultrip bowed, and limped toward the door; Gibbon made to follow him.

"Wait," Fitzgerald ordered, and poured out a glass. "Take a dram, Gibbon. Medicinal purposes. The good Lord knows you've earned it."

"That's good of you, Mr. Fitz," the valet replied, on his dignity; Fitzgerald's offer had undoubtedly shocked him — "but I should prefer a tankard of ale what Coultrip keeps in the cellar." He bowed, and followed the old man out of the room.

"Will you defy me, too?" Fitzgerald demanded of Georgiana. He heard the belligerence in his tone: *And me still the master of this house, by God.* He was feeling the strain of the day and night, biting down hard on a consuming fury.

She took the proffered brandy and drank it down in a single draught. "For medicinal purposes. As though you had the slightest idea what those might be!"

An antique settee commanded the middle of the room, its silk rotted like everything else at Shurland. Georgie lingered near the hearth, drinking in the warmth, firelight glinting on her dark hair. Her French twill gown was wretchedly spotted with marsh mud and seawater, and torn from the scuffle on the tenement roof; but Georgie never gave her appearance much thought. She was more interested in the flames at her feet.

"Why is the fire coloured, Patrick?" she asked, always the scientist. "I've never seen such a thing."

"Driftwood, love. The sea leaves its mark, and the flames remember."

"I suspect it's some sort of chemical re-action. And the smoke smells of salt." She glanced around suddenly. "What is this place? How do you come to . . . to . . ."

"Fight for any kind of welcome here?" he retorted bitterly. "Well may you ask. I shouldn't have brought you here. You knew I had a wife?"

Her eyelids flickered. "Well — she is everywhere recognised as a singular poet. I myself have read *Bohemian Odes.* And I understand she is quite . . . beautiful. Although she does not frequent Society of late."

"You know that we separated years ago — that we live apart?"

"Yes."

It seemed to Fitzgerald, as he looked at the young woman standing by the changeling fire, that his next few words must forever alter the feeling between them. Georgiana stood for a world entirely free of the suppressed violence of Sheppey, the sordidness of his marriage; she stood for order, and reason, and London, and the semblance of sanity he had found there. Now he had chosen to drag her through the barrier he'd set between present and past. Why had he done it? What reckless need had forced this meeting? He was about to speak — to find the words to explain Lady Maude Hastings Fitzgerald — when the drawing room door screamed on its hinges and Georgiana's countenance changed. Fitzgerald did not need to be told who stood there; she transformed the air of a room simply by entering it.

"Maude," he said, as he turned to face

her. "May I introduce Miss Georgiana Armistead to your acquaintance?"

CHAPTER
TWENTY-ONE

It was true — Maude had once been beautiful.

Fitzgerald could remember how she'd looked at twenty: her rich auburn hair dressed with flowers, her gowns too daring for an unmarried lady of good birth. Maude was tall and elegantly spare, her face a composition of oblique bones and green eyes. She was famous for riding punishing hunters; for stealing her brother's cigars; for the poems she wrote and circulated among her two or three hundred friends — and for meeting young men alone in Hyde Park. One of them had been the dangerous Patrick Fitzgerald.

She stood now in the wide doorway, staring at him as though he were a ghost. Thirty-eight years old, most of her hair and teeth gone, an open sore where her mouth had been.

"Patrick? Is that Patrick? I thought I heard

your brogue." Her voice was as insubstantial as dust. She moved toward him slowly, one hand extended. "A dream, I thought. *Patrick.* A memory of the dead."

"Hello, Maude." He took her hand.

"What are you doing here?"

She ignored Georgiana — perhaps she had not really seen her. It was hard to know what reality Maude distinguished from the chimera in her brain. At times she could finger the truth with punishing acuity; at others, she recalled nothing of what was said. Fitzgerald could not assume she was safe — he could tell her nothing of the true business that brought him here.

"Sure, and I was passing in a boat," he managed. "I couldn't help but call."

The hideous mouth opened in a smile; for an instant he was afraid she would throw her arms wide and kiss him. But some memory of their past inhibited her; she remained, swaying slightly, a few feet away.

"Armistead," she murmured. "I knew an Armistead once — Berkshire family. The assembly rooms at Bath. *Robert.* A fusty old-womanish sort of fellow." She turned away, an expression of worry crossing her ravaged features. "Don't let her drown, Patrick. The wind is up and the tide advancing. It will drown us all one night, in our beds. Our

192

sea-bed. Full fathom five thy father lies . . ."
She drifted toward the door, already forgetting him, her dressing gown trailing behind
her.

Coultrip was standing there.

"So charmed to make your acquaintance,"
Maude murmured to the butler, and floated
by him unseeing.

Fitzgerald watched the sway of her skirt
as it mounted the stairs, the bones of her
fingers rising along the baluster; he closed
his eyes abruptly.

"I did not know her la'ship was abroad,"
Coultrip told him steadily. "I thought her
retired some hours ago. Mrs. Coultrip has
prepared your room, Miss Armistead. Supper is served in a quarter of an hour. May I
show you upstairs?"

Fitzgerald had dragged a comb through his
unruly hair and straightened his cravat by
the time he rejoined Georgiana in the dining room. She had exchanged the twilled
silk for a fresh gown packed in her satchel.
Her hair was tidily bandaged and her face
washed. "I shall never take hot water for
granted again," she declared, as he pulled
out her chair; "and that wine is a luxury
past dreaming."

There was, as promised, the bread and

cheese and cold ham; but Mrs. Coultrip had added a tureen of cottage soup — a comforting concoction of turnips and braised mutton — and Coultrip a bottle of Burgundy from the cellars. It was half-past midnight. A profound weariness nipped at the edges of Fitzgerald's mind, and anxiety shouted its dim chorus; he ignored both. He braced himself for Georgiana's questions.

"How long has she suffered from syphilis?" she asked calmly.

"Nearly ten years."

"She takes mercury against it?"

"Twelve cures in the past decade. I suppose the torture has prolonged her life." He drank deeply of the wine.

"And her mind?"

"As you see. She passes in and out of dreams. Or nightmares."

"And you escaped it. The disease." Her tone was clinically neutral.

"Sure, and I did," he agreed. "We're a lucky race, the Irish. As I'm forever being told." That was the real question she was asking: *If you escaped, who gave her syphilis?* Behind the unspoken words lay the broken ground of his marriage.

He rose restlessly and turned before the fire, the wine glass glinting in his hand.

"Would you have me tell you all of it?"

"Not unless you want to, Patrick."

"But I do." He shifted a log with his boot. "I've kept the faith of lies and smoke, Georgie, so long — so long. Do you know what her high-born friends say, in their infinite wisdom? *She should never have married a dirty Irishman; that was her mistake.* I've allowed the world to believe it."

"Why — if that is untrue?"

"Because I've become a gentleman, for all that, and it's a gentleman's duty to lie." He emptied his glass, reached again for the decanter. "She was an earl's daughter, you know. Beautiful as sin. And so clever — all the power of life at her fingertips. When I met her, I thought Lady Maude was a girl the gods loved. And now look how they've broken her mind on their rocks."

"You still care for her," Georgiana said distantly; was it the knowledge of Maude's fate that pained her, or the unavoidable fact that Maude was Fitzgerald's wife? She had set down her fork. "How did you meet?"

"The Earl — her sainted father — hired me to defend his son when the buck killed his man in a duel. I kept the Viscount from hanging — that being my specialty — but young Hastings was forced to repair to the Continent, and there led such a life. . . . No matter. His sister watched the trial from the gallery. She fell in love, so she said, with my high courage; but faith, I think it was probably my voice."

Georgie smiled faintly. "Or your words. She writes poetry, Patrick."

"None of it comforting. She seduced me with poetry, you know." He finished his wine and reached for Coultrip's brandy. "Her verse could rip the skin off a man. As though her life was hollow, already consumed — an orange whose flesh she'd devoured, leaving only the pith. I think of her that way — her long, supple fingers clutching bruised fruit. The look of disappointment. That's what she felt in her life with me. I *disappointed*."

"Surely not!"

He snorted derisively. "She eloped with me, Georgie, because her father would never abandon his priceless girl to Irish trash. And God forgive me, I met her that dawn in a hired carriage with my whole heart in my hands. Did I think the tie between us would spur my career? Did I dream of a place in her perfect, peerless world? Maybe I did. Maybe I was already corrupted. But God, I loved her passionate mouth and her need for beauty and her lust for life in all its forms, lowborn and high, wretched and noble, ugly and gorgeous. I loved her greediness in drink and her flamboyance in dress. I even loved her petulant rages. I never understood they were signs of madness."

"Even before the disease?"

He shrugged. "Did the rot claim her? Or did she claim it? There are people — artists and poets — who believe syphilis is a gift that opens the soul to genius. My lady Maude believed it. She told me once that love was the only cure for living; and she pursued it in every slum, every house in Mayfair, in the back hallways of Pall Mall clubs, even in the open air — under the ramparts of bridges where the prostitutes dwell. Publicity gave the act spice, d'ye see? I don't know whether she took pleasure from her anonymous couplings or clawed art from debauchery — by that time I was dead tired of collecting my wife from every hellhole in London, each night. I gave her up, Georgie, to the glittering death palace she'd made of her life. And it was years before I saw her again — and then she was already sick past caring."

Georgiana was toying with her food, her face pallid in the candlelight. "How did she come to this place?"

"Her father leased it, when he understood

she was dying; and since he went to his grave, her brother's agents have managed the business. The family likes her marooned in the middle of the ocean — but convenient to Kent, should they wish to call." His mouth twisted. "I spent long months here, years since, when we hoped the mercury might cure her. The pain of it — the destruction — was horrific. She turned back to me, Georgie — she was in dire need of a friend. But when I see the enormity done to her, I bless the demon that destroyed her mind. Better that she not know — most of the time — what she has become."

Georgiana rose. "You haven't eaten a thing."

"No. I've no taste for food at Shurland Hall."

"Then we ought to leave this place."

He assessed her face. "Can you bear it here?" he demanded. "Did I do wrong to bring you?"

"I understand why you did. Von Stühlen will never find us. I'm just —" She leaned toward him, kissed his weathered cheek as chastely as though she were his daughter — "so *sorry*, Patrick. For her. For you. For the waste of two lives."

He watched the woman he loved mount the

stairs of his wife's house. And then he turned back to the bottle.

CHAPTER
TWENTY-TWO

Fitzgerald crawled into his cold bed after three o'clock in the morning, while the wind off the sea battered Shurland Hall. He awoke with a violent shudder of fear, as an enormous cosh whistled through the fog of his alcoholic dream and tumbled him from a pitched slate roof. When he collected his wits and his aching limbs from the floor, his pocket watch read eighteen minutes past seven o'clock. His mouth was foul with the memory of brandy. He stumbled to the wash stand. He rarely slept so late; it was his habit to greet his clerks each morning with a fire already burning in chambers. It was Sep who never appeared before noon, Sep who worked late into the night and of a Sunday —

The shock of water against his skin silenced his stuttering thoughts. There'd been no time, last night, to stop in Great Ormond Street and consult with Sep's doctor. His need to tear Georgie from the metropolis — from the threat of hands that had stifled the breath out of a young girl's lungs — had proved too consuming. He'd chosen to protect her as he'd failed to protect his oldest friend. Guilt and weariness flooded his mind. The summons to Windsor two days before had been followed relentlessly by fear and death. *Why?* What had he — what had *Georgie* done? If Sep should die —

He forced down the thought and stripped off his nightshirt.

Coultrip had taken away his filthy clothes and laid out some old things he'd left behind in a storage chest — country clothes a barrister never needed in London: tweeds and riding breeches. He put them on, and wondered if Maude still kept a horse.

The stable was empty, but he read the obvious signs in the fresh hay and water. *Theo.* Of course. He'd have taken the Chatham & Dover line from Oxford and then the ferry to Sheerness — but Maude kept his mount in readiness still. Or someone did. Coultrip, probably.

He set off in the grey light along the rough track to the shore, less than a mile north over the undulating sheep pasture. The rain was done, but tufted clouds hung low and dark over the sea, flattening the landscape.

The island was a horizontal world — strange and liberating after the vertical confines of London. The sharp air smelled of salt, of wet and matted wool, of the sourness of the marshes behind him. Fitzgerald was a hunted man, with the most powerful monarch in the world against him; but he was walking down to the sea in the early light and might have been returned for an instant to Ireland. Some part of his black mood lifted.

As he crested the line of dunes that bordered the shingle, a dull, rhythmic thudding came to his ears — the sound of pursuit. He wheeled, heart thudding and eyes straining up the coast toward Sheerness, in search of the men who had inexplicably tracked him and Georgie down. And there was the horse: a chestnut he did not recognise, although he had probably paid for it. On its back, slung low over the galloping animal's neck, was Theo.

The boy was not looking for watchers in the dunes, but at the endless stretch of empty shingle, the oblique line of advancing waves, the light of morning as he raced toward the east. Fitzgerald almost let him pass. He almost turned like a coward and shuffled back along his trail, to the despairing Hall and the tea that would be waiting there. But he had so little to lose. He ran pell-mell down the dunes, on an intersecting course with the chestnut, calling out his son's name.

"What are you doing here?"

The boy was scowling, his dark brows so like Maude's, all his fierce joy vanished in an instant.

It was the greeting Fitzgerald expected.

"I was passing by. So I gave a look in."

"Passing by *Shurland?*" Theo snorted, sounding rather like his horse. "Nobody does. You weren't expected."

"I never am," he said mildly. "How are you, lad? How's Balliol?"

"How long do you intend to stay?" The chestnut tossed its head, backing and prancing, and for an instant Fitzgerald saw the horse as Theo — fighting for control.

"Not long. Put that beast in his stable and walk with me. *Please.*"

Theo eyed him, unsoftened. "Clive's too fresh — he needs a good run. I doubt anybody's loosed him since Michaelmas. I'll come to you later, in the library — after breakfast."

"Sure, and I'll be there," Fitzgerald said. But Theo was already gone.

When he did reappear, at half-past ten, he was in a towering rage: the library door thrust violently open, and slammed to with equal force.

"I've just made that woman's acquaintance. What do you mean by bringing her here?" he demanded, as Fitzgerald rose from his chair by the fire.

"If you mean Miss Armistead —"

"I don't care what her name is! The *insult*, to Mama! Parading your mistress at Shurland with brazen disregard for everyone in the household —" Theo wheeled. "Do you know what they're saying in the servants' hall? Did you never stop to think how we might *feel*? No! You simply suited yourself, with your usual appalling —"

"Theo." Fitzgerald set down the roll of charts he'd been scanning. "Lower your voice, for the love of Mary. Miss Armistead is not my mistress. She's in the way of being my ward."

"Your —"

"*Ward.* Placed in my care on her guardian's deathbed."

Theo barked with laughter. "I don't believe it. She's thirty if she's a day!"

Fitzgerald paced toward him in a sudden gust of anger. "She is six-and-twenty, look you, and I'll not have her insulted."

"Tell me another story, Father," the boy said mockingly. "You always contrive so delightfully. But I suppose I should not be shocked. You've kept your light-skirts for years, haven't you? How else could Mama have come to the state she's in?"

Fitzgerald stopped dead. "What in the *bloody hell* do you mean by that?"

"I mean you gave her the pox that's ruined her life."

"Did she say that?"

"She doesn't have to," the boy retorted. "Do you think we're all *stupid?* All *blind?* How you have the *gall* to come here — Uncle Charles would take down his gun, did he know of it, and run you off the place —"

Fitzgerald shook him savagely; Theo's teeth rattled together. "How old are you, boy?"

"Se-seventeen," he stuttered, pale but defiant. "Eighteen next summer. Old enough to —"

"— Blister your parent with bitterness?" Fitzgerald released him. "Then you're old enough to know the truth. You've been sheltered too long."

"I. *Sheltered.*" Theo's lip curled in contempt. "Have you no idea how boys rag each other at school, Father? Of course not. You've never been near Harrow. You can't imagine the vicious things people say. I'm the half-bred whelp of an Irish bastard — didn't you know? Never mind that my grandfather's an earl; I'm the mongrel with a wild Celt's blood in his veins."

"Very well," Fitzgerald said furiously. "If you want brutal, I'll give it to you. Your mother got syphilis from a stranger when you were a bit child, Theo. That's why you were packed off to Harrow at seven. Because she was bound for Paris, and her first trial of mercury. We thought it might kill her."

"Your fault!"

"No. I've been spared her curse, God help me. *I do not carry the disease,* Theo. I shan't tell you how your mother contracted it; that's her story, the only one she has left. Perhaps she'll spin it for you one day."

"She's long past making sense," the boy spat out. "Which means you can tear her reputation to shreds, without the slightest possibility of argument. You vile, *unfeeling* blackguard — If I weren't your son —"

"What?" Fitzgerald reached for a decanter of brandy, poured himself a glass. His mouth was filled with bile and his stomach

206

churning; for all he loved Theo body and soul, their meetings always ended like this. Dust and ashes and the two of them screaming at each other. "You'd put a bullet through my heart, like the noble lad you are? Watch the cur die and avenge your Mama? Don't be a *fool.*"

He tossed down the brandy in one gulp, wiped his mouth on his sleeve.

"Talk to a doctor, Theo. Read a medical book, while you're idling away at university. You're safe from her illness — she was free of it when she had you — but you need to know what's coming. Maude looks to be in the last throes of the disease and I don't think her frame could stand another treatment. You'll have to cope with her dying in a very few weeks more."

There was an ugly silence. The rage had fled Theo's face, to be replaced by uncertainty; he looked suddenly too young for Oxford. As indeed he was. Theo had always rushed his fences.

"Madame duFief —" he said.

"Is paid to look after your Ma, but she's not a nurse. Get Thornton from London when Maude starts to rave. He's helped her in the past."

"You won't be here." Theo's hands balled into fists. "You'd desert her at the end?"

Fitzgerald sank down wearily by the fire, and put his head in his hands. *Theo.* She had named him for faith, after all, at a time when they both still had some; and the boy would be loyal to his mother to the death. He had to believe in something. It had never been his father.

"When do we get the newspapers?" Fitzgerald asked.

"Coultrip fetches them from Sheerness — they're sent across on the ferry. Why?"

"You'll know already of the Consort's death?"

"Of course."

"I'm forced to leave England on a matter of business," he said slowly. "No telling when I'll get back."

"And your *ward* goes with you?" Theo taunted, his contempt on his face. "Where are you bound, Father — for Paris?"

"That's why I spoke of your Ma as I did," Fitzgerald persisted. "You'll need help."

"I shan't attempt to reach *you,* if I have news," Theo said curtly. "I'm *done* with you. For good."

Fitzgerald started out of his chair. "Hate me or no, Theo, I'm your father forever, lad. When Maude goes —"

"I'll have no reason to see you, ever again. Uncle Charles is naming me heir to the

earldom — all he's turned out is girls —
and as far as I'm concerned, you've nothing
to do with my world."

Fitzgerald grinned derisively. "You'd need
an Act of Parliament to follow Monteith,
lad. You're descended on the distaff side."

"Uncle will get one," Theo retorted, his
lips white with anger. "He's already had me
change my name."

"You're to be a Hastings?"

"*Fitzgerald*-Hastings," Theo corrected self-
consciously. "Mama insisted."

"I shall have to thank her for that,"
Fitzgerald said bitterly.

"Don't," Theo tossed over his shoulder.
"Don't go near Mama. Just leave Shurland.
We've never wanted you here."

CHAPTER TWENTY-THREE

. . . hope this letter finds you improved in health and spirits, relative to when I saw you last. You will know by now, my dear Septimus, that our chambers were exceedingly disordered by the rogues who saw fit to strike you down. I suspect that I was the unwitting cause of both the disorder and the attack upon your person, *viz.,* that it was me they meant to strike — the violence due to my refusal, while at Windsor on the night of the fourteenth last, to sign a forced confession of willful deceit in the ancient and near-forgot matter of Edward Oxford. . . .

Fitzgerald frowned, and set down his pen.

He had no idea whether Septimus Taylor had regained consciousness — or ever would. His words, like prayer, traveled straight into a void.

. . . Miss Armistead being encompassed in my troubles, I thought it best to quit London before further violence was done . . .

There it was again: the sharp sense of his own bewilderment, his profound ignorance. Why, *exactly,* had all this happened? Why was he, Patrick Fitzgerald, a source of injury and death to his friends — even to complete strangers?

He closed the letter abruptly, with a plea for any information Sep might consider significant, to be forwarded to Shurland; and then, in a fit of petulance and frustration and profound self-pity, went looking for Gibbon.

He found him in Mrs. Coultrip's scullery, running a stiff boar brush over yesterday's trousers.

"Will they do?"

"Aye," the valet said dubiously, "but only for second best, mind. Were you shoveling coal on your knees yesterday, afore you saw fit to take ship down the filthy Thames?"

"I was set upon by ruffians. While attempting to scarper across a tenement roof. Sure and you found blood on the cloth. You'll have guessed, Gibbon, that life has taken a surprising turn."

"Miss Armistead did just mention the overturning of your carriage in Hampstead," the valet conceded, "when I took up her breakfast tray — me having presumed to inquire after the nasty bruise on her temple. When considered together with Mr. Sep's unfortunate accident —"

"As you say. We live in terror for our lives."

"Pity you didn't think to mention that in all your haste at quitting London," Gibbon remarked matter-of-factly. "I might just have placed your pistols in your leather grip. As it is —"

"Ask Coultrip for the keys to the gun room. Master Theo will have kept some pieces in working order, no doubt. We might borrow them for our — for the duration."

"Right you are, Mr. Fitz. And what *is* the duration, if I may be so bold?"

"I hardly know." Fitzgerald glanced at the letter still clutched in his hand. "I've asked too much of you already, my Gibbon, without so much as a by-your-leave. Better, maybe, if you took the *Dauntless* back to London and waited on my pleasure in Bedford Square?"

"I'm not nearly so pigeon-hearted as you think me, seemingly," Gibbon said with withering contempt. "Will you be wanting that letter posted in Sheerness?"

"Yes." Gibbon was intimate enough with Shurland's habits to know that there was no post in Eastchurch, the village on Shurland's edge, but that the ferry collected letters for the mainland at its dock in Sheerness, a good eight miles distant. "Mr. Theo might be willing to go — his mount is said to need a gallop; or perhaps I can roust Coultrip and his trap."

"Coultrip can drive me just as easy, and I might fetch a London paper while I'm about it. You bide where you are, Mr. Fitz — and look to Miss Georgie."

Something in the valet's tone brought Fitzpatrick's head around. He had not yet seen Georgiana that morning; he had been preoccupied with the letter. And Theo.

"Is she ailing?"

"Sickening for an inflammation of the lung, by my thinking," Gibbon answered succinctly, "but you can't tell the ladies anything, bless them — particularly once they've been to school in Edinburgh."

Drawing room, library, billiards table were all deserted, and the fire dying to embers in the morning room. Her bedroom door was ajar, and the interior equally lifeless — although, he was relieved to see, presentable enough for Shurland. In her better

213

days, Lady Maude had been a devotee of the fanciful — and though the Hall was indeed twelfth century in its foundations, she had plastered and painted the interiors in an exuberant riot of shades: burnt umber and Carrera gold and dusky peach, picked out with startling greens and blues. Fitzgerald could still recall the distant summer when a boatload of Maude's friends — theatre people, brought in from London — had set to painting scenery all over the walls; and now, a progression through Shurland's upper storey was a trip through Indian jungles and Oriental landscapes, across the Russian steppes and onto the shores of Tahiti. Georgiana's room was more restrained — the chamber offered Shakespeare's Globe to the wondering eye, with a quotation from *As You Like It* running in gold script about the perimeter of the ceiling. Mrs. Coultrip had placed a bowl of nuts, a clutch of apples, and a ewer of water on a side table as a hasty form of welcome. Georgie's bags still sat on the carpet — she had not fled from him entirely, then.

He glanced through doorways, a kaleidoscope of set-pieces, all empty and sadder in this barren December than he had ever found them — and paused in the hallway to think.

"You are in search of your *chère amie,* Monsieur Fitzgerald?"

"She is not my *chère amie.* She is my ward." He turned his head to stare down the corridor in the direction of the West Wing — where Lady Maude spent her hours of nightmare and waking. A figure stood there, quite still, the folds of her long green gown disappearing into the scenery against which she was arranged. "Madame duFief. Top o' the morning to ye. I trust you're flourishing?"

She inclined her head. "I cannot complain — being a daily witness to the most *frightful* suffering in another. I do not need to inquire after your health, monsieur; you have never looked better."

She was a woman he could not like: fierce in a subtle and unforgiving way; avaricious in petty things; prone to the special hypocrisies of the paid companion. She remained at Shurland because she had little choice — the Hastings family trustees paid her too well for her service to Lady Maude. Odaline duFief preferred to pretend, however, that it was loyalty and love that kept her marooned at Maude's side; that she, alone of all the world, remained true as more

215

exalted friends fell away. She regarded Fitzgerald with a special contempt for neglecting his wife.

"Such a sweet creature as Miss Armistead looks," she said now. "I conducted her myself to Lady Maude's apartments. She wished most earnestly to see her. I suppose she is conscious — as who could not be, that possesses a heart? — of the tragic genius confined and wasting in these rooms."

"I am sure she thinks her ladyship a fit subject for observation," he returned impatiently. "The lass is trained in medicine, look you."

He uttered the words too harshly; Madame duFief drew a breath, on the verge of retort; but they had reached Maude's doorstep now, and all conversation was suspended.

She lay on a divan, with a shawl about her shoulders and an expression of ecstasy on her ravaged features; Georgiana's look was alert and intent, the scientist collecting data.

" '. . . the drumbeat quickens, the deathless partners race/to meet that heartfelt orison/on hellish carapace . . .' "

"Poetry," Fitzgerald said quietly. "That'll be a new bit, surely, me darlin'?"

" '. . . until the dawn of . . .' something . . .

and *something something* face . . . Is that you, Patrick? I have been declaiming my odes. For the girl. But I cannot remember her name. Or what comes next. Perhaps there are no more words —"

"Miss Armistead," Georgie supplied; her expression was closed, unreachable, and she did not look at Fitzgerald.

"Armistead! That was it!" Maude turned her head toward the voice, eager and reaching, once more on familiar terrain. "I knew a Robert once — I don't suppose he is any relation? — in Bath. He refused my invitation to take his clothes off; unaccountable behaviour."

"He cannot have understood the honour you did him," Fitzgerald said.

"Years ago. When I was a Beauty." Her head swiveled once more, in Fitzgerald's direction, and she extended one claw of a hand. "Dear Patrick! How I *longed* to see you! How happy I am you are here! But I am tired now; you must all go away and leave me with my odalisque. That is what I call duFief, you know — my odalisque."

"And the honour, your ladyship, is *always* understood," Madame duFief said quickly.

She was kneeling at Maude's side, pressing a folded square of linen against her brow, when they left her.

"You know she has gone blind?" Georgiana asked.

"I suspected it," he answered. "The way she turns to follow a voice —"

"Yes. She can barely make out shapes." Georgie paused at the threshold of her room. "I should apologise for my presumption, I suppose — you didn't ask me to examine her."

"Did *she?*"

"I don't think she had the slightest idea what I was doing. I didn't attempt to take her pulse or listen to her heart — just studied her. Patrick, your wife is in an advanced stage of decline. She should be admitted to hospital — or a private nursing home of some kind. She is so isolated here, and that companion — perhaps she means well, but —"

"Hardly."

She studied him soberly. "Did *you* hire Madame?"

"Me?" He affected astonishment. "But no. I am forbidden to make any financial arrangements for my wife, of any kind. That cat was chosen by Maude's brother Monteith, the present Earl."

"Then tell him that his sister is slowly being poisoned with opium. I imagine Madame is the one who gives it to her."

"Did duFief spit at you? With her venom?"

"She said some vile things, certainly — but all insinuation. I have hardly raised your credit by coming here. I do apologise, Patrick."

"You!" He reached for her hand. "To apologise —"

"I think I will just lie down," she hurried on, clutching at the doorknob with painful force. "The excitement of the past two days seems to have caught up with me."

He released her, stepped backwards. "Gibbon says you're sickening for something."

She smiled. "An inflammation of the lung. I happened to clear my throat too loudly in his hearing. Now, if only Lady Maude had a *Gibbon* to look after her —"

He stood outside her door for several moments after she'd closed it, yearning for vanished warmth.

219

CHAPTER
TWENTY-FOUR

Palmerston assures me that I do very well
— that I go through the forms of living,
despite Albert's loss, with composure and
dignity. My Prime Minister observes that
regardless of the paroxysms of grief that
sometimes overcome me (so that I am
forced to retire for a period of solitary
reflection), I have done my utmost to perse-
vere *for the sake of He who is Departed.* How
strange a force is national character! And
how well the sovereign of the nation embod-
ies it! Whereas in the princedoms of India I
should be expected to immolate myself at
my Beloved's death, in England I am to be
commended for *fortitude.*

It is difficult to like Palmerston, however
much one may admire him. He is not the
Prime Minister that Melbourne was. There
is an arrogance to the man's manner that
must disgust. In his early years he was
infinitely charming — possessed of intel-

ligence and wit — a handsome fellow who
brightened a room merely by entering it —
but now that he is gouty and walks only
with the assistance of two canes, I cannot
forget how he attempted to force his way
into Lady ——'s bedchamber one night
here at Windsor, years ago, when he was at
least sixty, with the intent of seducing her
— and when betrayed by the lady's indignant screams, offered as his excuse that he
had often been in the habit of sleeping in
that room in the past — presumably with
its previous occupant! — and had mistaken
his way in the dark!

Albert refused, categorically, to forgive
him for the affront — and could never meet
him thereafter without distaste. And it is
Palmerston who is to commend me for
conduct becoming a Widow and a Sovereign!

Being tired of prime ministers and their
prosiness this Monday morning, and having
signed a ridiculous number of papers I did
not attempt to so much as read, I pleaded a
paroxysm of grief, and quitted Lord Palmerston after only an hour.

Yesterday's rain having quite left off, and
the chill being not too great, I determined
to set out on a walk through the Home Park
— for refreshment, and the easing of disor-

dered spirits. I succeeded in avoiding the Duchess of Atholl, and Lady Augusta Bruce; and should have accomplished my objective of exiting the Castle unobserved — had it not been for Alice.

I did not apprehend, at first, that she had followed me.

I thought myself quite alone as I made my way through the Lower Ward of Windsor, and slipped out by Henry VIII's gate; wandered through the dying remains of the garden, so desolate in winter, particularly after rain; and chose the path toward Frogmore.

Frogmore House will be eternally blessed as the final residence of my dear departed Mama — who died there, but seven months ago, and to which I am given to wander when at leisure, in my grief for and profound communion with that excellent parent, whose loss must forever cut a chasm through my existence. The house, a fine white edifice, is perhaps a hundred years old — and once served as a sort of retreat for my grandmama and aunts, when they tired of Windsor and Grandpapa's mental infirmity. Here they held fêtes, for a select number of their intimate friends, and behaved rather as Marie Antoinette might have done, among her milkmaids — with the principal difference being, that they kept their heads. It seemed the aptest place to lodge Mama, when she had grown too old to manage in Belgrave Square; within the Home Park of Windsor, but not within the Castle *itself.*

She is buried now in Frogmore's grounds — and the place seems a likely choice for Albert's mausoleum, which I intend to be very grand, in the Italianate style, with frescoes reminiscent of Raphael — a painter of whom my Beloved *entirely* approved. It is essential that no expense or effort be spared in the construction of this blessed Valhalla. I will have no one — exalted or low — question my devotion to that Angelic Being. I merely command them to marvel at this evidence of my *fortitude.*

At Frogmore, I might visit Mama and Albert both, and weep over the betrayals and misunderstandings that divided us — the meddling of vicious interlopers — the loss of trust when *love alone* ought to have guided us.

It was as I contemplated the idea of myself, bowed low before the awful entombment of my heart, admired in the eyes of a sorrowing and grateful nation — that I became aware of a Presence near me.

Not Alice; I had not yet perceived her

black-garbed and ruffled form as I descended the steps of Frogmore House. I ought, perhaps, to have gone first to Mama's grave — but I preferred to sit instead in her dear yellow sitting room, shrouded in silence. It was here in the first days after her death I relived, with what fresh agony, every particular of my childhood; for it was my Duty to go through her things. To read her letters. Her journals. To comprehend, once again, in turning the pages of her account books, how deeply exploited I was by one who ought to have made my protection her sole object in life.

It was not her shade who troubled me now. The Presence I discerned, on the fringe of sight, was living enough — one of Windsor's under-gardeners. He had been scything the dead grass at the base of Mama's rose bushes, and had built a little pyre of sticks on which to burn the rubbish. Having already lit this bonfire before my solitary and august figure appeared to disturb his honest labour, he now stood in confusion, cap in hand, all but disguised by acrid smoke.

I approached him unwaveringly.

"What is your name?"

"Albert, Ma'am."

Divine Token! I was moved — I was

startled — I reached out a hand as if to touch his shoulder — and said: "We observe that you are already gone into black. That is very well done of you . . . Albert. We are deeply moved, for His Sake."

The lad bent on one knee, his eyes fixed on the ground, his entire frame trembling. While he was venerating his sovereign thus, I reached into the capacious pocket of my black bombazine and withdrew a small clutch of artificial flowers — replete with bright leaves picked out in Scheele's Green — and cast them onto his bonfire.

Had I known Alice observed me, I might have chosen another time and place.

"Mama." She emerged from a little coppice as I processed back up the path through the Home Park, my cloak drawn close about my shoulders against the cold — which, with the advancing afternoon, was now penetrating in an unusual degree. Her countenance was extremely pallid, and the shadows beneath her eyes as profound as though etched in charcoal. She wore no bonnet or cloak, and was shivering.

"Alice, my dear child! What are you doing there, loitering in the woods?"

"I saw you leave the Lower Ward from my bedchamber window. I was — anxious. I did not like to see you quite alone, Mama."

"And so you determined to spy upon me?"

"— To ensure, merely, that you came to no harm."

"And is the threat of violence so general, on Windsor's grounds?"

Her hands twisted nervously. "Your ladies-in-waiting are searching everywhere for you, Mama. Conceive their apprehension — that in the depths of despair — in the first agony of Papa's passing — you might quite unconsciously do violence *to yourself.* When it was discovered that you were gone from the Castle —"

I drew myself up as much as possible, given my lack of inches. "I have been in the habit of visiting your dear grandmama's grave, surely, on any number of occasions since the Sad Event. I do not recollect that I have ever made of such visits a *grand party.*"

"No, Mama." She studied my visage intently, her expression doubtful. "Can you assure me that you are *quite well?*"

"Despite the trifling matter of having lost my *All-in-All* — I am perfectly well."

"You spoke to the under-gardener, I collect."

"Consider of this, Alice: His name is *Albert.*"

"How very singular!" She stepped backwards a pace. "Was it for that reason you placed some artificial flowers on his fire? I observed you. Were they *my* flowers? Those Violet reported as missing?"

"Perhaps." I shrugged. "I have no way of knowing."

"*Burnt* them, Mama?" she cried, her pent emotions bursting forth in a hideously uncontrolled manner. "Did you think to save me from my worse nature? Can you truly believe me capable of wearing such gaudy stuff, when plunged in the deepest mourning for beloved Papa?"

"Alice, do you know where I found those flowers?"

She looked all her bewilderment. "In my dressing room, I must suppose."

"I found them in Papa's little study — his cabinet, as he called it. Set into a vase of water. Is that not extraordinary?"

She turned her head abruptly, as though I had hurled an insult. "It is altogether absurd!"

"Yes," I agreed. "Quite so. If you think a little — you will understand why I thought it expedient to burn your flowers."

She met my eyes then, but doubtfully, and not without fear.

I swept on my way back up to the Lower

Ward. I must hope that Alice will take from this a useful lesson — that she will no longer presume to dog my footsteps and overlisten to my private conversations. Or to suspect *me* of such a despicable crime as suicide.

"Have a care, Alice," I threw over my shoulder in parting. "The air grows cold, and the place far too lonely. You might just catch your death."

CHAPTER
TWENTY-FIVE

The door knocker of the house in Great Ormond Street was wrapped in black crepe, but von Stühlen thought nothing of this; most of the houses in London were similarly shrouded with dusky bunting hung from windows and gas lanterns. Strange, to think that this morning an entire Kingdom wore black for Albert. Von Stühlen could no longer mourn him; his Albert had died long ago.

It was Tuesday, the seventeenth of December, and until the Prince Consort was buried on the twenty-third, no sign of gaiety or Christmas cheer would break the City's ochre-coloured gloom. That was a pity; because Albert had always loved Christmas. Loved winter. Von Stühlen had known him to build snowmen twice as high as himself — to pull his children shrieking on sledges — to challenge von Stühlen to bouts of ice hockey: the two of them slashing at each other's heads, shouldering each other into drifts as they'd done on the river in Bonn during their student days, their skates carving deep rifts in the soft English ice. Albert furious and laughing as he fell on his backside, until the early northern darkness made concession possible.

He felt a sharp stab of yearning for that vanished boy, who'd been awkward and tongue-tied as von Stühlen himself had never been; the boy so lost in ideas he'd found it difficult to speak. Albert had never made friends easily — so they meant the world to him. He'd cherished his rare connexions, accorded them an insane loyalty; there were times von Stühlen was convinced Albert would die for him. He understood nothing of that impulse; Albert's ideals were like another language, foreign to his friend's ear from birth.

Contrary to what the world believed, Albert and Wolfgang had almost nothing in common — except circumstance. They were both second sons of German nobles. Both raised without expectations by impoverished and high-living fathers. Wolfgang's had communicated almost every conceivable vice, along with an air of impeccable fashion and a refusal to be bested; Albert's had left him as innocent as a stray pup. Why they formed their inexplicable bond during their school-days, von Stühlen could hardly say. *He* had been the leader, then; it was Wolfgang — popular, wild, confident — who had singled out the silent boy and carried him carelessly along in the train of his perpetual entourage, exposing Albert to the vagaries of the world with ruthless enthusiasm. The Duke's second son was an unwilling pupil. *His virtue,* von Stühlen remembered someone saying, *is indeed appalling; not a single vice redeems it.*

When he'd learned that Albert was to be sacrificed at twenty to an ugly little harpy — torn from his studies and shipped off as the British Royal stud — he'd tried to get his friend drunk and tuck him up with a whore. Albert had partaken sparingly of the wine and paid the woman off with gentle courtesy.

Why? von Stühlen demanded of himself now. *Why did I ever waste a thought on so drab a soul?* Albert's brother, Ernest, was far more his kind — a rakehell already nursing a mortal case of pox. Albert was kind-hearted and gentle, qualities von Stühlen despised. He intrigued and confounded von Stühlen; his pursuit of the ideal — his unswerving devotion to its demands — suggested something dangerously like the existence of God.

In all the stupidity of twenty, von Stühlen had actually pitied Albert as he sailed that October from Antwerp. He had rejoiced in his own freedom to make what he could of his fortunes. It was only later, watching as his friend came into his Kingdom — as all the realms of heaven and earth opened themselves at Albert's feet — that von Stühlen understood how bitterly Fate had cheated him. He was still an impoverished second son; Albert commanded the world.

He glanced the length of Great Ormond Street as he stepped down from his equipage and handed the reins to his groom. It was empty of life. Why leave the fire, when most of the shops were still closed? Ladies of quality collected in one another's drawing rooms, linen handkerchiefs at the ready, to debate the proper mode of mourning dress and how best to salvage the Season; their men posed uneasily in clubs. Talk was solely of this death: Even the bloody civil war in America had been consigned to the ash bin. Most of the predictions and chatter skirted one essential fear. Von Stühlen tasted it in the silence of every room he entered: All London was dreading the future with Victoria.

She was rumoured to be mad. Whispered

reports from the intimates of Court let it be known that grief — the loss of a loved one — completely unhinged her. That she reveled in melancholy, retreated into sorrow, obsessed over death and her own pitiable loss until nothing and no one — particularly her children — could reach her. *How would the Queen rule without the one man who had forced her to do so?* That was the chief question in Pall Mall; neither Whig nor Tory had a cheerful answer.

She will follow him soon to the grave, von Stühlen said, when pressed for his opinion. *That is all the consolation left her.* His audience always nodded in relief.

He mounted the broad front steps of Septimus Taylor's house and lifted the muffled rod of brass.

"It's good of you to come, Count, I'm sure," said the butler as he studied von Stühlen's card doubtfully in the front hall. "Are you a client of my master's, perhaps?"

"More of a social connexion. We have been in the habit of dining together at the Reform Club."

"Ah! The Reform! Naturally, sir. I was forgetting Mr. Taylor's numerous cronies. Thus far this morning it has been only family — Mr. Taylor's nephews, and Mrs. Rutledge. You'll be the first true call of condolence; I'll make certain Mrs. Rutledge sees your card."

"And Mrs. Rutledge is . . . ?"

"His daughter, sir."

"Ah." Von Stühlen's good eye flicked around the narrow hall, which offered a handsome staircase and nothing more; the principal rooms were above. A marble-topped table, claw-footed and carved in walnut, stood beneath the stairs; there was a porcelain bowl ready to receive callers' compliments, a small pile of post. "When did Mr. Taylor —"

"At twelve minutes past two o'clock in the morning, sir. He went very quietly — never regained consciousness, though Doctor remained hopeful to the last. A great loss, sir — and to depart in such a way!" Overcome, the butler withdrew his handkerchief from his coat and buried his nose in it. "Those ruffians! Hanging's too good for 'em!"

"Indeed. And the police — ?"

"Are at sixes and sevens." The butler's indignant face emerged from his linen. "They wished most earnestly to speak to Mr. Fitzgerald — he's Mr. Taylor's partner, and found him at death's door in chambers — but Mr. Fitzgerald has been called away!"

234

"Very odd," von Stühlen observed. "Have you an idea of Mr. Fitzgerald's direction?"

"I received it only this morning, in the post." The butler lifted an envelope from the stack of correspondence and peered at it nearsightedly. "Shurland Hall, Eastchurch, Isle of Sheppey. Perhaps Mr. Fitzgerald is spending Christmas among friends . . . ?"

It was clear, by that Tuesday morning, that Georgiana was ill — so ill she was unable to leave her bed, and Mrs. Coultrip was obliged to wait upon her.

Fitzgerald loitered in hallways, anxious for news of her condition; heard the sound of ragged breathing through her open door; sent queries and good wishes by Mrs. Coultrip; and finally salved his restless spirit by sitting in the library and poring over Channel charts, decanter near at hand. He had just determined to drive into town and find a doctor to examine Georgie, when Theo wandered through the library door.

"Are you fleeing your creditors, Father," the boy demanded, with an eye to the charts, "— or are clients so thin on the ground, you've no reason to tarry in London?"

He's determined to offend, Fitzgerald

thought. *Don't take the scent.*

"With the Prince dead, little will be heard at the Bar in coming weeks," he replied mildly. "Tell me of Balliol, Theo — how do you get on? Read anything good this term?"

"Social theory," the boy drawled. He hadn't bothered to take a chair. "Ethnology and anthropology. James Hunt. Robert Knox. Mackintosh. Ever heard of them?"

"Can't say that I have."

"But then, your education was always deficient."

"That it was," Fitzgerald returned, keeping his temper in check, "but I put enough by, all the same, to send you to school. What do these Hunts and Knoxes teach you, then?"

Theo smiled faintly. "That England and Ireland are forever divided by the national character of their peoples — the reasoned, ordered, civilized Anglo-Saxon having nothing in common, by blood or habit, with the savage Celt. Mackintosh adds that where the Anglo-Saxon is a model of prudence, self-governance, and industry, the Celt is utterly alien — being prone to wild rages, persistent melancholy, indolence, and an undue veneration for the whip." He eyed the half-empty decanter. "Not to mention drink. What do you say to that, Father?"

236

Fitzgerald sank back in his chair and stared up at his son. "I'd say that any people as subject to the English whip as the Irish have been, for time out of mind, *ought* to be melancholy and enraged. Do you enjoy this kind of study, Theo?"

"I suppose it helps to answer youth's eternal question," he retorted. "*Who am I?* I can't help but wonder, with such parents as mine."

"You're a good deal more than the sum of Maude and me, lad."

"True. As I've said — every man is the result of generations of bloodline and history. Mine is both aristocratic and mongrel — so I repeat, Father: *Which am I?*"

"Whatever you aspire to be," Fitzgerald answered bluntly. "Or so I have always found."

His son's eyes danced over him mockingly, in search of something Fitzgerald could not see in the outline of his features. "In the prognathous jaw and dusky skin of the black Irish, as they're called, one can trace the descent from a common ancestor of the Negroes. But Mama spared me *that* indignity. I will always be recognised for a Hastings."

"Not entirely." Fitzgerald said it bitterly. "You got my temper, my implacable hatreds, and my taste for argument. You'd make a brilliant lawyer, look you."

"I'd rather die first."

"Sweet Jesus, boy, does it give you so much pleasure to cut at me?"

"Of course!" Theo cried. "It's almost the only pleasure I have! You made sure of that, Father — by stealing my birthright from the moment I was born! Do you know what it's like to be a *Paddy*'s son?"

Fitzgerald did not reply. He had seen, over Theo's shoulder, Odaline duFief in the library doorway. She made no sound, her whole form listening.

"— the friends that daren't invite you home. The girls who cut you direct, once they learn your name. The whispers and looks that follow you across the room, every time you suffer failure. It's almost worse when you succeed! The Paddy's son is *supposed* to fail!"

"Stop it, Theo," Fitzgerald said blindly. "Stop it *now*. How may we help you, Madame duFief?"

"Your little friend, monsieur," she said with deceptive sweetness. "She has taken a turn for the worse."

CHAPTER
TWENTY-SIX

"The cold itself should be a trifling indisposition," said Harris, the Sheerness doctor, as he descended the stairs at Shurland that evening, "but when complicated by fever, is necessarily of concern. Miss Armstead must be kept warm and quiet for a se'nnight at least, if we are not to see an inflammation of the lung. That would be most dangerous, Mr. Fitzgerald, as I am sure I need not tell you. If only Shurland were not so draughty!"

Fitzgerald had driven the pony trap from the barn, his anxiety for Georgie spurred by his need to be free of the Hall and its ghosts. The chill air, laden with Channel salt and the scent of sheep dung, whipped his cheeks as it swept the length of treeless Sheppey — and he understood why Theo was so often out-of-doors, on Clive's back, during these end-of-term vacs. The boy could be free of anything — even social theory — on these moors.

"I have known just such a healthy young woman carried off in the past, from an inflammation of the lung, when insufficient care was taken," Harris persisted. "I should have bled Miss Armistead, had she not strenuously set herself against it; and I will not undertake to promise *never* to bleed her, if the fever persists."

"Sure and I'll do my best to support you, Harris," Fitzgerald returned, "but Miss Armistead is by way of being learned in medicine herself, and will object to meddling."

"Learned!" the doctor snorted. "The dear ladies will always believe they know best, in all matters of health, regardless of their limited experience and education — it is the maternal impulse, instilled by the Creator — but in Miss Armistead's case, it is for her natural protectors to steer her between the shoals of over-confidence and willful conceit. I shall call again in the morning, Mr. Fitzgerald. Pray see that Miss Armistead swallows the draught I have left in Mrs. Coultrip's keeping, at bedtime and again at two o'clock in the morning. I shall leave instructions as to gruel and fortifying broth."

Fitzgerald promised faithfully, and showed Dr. Harris the door; then stood in the chill

240

Hall for an instant considering his position.

In choosing Shurland as a point of refuge, he'd never intended to make a prolonged stay. Now he was trapped until Georgiana's health improved — unless he left her behind, and went on to France alone.

"What did the doctor say, begging your pardon, Mr. Fitz?"

"He says you're a grand sort for a doctor's clerk, having spotted Miss Georgie's illness before she did herself. I'm afraid we're tied to Shurland until she is well, Gibbon."

"That means a few days, at the least. And what of these murderous folk who're after your blood, if I may be so bold?"

"We shall have to hope they've lost me altogether."

Gibbon shook his head, and held out the London *Times.* "I took the liberty of ironing the newspaper you brought back from Sheerness, as is usual — and I don't like the look of *one* item."

Fitzgerald glanced at the column under Gibbon's blunt thumb. *Noted Barrister Dead After Attack in Chambers —*

"Sep," he whispered, and took the paper from Gibbon's hand.

It was a sordid little piece, full of innuendo and speculation. Mr. Taylor had been known

241

for his Radical views; an outspoken anti-
monarchist; given to pursuing his affairs
even on the Sabbath, and disinclined to
alter his habits in respect of the Prince
Consort's tragic passing; almost justifiably,
attacked and laid low in chambers — dying
barely twenty-four hours later — and the
summary capped with a pious little dismissal, that Septimus Taylor would be
chiefly regretted among the miscreants of
Newgate, whose interests he had principally
served.

You deserved better, Fitzgerald thought;
and wished the obituary scrivener a special
rung in Hell.

It was the suggestion buried within the
body of the article, however, that brought
his brows together: that Mr. Taylor's partner, one Patrick Fitzgerald — having discovered the victim when he, too, profaned the
Sabbath by venturing to visit chambers on
the Sunday — had quitted London without
consulting the police, who greatly desired to
speak to Mr. Fitzgerald in connexion with
Mr. Taylor's death . . .

"Have you read this?" he asked abruptly.

"My sympathies, sir. I know how you
valued Mr. Taylor."

"I shall have to leave Shurland at once."

"With Miss Georgie —"

"Impossible. She'll stay until she's well — and you with her. It's myself the police are wanting. With Bedford Square empty, they'll look to the Inner Temple. And no doubt my chief clerk will help them kindly — he'll have received my bit letter from Shurland this morning. Faith, and the Law might arrive at any moment."

"Beggin' your pardon, sir — but would it not be best to answer their questions? Surely you've nothing to fear — having done your utmost to save Mr. Taylor?"

Fitzgerald laughed. "Haven't you read it in the paper, man? The wild Irishman is to be charged with murder! Even did I prove my innocence, only think of the delay — the thwarting of our plans, the stripping of all protection from Miss Armistead, the frustration of our object —"

"May I presume, sir, to ask what that object might be?"

"You may not. You can't betray what you don't know." He mounted the stairs, two at a time. "Be a good fellow and pack my things. We drive to Sheerness in half an hour's time."

"Then let's hope the Bobbies give us so long," Gibbon muttered.

Her door was ajar, so that Mrs. Coultrip

might glance in from time to time without disturbing her patient; and as he stood in the glow of her single candle he could hear the laboured breathing. He ought to have continued down the hall to take his leave of Maude — he ought to have tiptoed past and allowed Georgie to discover his flight in the morning, when he was too far away to be persuaded. But he paused, staring at her. Her cheeks were too flushed above the white lace of her nightgown and he could sense the burning fever as though her skin were actually beneath his hands.

And suddenly what he saw was not *Georgie,* but another girl — a younger girl — her clenched fists raised to fight off the horror of night, in the form of a suffocating pillow —

A shout from below, ripe with anxiety.

"Mr. Fitz!"

He wheeled and made for the stairs.

Theo was standing before Gibbon, hands on his hips and mutiny on his face. But it was to Fitzgerald he spoke.

"You lied to me! But why am I surprised? When have you ever done anything *else?*"

"What are you talking about?"

"I asked if you were fleeing debts. You said not. But you *lied.*"

"Theo —" Fitzgerald moved impatiently

down the stairs to his son.

"Appleford told me." This was the Eastchurch blacksmith. "I took Clive over to be shod a few hours ago and he said the whole of Sheppey is buzzing about it —"

"About *what?*"

"The party of duns who're asking everywhere for Shurland Hall. A right pack of toughs Appleford said they were — led by a gent in an eye patch."

Fitzgerald went cold. "A German? Dark-haired?"

"You see," his son crowed in triumph, "you *do* know what I'm talking about."

"But if they've been here all day," Gibbon muttered, "why haven't they come to the Hall?"

"They're waiting for darkness."

Something in the tone of Fitzgerald's voice stopped even Theo's words in his mouth. It was half-past four in the afternoon, and would be dark in a matter of minutes.

"Quickly," Fitzgerald said. "I'll rouse Georgiana. You gather my things."

"Father —"

He grasped Theo by the shoulders. "Listen to me, lad. Put Madame duFief and your mother in Coultrip's trap, and send them all to Sheerness. You can ride alongside.

Take a gun."

"Clive's feet are sore! I shouldn't mount him for at least a day —"

"Lead him at a walk, if need be, but get him and the rest away while there's still light. You've no thought what these men are capable of."

"You make them sound like murderers," Theo spluttered.

Fitzgerald glanced at him as he turned back to go up the stairs. "They are," he said.

CHAPTER
TWENTY-SEVEN

The dressmaker came direct from London today, with a fellow from Robinson's — the mourning warehouse most patronised by persons of Quality — and so I spent the better part of three hours in being fitted for my widow's weeds: a quantity of detestable caps, with a peak over the forehead; black flannel petticoats; gowns of black velvet, watered silk, and black bombazine, with its ostentatious rustle; black bonnets and shawls; black capes and undergarments; black feathers and black lace. I already possess several stout pairs of black boots, which must be a source of comfort; I detest being fitted for shoes.

And then it was for the girls to stand, and be dutifully measured for ells of mourning cloth: Alice and Louise, Helena and Beatrice — to see a child of four so sunk in mourning, is to cry aloud for Heaven's mercy. I took the fatherless child in my arms and thought what a picture we must make — I so oppressed with loss, she a vision of bewildered innocence. I must direct the Court photographer to consider of our poses.

The dressmaker dared inform my maid that all of London is submerged in black — no other shade is to be had at the linen-drapers' — and that those who engage to dye lighter stuffs to mourning hue are doing a brisk business the length and breadth of the Kingdom. Robinson's cannot fill its orders fast enough, and must dispatch its goods by railway and private carriage. How extraordinary to think that Albert's death should occasion a surge in commerce. . . .

"Alice," I said idly as she turned beneath the dressmaker's hands, "how do you like your new maid?"

"Not as well as Violet," she replied. "But you must have suspected that, when you dismissed her."

"Margaret is from the Highlands. She is one of our Scots. Her influence on you must be far more salubrious than that chit of a girl's."

"Margaret drinks."

"All our Scots are prone to . . . their ways. It is a part of their natural simplicity."

"She no more understands how to dress a

lady of fashion than would a cow."

"That is as well — for you cannot be thinking of fashion in the depths of your loss."

The dressmaker's hands faltered in their industrious fitting; I must suppose the creature, with unflagging impertinence, overlistened to my intimate conversation with my daughter — and heard my gentle words as a rebuke to her profession. I quitted the room immediately — for I have a horror of encroaching ways on the part of any of my dependents.

Alice found me out, however, an hour later, as I drank tea in the seclusion of the Blue Room — which I have strewn with bouquets of fresh flowers, sent daily from the London florists. I like to sit here, and *shall* sit here a great deal in future. I shall read what Palmerston gives me, and perhaps His Spirit shall guide whether I sign Palmerston's papers or no.

"Mama," Alice said, "is that Papa's cast you are holding?"

The cast of Albert's arm, that we had made when the children's were cast, a few years ago. I rest it in my lap from time to time, the fingers clutched in mine.

"It feels so very like," I said. "Particularly when the warmth of my body has softened the plaster."

She turned her face aside, but not before I caught the expression of repugnance. Alice has never been a careful child; she is not like Helena, who presents a dreaming visage to the world and allows no hint of what she truly feels to be read by its multitudes. Alice betrays everything.

"You know, Alice, I am not sure that you truly *love* your Louis," I observed. "But then — what can a girl of eighteen understand of love? An infatuation, merely. A flight of impetuous fancy."

"Mama, why did you order Violet dismissed from my service?"

"I believe the girl was in *my* service, Alice — not yours."

She gestured impatiently. "Even so. You sent her away without a character, but a week before Christmas. Was that just? Was that kind?"

I placed the cast of my Beloved's arm carefully on the desk that stands in the Blue Room; it shall weight down Palmerston's papers, when he brings them. "Violet was impertinent."

"Impertinent! Because she reported my silk flowers to be missing — the same flowers you later burned in the garden? Mama, I must and will know why those flowers disturbed you so!"

"Because of where they were found. Natu-rally."

"In Papa's study?"

"In a vase of water."

"But how is that to the purpose — what can *that* have had to do with Violet?"

"It is possible . . . that she colluded with him. That she gave him the flowers. And told you they were missing only when you should have perceived it for yourself — when the review of your wardrobe was made, in preparation for mourning."

Alice looked her bewilderment.

And now, I thought, *she will tell everyone that I have gone mad.*

I withdrew the one letter I had saved from burning, in the midnight destruction of my Beloved's correspondence — the letter from Baron Stockmar, written over a year ago — and offered it to Alice.

"Read it," I commanded. "You will know better what I am about, once you have understood the words."

CHAPTER
TWENTY-EIGHT

The need to run hammered in Fitzgerald's brain. Georgiana moved only slowly across the mile of bog and meadow between the Hall and the *Dauntless*. Fever made her stumble and her breath tore through her ragged throat. Already, the dusk had fallen.

Between them, Fitzgerald and Gibbon tried to support her; but there was baggage to carry — their clothes, and Georgie's satchel of instruments. The grip of Fitzgerald's hand on her arm was so tight it must have hurt her; but she said nothing, her jaw set, as their boots squelched through the stinking marshland.

"You might consider, Mr. Fitz, an improvement to your mooring when next you're at Shurland," Gibbon suggested. "A gravel path, mebbe, straight down from the house. Or moor the steamer at Sheerness, however inconvenient."

Fitzgerald said nothing. They had come to

the head of the brackish creek where they'd anchored the *Dauntless.* His eyes searched ahead, straining against the gathering dark; strained again.

"I reckon we're dead nigh," Gibbon said uncertainly.

Fitzgerald stopped in his tracks and released Georgie's arm. She sagged against him.

"Patrick — what is it?"

The *Dauntless* was gone.

Theo had done as he'd agreed, and escorted Coultrip's trap as far as Brambledown, a mile and a half west of the Hall; but as the cavalcade entered the small sheepherders' village, Clive pulled up dead lame.

"You'll have to go on alone, Coultrip," he said as he slid out of the saddle and lifted his hunter's foreleg. "I'll follow tomorrow. Clive's done in."

"Your father won't like it," the old man said bluntly.

Theo raised his head. "My father's on his way to France. What has he to do with anything?"

"Theo, *darling,*" murmured Lady Maude, "Patrick did his best. I was bloody to him, always. Poor lamb."

"Go on," Theo persisted, ignoring her.

253

"Put up at the Britannia. I'll call for Mother tomorrow."

"It's no druthers to me what you do, lad," Coultrip replied, snapping the reins over his nag, "so long's you lock up t'Hall tight."

Theo stood for a moment, watching them go. Then he turned and began to lead Clive back along the road they'd come.

He did not believe his father's warnings. He was alone, and free, for the first time in days. He would build a good fire and spend the night reading a book. His heart felt lighter than he could ever remember.

Von Stühlen had pulled up his hired fly in the sole clump of trees Eastchurch boasted. The wind off the sea, two miles distant, was bitterly cold and the driver thinking of his horses, the way muscle and bone stiffened dangerously in such weather when the animals weren't moving.

They had been waiting for over an hour on the approach to Shurland Hall, the fly screened by the coppice's branches, blankets tossed over the horses' backs. After half a day on the island, von Stühlen knew a good deal about the isolated and poorly-secured house. He knew Fitzgerald was inside, and Georgiana Armistead with him. That an invalid and her companion were the only other occupants. The servants, an elderly couple.

He set aside the volume he'd been reading — Tennyson's *Idylls of the King* — and consulted his pocket watch. Nearly six o'clock. He would have preferred midnight, the household sleeping, and the cover of darkness complete; but he could not keep his men hunched in the cold any longer.

Idylls of the King. Albert had recounted once a visit he'd made to Tennyson's home at Freshwater, not far from Osborne — how he'd surprised the poet laureate in the midst of unpacking at the new house, Albert standing awkwardly by a window to gaze out at an indifferent view, praising everything in his correct German way as Mrs. Tennyson disposed of her china . . . Victoria did not deign to visit Freshwater, but summoned Tennyson to Windsor instead, and made him spout his poetry as though she were Elizabeth, and Tennyson Shakespeare. Such scenes reflected poorly on each, von Stühlen reflected.

Why did he *hate* Victoria so deeply? — Because she had given Albert everything in the world, when his heart whispered it might as easily have been him? That it *still* might be Wolfgang, Graf von Stühlen, who inherited this English earth? Provided he

255

steeled himself. Refused to let her sap his strength, as she had sapped Albert's —

Jasper Horan, his face pinched with cold, tapped on the fly's window. Von Stühlen opened it a crack.

"Oi, guv'nor — summat's coming along the road, bound for the house."

They had scattered five men in the sheep meadow as lookouts, against just such an eventuality; one of them must have raised his arm in warning.

Von Stühlen felt for his pistol; it lodged snugly against his ribs, hidden by his cloak. He thrust open the fly's door and walked at a leisurely pace into the middle of the road, leveling his gun on the approaching horse, his gauntleted right hand raised.

And if it were Fitzgerald? Georgiana Armistead with him?

He could carry them both back to London, and the Metropolitan Police. But the Queen would dislike that; it would place her enemies immediately beyond her control. Charges, imprisonment, a trial — all of these would attract the attention of the newspapers, and give Fitzgerald a platform for protesting his innocence. Exactly what Victoria dreaded.

Sick excitement filled von Stühlen's throat, and his fingers gripped the pistol more tightly. He would force Fitzgerald and his woman into the fly and later, in private, he would extort from them everything they knew about Victoria. He would learn, at last, why she feared and hated them so. And then — and then, he would destroy them. . . .

No horseman, but a boy leading a rangy hunter at a walk. He stopped dead when he saw the dark figure with the gun raised.

Von Stühlen's eyes roamed over the tense, whipcord body; no Fitzgerald. No Georgiana Armistead. It was *she* he had principally hoped to meet with in the dark; *she* he wanted to watch, as he killed her lover.

He swallowed his disappointment, mind raging, and walked toward the boy.

CHAPTER
TWENTY-NINE

"Stolen, I reckon," Gibbon said tersely. "That boat will never have simply floated away. I made sure the rope was knotted good and tight."

"Here," Fitzgerald said. "Support Miss Georgie." He walked forward a few paces through the pitch black, craning over the tussocks of marsh along the creek bed. In the darkness he struck his shin against a mooring stake — and stifling a curse, felt along its length. Part of the *Dauntless*'s painter dangled from the iron ring.

"Somebody's cut it loose."

"Von Stühlen?" Georgie faltered.

The hair prickled on the back of Fitzgerald's neck.

He could just faintly catch the sound of plashing oars, familiar since childhood. It came from farther down the channel.

"We might strike out for Brambledown," Gibbon was saying. "There's a few sheep farmers there'd take us in, mebbe."

Fitzgerald began to run toward the sound of the boat, tripping and stumbling wildly over the uneven ground. The pale glow of a shuttered lantern shone out some distance ahead, and he had an idea of the thieves, waiting for the cover of darkness, unwilling to fire the steamer's engine out of fear of the noise —

A hand grabbed for his ankle, and he went down hard.

The man was upon him in seconds, all his weight on Fitzgerald's back, forcing his face into the black muck of the marsh.

Gasping, he reached backwards and clawed at the unseen killer, struggling to raise his nose from the bog. No good. The weight shifted and rolled but would not be shed. Fitzgerald's brain screamed with panic and he knew the impulse to suck the marsh deep into his lungs, desperate as he was for air. Something struck the crown of his head, but glancingly — a blow meant for another. And then the weight was gone and he could raise his face from the stinking muck.

Gibbon, cursing gutturally as he rolled in the salt hay, his hands at their attacker's neck.

Fitzgerald thrust himself to his feet, his senses singing, and staggered toward the two men. He began to kick the one that was not Gibbon, hard, in the small of the back. And then he remembered the pistol he'd taken from Shurland's gun room.

With shaking hands he pulled it from his coat. If he fired it, von Stühlen would know where they were. If he fired it, he might hit Gibbon.

He lifted the butt of the gun and brought it down hard on the killer's head.

The man went limp.

"You look like your mother," von Stühlen observed, as he stopped short in front of Theo. "I knew her once, you see. Long ago. When she still went about in Society."

"That doesn't give you the right to hold me up like a common highwayman," Theo said. "May I have the honour of your name, sir?"

"Wolfgang, Graf von Stühlen." He thrust the pistol into his belt. "And yours?"

"Theo Fitzgerald-Hastings."

"Ah. An improvisation, I suspect."

The boy ducked his head. "I'm Monteith's heir. My uncle."

"So. You will be an earl one day, and I am a count. We may speak as one gentleman to another." Von Stühlen held out his arm in a gesture of invitation. "May I accompany you to the house? There is a matter I must urgently discuss with your parent. Mr. Fitzgerald."

Theo tugged on Clive's rein, and trod warily forward. "No one's at home, I'm afraid. They've all gone but me."

"Impossible," von Stühlen said easily. "I've been watching the road."

The boy stopped short.

"Forgive me. Such measures are sometimes necessary, when one is in service to the Queen."

"The Queen?" Theo stared at him. "What has the Queen to do with Shurland Hall?"

"I'm afraid that is your father's question to answer," von Stühlen said gently. He began to walk again toward the house. Jasper Horan fell in with the pair of them, a few feet behind his master, and others — emerging from the trees — gathered inexorably. Three men, then five . . .

"What do you want with him?" Theo demanded roughly.

"We are looking for Mr. Fitzgerald . . . it pains me to say it . . . on a matter of possible treason . . ."

"Rubbish!"

Von Stühlen inclined his head. "Taken together with the unfortunate murder of his partner in chambers — and your father's sudden flight from London — there are any number of questions to be answered. But only *one* that I must put to *you:* Where is your father now? At precisely this moment?"

Theo studied von Stühlen's face, the tension in his frame gradually easing; and then, he told him.

"Georgie!" Fitzgerald muttered in a half-whisper. "Georgie!"

She was sitting on the rock where Gibbon had left her, near the *Dauntless*'s old mooring. Beside her stood a man hunched with age, a lantern raised in his right hand. Both of them turned to look at Fitzgerald and Gibbon as they emerged from the marsh.

"This is Mr. Deane," Georgie said. "He says he's your neighbour. He has a boat, Patrick."

It was a fisherman's dory, the oars shipped in their locks — the boat Fitzgerald had heard, before tumbling in the dark.

Fitzgerald reached for his purse. "Could you take us around to Sheerness, Mr. Deane?"

"He left this morning for France?" von Stühlen said as they halted in Shurland's courtyard.

"Yes. He wished to take his mistress there,

for the Christmas season," Theo said indifferently. "Not particularly kind in him, to break his journey under Mother's roof — but Father has always had a curious notion of propriety. All my people have, to be frank."

"I see." Von Stühlen scanned the Hall's weathered façade. "How exactly did your father quit the island?"

"On his steamer. The *Dauntless*. He moors it at the head of the creek, a mile or two south of the Hall."

"I know. Your blacksmith — Applefield? Applewood? — told me as much. Which is why my men cut the boat adrift this evening."

Clive's head jibbed suddenly; Theo's grip had tightened on the lead. "Then I must be mistaken. I was out riding when Father left. Perhaps he took passage from Sheerness after all. It would be the safer choice, for a winter crossing."

"I don't think so," von Stühlen mused. "I think, rather, that you are lying." He drew the pistol from his belt and leveled it at Theo in one swift movement, the muzzle hovering between the boy's eyes.

Theo stepped backwards, dropping Clive's lead. All around them, a casual circle of men, intent and watching. For an instant von Stühlen was swept backwards, to Bonn — another circle of watchers, in academic gowns this time, Albert attempting to quell the violence as a pair of peasants cowered in their midst — but he thrust the image firmly away. Mercy had triumphed that time; but mercy had no purpose here.

"Tell me the truth."

"I have!" Theo cried hotly.

"No." He cocked the gun. "You've lied repeatedly. Where is your father?"

The boy's eyes were trained on the pistol's mouth. Clive nuzzled his hair, the great nostrils blowing gently on Theo's scalp, and unconsciously he reached up to steady him.

"I shall count to three," von Stühlen suggested wearily. "One. Two —"

"He went down to the *Dauntless* an hour or so ago," Theo said quietly. "Did you really leave the mooring unguarded?"

"No. I didn't. Horan!" Von Stühlen turned, his gun hand relaxing. "A party to the creek — and quickly!"

Theo lunged for the dangling pistol, his fingers clawing at von Stühlen's wrist. The element of surprise helped him, briefly, before the older man reacted and the others closed in. But von Stühlen was strong, and experienced, and unafraid — as he turned the gun on the boy and his plunging horse.

264

CHAPTER THIRTY

The very day that she was dismissed from the service of the Queen — a position she held because of her uncle, who before his retirement had been one of the Duchess of Kent's people, and had known Victoria from a child — Violet Ramsey fulfilled the errand with which HRH Princess Alice had charged her.

She walked into Windsor and placed in the general post a plain white envelope addressed to the offices of the London *Times*. It was upon her return that the Master of Household informed her she was dismissed; she was not to see or speak to Princess Alice again, but to gather her few belongings and three days' wages before quitting the Castle for good. Violet might have protested, but she assumed her transgression — the posting of the Princess's letter — had somehow been witnessed or betrayed.

■ ■ ■ ■

On Wednesday, the eighteenth of December, the following notice appeared in the *Times,* in the midst of the column headed *Personal:*

PRIVATE COMMUNICATION TO DR. ARMISTEAD. VITAL INFORMATION REGARDING A FORMER PATIENT. REPLY IN PERSON, THE KING'S ARMS, PORTSMOUTH, NOON 19 DECEMBER.

Georgiana Armistead, for whom it might have been intended, never saw it.

"You *will* write to me," Alice urged, "when it's all over — and tell me how it was done?"

"Of course." Bertie lifted his hand, let it fall again. "It seems strange — all of us so scattered, when Papa —"

Her brother stood awkwardly in his dark mourning clothes beside the carriage that was to take them to Osborne. The Queen had managed to quit Windsor quite early that Thursday morning: It was plain that she was desperate to be free of the place as soon as possible. She had not even looked at Bertie as she entered the carriage; a shudder had served as goodbye.

Alice ran a delicate hand the length of his

sleeve — Bertie was always impeccably turned out — and then, impulsively, stood on tiptoe to kiss his cheek. "I know you will do as you ought. Think of me — I shall be thinking of you — on the twenty-third."

"Good luck with Eliza."

"Yes." She glanced at their mother measuringly. Under the absurd peak of her widow's cap, her countenance looked oddly childlike, vulnerable.

It was, Alice thought, the perfect mask.

They reached Portsmouth at half-past eleven.

It was the custom for the gunnery staff at the Naval Academy to salute the Queen with a volley of cannon, before she embarked upon the Isle of Wight ferry; but today the guns were silent, out of respect for grief.

Alice knew she would have at most an hour at the King's Arms. Mama would take refreshment in her private rooms; and she had only to plead a bout of sickness to be left alone.

"Of course you are indisposed," Mama said coldly, when Alice wavered unsteadily in the doorway. "You could expect nothing less, from having crammed yourself into the nursery carriage. Five of you, and Beatrice most unwell! I do not know what you were thinking of. I was forced to attend to the Duchess of Atholl's expressions of sympathy for a full two hours — and she is exceedingly tedious, as I need not remind you. I have no patience with you at all, Alice."

Mrs. Thurston, who had guarded the infancy of most of the Queen's children, was calling trenchantly for warm milk and beef broth; Helena and Louise, far from retiring to rest as their mother would have wished, appeared to be bowling in the passageway; various maids and footmen were tramping through the upper floor of the inn as though it were a public footpath; and Lady Caroline Barrington, the Lady Superintendent of the Nursery, could faintly be heard adjuring the younger girls to pray partake of refreshment before embarking on the ferry, as the sea air would otherwise make them most unwell.

Alice unlatched her door and peered into the passage. It was empty save for Madame Hocédé, the French governess, who disappeared into the private parlour as Alice watched. She closed the chamber door behind her and descended the main stairs, searching for the taproom. It was possible that Papa's unknown doctor might be waiting there — and she was desperate to speak to him, to hear him soothe the terror that had gripped her since Papa's death, to know that her life was not destined to be tragic, after all.

But the inn was closed to all but the Royal party. Though she wandered the main floor until the carriages were brought round, and she was forced to submit and enter one — no one appeared to answer Alice's prayer.

■ ■ ■ ■

PART TWO
THE CONTINENT

■ ■ ■ ■

CHAPTER
THIRTY-ONE

The donkeys were named Jacques and Catherine — pronounced in the French fashion, *ka-TREEN.* They were picking their way with complete certainty among the stone pines and the arbutus scrub, toward the mouth of the waterfall, and the sun was hot on Louisa Bowater's neck.

She shaded her eyes with one hand and looked back down the precipitous trail. She had never seen such a landscape before, had never felt such an exultant rise of spirits at the unexpected glimpse of the sea; had never ridden a donkey, if it came to that, before this sudden descent into the south of France. She was nineteen years old, surrounded by strangers, and in deepest mourning. But here, on the dusty path cut through the olive groves, she could almost believe in the possibility of happiness.

Leo had never ridden a donkey, either. He had barely been allowed to mount a pony at home — and that, only in Scotland, where he was hedged about with burly attendants. He injured himself so easily that if the donkey stumbled and tossed him onto the rocks — or if he slipped out of the saddle through sheer inattention — he might actually *die.* A careless bump in a railway carriage on the way to Avignon had rendered his arm useless for weeks. But he seemed unaware of the ridiculous risks he ran today. He trusted Gunther. And Gunther had told Leo, in his positive German way, that he would never be well unless he exercised.

Louisa had no intention of contradicting the doctor — of burdening Leo with exclamations or sanctimonious warnings. They had long since moved beyond the stilted conversation of hired companion and dutiful child, to something more like the easy relationship of a brother and sister. Indeed, at nineteen, Louisa might have been Alice or Vicky — Leo treated her much as she guessed he had once treated them, before engagements and marriage and sudden exile had changed everything.

He was holding the reins loosely in his right hand, and with his left, whacking at passing rocks with a bit of stick. He sang a tuneless little song as the donkey — he insisted on riding Catherine, always —

lurched upwards. It was Christmas Eve, and they had come in search of a proper tree. Gunther carried the axe.

It was the first fine day since Sunday, when the mistral had howled in off the sea, past the Îles de Lérins and the Esterelles jutting whitely into the foam, slamming doors and whirling dust into every corridor. That night, Louisa could hear voices crying in the old house's eaves. Lost souls, beseeching and desperate; she had not dared to ask Leo whether he heard them, as he lay in his narrow iron cot in the high-ceilinged room. She simply ordered fires to be lit in the bed-chamber hearths, for a bit of comfort. This was, after all, her first experience of death and its hauntings.

They had come to Château Leader, the grand pile of limestone fronting the Toulon road in the heart of Cannes, more than a month ago. Louisa had recorded the trip almost hourly in her journal: the landing at Boulogne, and the burly French peasant women who strapped baggage to their backs; the few days in Paris, as guests of the British Embassy; and then the slow, erratic descent to Avignon and Fréjus. The weather had grown steadily warmer and drier, the familiar vegetation of the north replaced by resinous stone pines and olive groves, arbutus and juniper. There were lizards on the rocks, and carts full of wine casks filling the narrow roads through the hills. Louisa's papa, Sir Edward Bowater, had been reminded more than once of his years with Wellington in the Peninsula, fifty years back; and he'd told the most exciting tales of war, Leopold hanging on his words in the tedium of the carriage, so that the boy and the elderly soldier had grown quite comfortable with each other — Leo going so far as to call Sir Edward *Grandfather.* He could not remember his own.

But Papa had fallen ill in Avignon. By the time they reached Cannes, it was evident he would not be capable of caring for the child. Gunther — the young German doctor Prince Albert had sent as Leo's tutor — had looked increasingly anxious. His medicines helped Papa not at all. Hurried communications flew between Windsor and the consulate in Nice. Mama — who was Papa's second wife, and years younger than Sir Edward, with her daughter to think of; Mama, who had borne with the loss of the estate and the money troubles and this sudden uprooting to the Continent as a Royal guardian — had sunk daily into greater depression. Leo's amusement and care had fallen almost entirely on Louisa's shoulders

— and she hadn't minded, really. It was a relief to put the sickroom to their backs, and head out on the donkeys into the vineyards and terraces. Together they discovered aqueducts, or the ruins of them. They took picnics with Gunther into the mountains. They climbed the rocky cliffs, Louisa's skirts bunched in one hand, and talked of botany.

And then Papa had died.

Leo was sent to a hotel while Sir Edward breathed his last, but the next day — another Sunday, Louisa remembered, with bells ringing from the churches among the dreaming white houses of Cannes — he had unexpectedly returned with Lord Rokeby, who'd arrived from the consulate in Nice. At first she thought Rokeby had come to take leave — that Leo would be torn from them, she and Mama left alone in this sun-baked foreign town to bury her father. But what Lord Rokeby had brought was Alice's telegram from Windsor.

It became an unspoken bond between Leo and Louisa, this loss of their fathers on the same day.

Mama was beside herself — unable to credit the working of Providence, which had bestowed Royal favour with one hand, only to take Sir Edward with the other, and

277

abandon them in exile. Louisa, however, did not bother abusing the Fates. There was a quality to the light and air of Cannes that suspended time; she might exist solely in this moment, the creak of saddle leather and the pungent smell of sweating animal; the hot breeze tugging at her hair. Without the dizzying view beneath her she might think, instead, of the future — and she dreaded that almost as much as Leo did.

He had pulled up his donkey on the trail ahead, and was almost standing in his stirrups, staring at Gunther. "What is it?" he demanded excitedly, in his high, cracking voice. "Have you found a tree?"

Dr. Gunther — who was only in his twenties, absurdly formal in his German way, and lonely, Louisa thought, as all men of limited means must be — was standing stock-still in the middle of the trail. He held one hand at waist height, in a silent gesture of warning.

She kicked Jacques forward and looked.

They had reached the summit of the trail, which gave out onto the Fréjus road. Directly opposite, the waterfall tumbled whitely through a scattering of boulders spiked with juniper; it was one of these Gunther intended to cut. And to the left, on the brow of a hill, was a traveling coach pitched at a crazy angle. One of its near wheels was missing, and two men in shirtsleeves laboured with the axle. A young woman stood at the horses' heads.

From something about the party's dress and general appearance, it was clear to Louisa that these people were not French. She caught a few words indistinctly on the breeze, and said aloud, "Why, they're English!"

Leo came up to join her. His face was very white, suddenly, under the blazing sun; it was more than usually ugly, with fear.

"I know that lady," he whispered. "I've been to her house, in Russell Square. She's . . . acquainted with Papa."

He reached across the saddle horn and grasped Louisa's hand tightly in his icy paw.

He's terrified, Louisa realised, *that they've come to take him home.*

Together, they waited.

Gunther hailed the strangers in his deliberate German way. One of the men straightened, and came forward to meet him; the other doggedly persisted in repairs to the carriage. Handshakes, gestures followed; Louisa interpreted a broken lynchpin. It ended with them all sitting down near the waterfall to share the food she'd brought in panniers strapped to Jacques's back. The French driver walked into Cannes to fetch a wheelwright.

"Did Mama send you?" Leo blurted out almost as soon as they had sat down. "Is she desperately unhappy because of Papa?"

"I am sure she must be," the woman said. "But no. I have come to the south of France for my health — not on behalf of the Queen."

She was certainly thin with illness, and her voice was guttural in her throat.

"You're looking remarkably well, Your Royal Highness. Cannes agrees with you. I should not have known you for the boy I saw in Russell Square."

"It is all the exercise I'm taking," Leo said proudly. "Gunther insists upon it. He's a doctor, too."

"Too?" Louisa interjected.

"I qualified in Edinburgh," Miss Armistead said apologetically. "The Consort was so gracious as to request that I . . . visit with Prince Leopold. But that was at least a year ago. How extraordinary that we should meet again, in a foreign clime!"

"Yes," Gunther murmured. "Quite extraordinary. I once spoke with your late guardian, Miss Armistead — I should say, *Dr.* Armistead — regarding the statistical manifestation of scrofula among able sea-men in the Royal Navy . . ."

They walked off a little way together, among the junipers.

The Irishman called Fitzgerald smiled down at Leo. He was too old to be hand-some, Louisa decided — forty if he was a day — but there was a charm to his tousled head and a humour in his looks that were oddly winning. Was this what Mama termed a *rake?* she wondered suddenly. Was the stranger, despite the decent cut of his clothes, not *quite* a gentleman?

"What if the three of us were to find this Christmas tree, while the others talk of Science?"

Louisa smiled. She could see that the roguish Mr. Fitzgerald did not approve of women pretending to medicine.

After that, they were able to enjoy the piney sunlight and the cool sound of water over stone. Louisa felt perfectly comfortable inviting the strangers to Château Leader, for Christmas.

CHAPTER THIRTY-TWO

I am tired, and the hour is late; but I must not sleep: I must not drink the sedative dear Jenner has sent to me. In the silence of an Osborne Christmas Eve, I may compose myself, and write, as I must, to the precious ones who are far away. Vicky, of course, in whom it is as natural as breathing to impart the most sacred thoughts of the hidden soul, and to Affie at sea, and to Leopold.

My wretched, miserable existence is not one to write about, I began — and then set down my pen.

Poor orphaned boy! To be left fatherless, at such a season and at such an age — when one is far from home and lodged among strangers, however kindly disposed toward one — however well paid! What to say to little Leo, of the *awful stillness* of the Blue Room, when once that dear soul had departed? He is unlikely to comprehend very much, after all.

You are an affectionate little Boy — & you will remember <u>how</u> happy <u>we all</u> were — you will therefore sorrow when you know & think that poor Mama is more wretched, more miserable — than any being in this World <u>can</u> be!

Impossible to write the truth. I have never regarded Leo as particularly intelligent. His temper is so *very bad;* he is unlikely to feel his loss as he ought. He is the least dear to me of all my children — being so delicate, and giving rise to such anxiety and trouble in his father's breast *and* in mine, he has never been anything other than tiresome.

I pine & long for your dearly beloved precious Papa so dreadfully . . .

I do not think poor Leo ceased crying in rage from the first hour of his existence until the close of his first twelvemonth; and even at two, he was so frequently given to fits of screaming that I once remarked he ought to be soundly whipped. He resembles a frog in his features, and his posture is generally stooped, so that I have never been moved to sketch him in any manner other than the grotesque — Indeed, I avoid the necessity of drawing him *at all.* I find better subjects in Arthur, who is so charming and well-favoured that everyone adores him; and in the pretty ways of Louise and Beatrice.

Leo's frequent clumsinesses and the resultant confinements to bed — here with bruised knees, there with an oozing lip, yet again with a swollen elbow — make him a pitiable object; but one cannot help feeling exasperation at his endless demands for attention. Not even the best of governesses could make him more like other children — by the time he reached the age of five, I had despaired of any improvement in looks, bearing, manners, or disposition. His speech was marked by an impediment, and his tantrums not to be endured. These past several months in which he has been absent, in the south of France, should have been the most restorative of my life — but I am doomed to find the prospect of peace and happiness forever set at a remove. They are not for me; or at least, not this side of the grave.

I shall enclose in Leo's letter *2 photographs of beloved Papa, wh you can have framed — but not in black, — a Locket with beloved Papa's hair & a photograph — wh I wish you to wear attached to a string or chain round your neck . . .*

Leopold is flawed — dreadfully flawed, in every aspect of body and soul. My darling

Albert searched, to the very hour of his last breath, for causes he could name — enemies he could accuse — demons he could exorcise. My heart whispers that in pursuing the Truth — in daring to question the goodness of Providence — Albert tasted a bitterness that broke his heart. But for Leopold, we should all have gone on as before — innocent in our happiness.

Is it any wonder I quite detest the child?

CHAPTER
THIRTY-THREE

"Have you ever seen a sea so glorious?" Georgiana exulted as they walked up the Toulon road together at noon the next day. Her voice was still husky with disease, and she had certainly grown thinner; the bones of her face looked fragile as porcelain beneath the tissue-wrap of her skin. Illness had honed her beauty so that it became almost terrible. Fitzgerald could not stare at her enough.

"Never," he said, "though I will always prefer the view from Cobh."

"You miss Ireland so much?"

"The view was precious, because I was looking *away*."

She grasped his hand and shook it slightly; the warmth ignited his fingertips, and for an instant, he could hardly breathe. The need to take her in his arms — potent and ravaging — had been growing in Fitzgerald for most of the past week, when Georgiana had never been out of his thoughts and only rarely out of his company.

We'll tell people I'm your niece, she had suggested when they landed at Calais, *so that no one makes a fuss about arrangements.*

Arrangements. Train compartments and carriages. Tandem hotel rooms. Fitzgerald lying awake during the long hours of the night in the hope of hearing her movement through the wall.

"That's how I feel right now," she said. "That I've escaped. *Everything.* I'd no idea life in London had grown so dreary."

He tried to smile at her, tried to catch her lightness of tone; but most of him was still on guard, for von Stühlen and the men who did his killing.

They had taken ship by night in Sheerness — a private vessel, the skipper quite willing to cross the Channel once Fitzgerald showed him his purse. No papers were required to enter seaports, which were open to all for purposes of trade; but once in Calais they had to stop at the town hall, and list the villages they intended to visit — an internal passport being necessary for travel through France. Fitzgerald hated this unavoidable disclosure of their plans: It left a calling card, he thought, for anyone who might follow them.

He had been to Paris a few times before — but in Maude's company, Maude's circle: buffered from want and responsibility. He avoided the capital altogether this time, heading south from Calais, feeling his way toward Cannes, with Georgie persistently sick, unable to travel swiftly. In this Gibbon was invaluable: He struck up conversations in back rooms, accepted the wisdom of pot-boys and ostlers. Gibbon found them good inns at modest cost, in Orléans and Avignon and Vidauban. He chose horses when they needed them. Fitzgerald guessed that he also watched their backs — he, too, was tensed for the first sign of pursuit. None had come.

The absence of threat made Fitzgerald's skin crawl.

"My deepest sympathy, Lady Bowater, on the loss of your husband," he said, as he bowed over the hand of the faded woman in the Château Leader's drawing room. In her black silk dress and crinoline, hastily procured from an establishment in Nice, she would not have looked out of place in a great English country house — a dark paneled room with heavy red hangings, fussy with ferns. Here, awash in strong sunlight, marooned in the midst of a marble floor, she was as anomalous as a bat among butterflies.

"How delightful," she breathed, clasping his hand between two of her mittened ones, "to hear a voice from home, even if you *are* only Irish! One grows so tired of French! Is that not so, Lord Rokeby?"

This gentleman had driven over from Nice to wish his compatriots a happy Christmas; a peer's younger son — elegant and distinguished. All that Fitzgerald was not.

"I am pleased to make your acquaintance," Rokeby observed somewhat distantly, "— and may I add that the *lady* requires no introduction. What a pleasant surprise, Miss Armistead, to find you in the south of France! And Mr. Fitzgerald is by way of being . . . a *relation* of yours?"

"I call him my uncle," Georgiana said simply, "as he has served as guardian since the untimely death of Dr. John Snow. But I might as fondly call him a father — for all the consideration he has shown, in recent years. It was anxiety for my poor health which urged Mr. Fitzgerald to bring me to Cannes."

A father, Fitzgerald thought violently. *A father, by all that's holy.*

"Ah," Rokeby murmured. "Exactly so.

289

And how was London, when last you saw it?"

"Plunged in mourning, I need hardly say."

They moved toward the hearth, engrossed in the kind of polite nothings which Fitzgerald found so difficult to master; Georgiana managed them effortlessly, an artifact of her breeding — or the finishing school she had abandoned as soon as she was decently able.

"Lord Rokeby is attached to the consulate in Nice," Gunther supplied, "and was charged with breaking the news of the Consort's passing to young Prince Leopold. I believe he may take the child off Lady Bowater's hands, with time. In the meanwhile, his delightful manners and conversation are a great comfort to her ladyship — in being less foreign than my own."

The German doctor gave no particular edge to the words, but Fitzgerald detected a circumstantial bitterness. He had worn Gunther's boots in his time. He would have liked to have drawn the man out — established a certain understanding — but Georgie had made her tactics plain. *You had better leave Gunther to me,* she had said. *It is fortuitous that he was acquainted with Uncle John; and besides, I shall know what to ask him about young Leopold.*

"Have you seen my fretsaw?" the boy

asked Fitzgerald suddenly, holding out the tool. "I have all sorts of building things. Gunther gave them to me as a Christmas present. But Papa ordered them, he said. Papa thought of me. Though he was quite ill."

The boy's fingers were clenched on the saw's handle. Fitzgerald took it from him: a well-balanced tool of wood and steel, proportioned for small hands. The blade was a marvel of precisely jagged teeth.

And they had given it to a child who bled at the slightest provocation.

He glanced at Leopold. "It's grand! Have ye tried it yet?"

"No." He looked uncertain, half-scared. "I have some wood, though — on the terrace."

"Then let's show your papa," Fitzgerald suggested, smiling, "what his saw is made of. Come along, lad."

There were other gifts as well, which Gunther had procured on instruction from Windsor, well before the seriousness of the Consort's illness was understood. Lead soldiers, a pocket compass. A battledore and shuttlecock. Numerous books, some in German. A fabulous kite, fanciful and clearly French, made of silk and covered in fleursde-lys. A miniature violin, perfect as the fretsaw, for an eight-year-old's hands.

"Ten pounds I was given!" Gunther exclaimed, clearly shocked. "Ten whole pounds, for a child's gifts!"

Princess Alice had sent a game of table croquet, all the way from London.

"She must have read Leo's letters," Louisa explained, as though this were unusual among the Royal Family. "He has developed a positive *mania* for croquet. We play tournaments, in teams, when the weather is fine. You must join us tomorrow."

"I've been winning," Leopold observed. He looked up from the small wooden box he was crafting carefully with hammer and nails. "Gunther and I are allies. The French know nothing of the game. Fancy being ignorant of *croquet!*"

After dinner — beef and an approximation of Yorkshire pudding, which failed miserably to suit, owing, as Lady Bowater said, to the "*stupidity* of the servants, who *insist* upon cooking in the French style," — there were charades, and *tableaux vivants.*

Lord Rokeby began, with an interpretation of *The Sorrows of Young Werther,* which the entire party comprehended almost at an instant. Louisa followed, animating the word *belle,* by alternately swinging her skirts vigourously and pretending to flirt with every gentleman in the room, to the visible disapproval of Lady Bowater. Leopold disappeared after this, and when the drawing room draperies were once more parted, materialised in a black cape and the heavy worsted cloth of a French peasant, stooping and shuffling about the room in search of alms.

"It is that beggar who followed us," Louisa whispered soberly to Fitzgerald, "the whole of our first day in Cannes. Leo and I were quite alone, and this sinister figure — we knew not whether man or woman — dogged our footsteps, muttering scraps of French, hand held out all the while. It made quite an impression on Leo; he could not shake the idea that the figure was Death. And indeed —"

Her voice trailed away uncertainly.

And indeed, Fitzgerald thought, *the boy's instincts were not far wrong.*

". . . made for the stage, Your Highness," Georgiana was saying, on the far side of the room; and then she broke off in a fit of coughing that brought an expression of alarm to Lady Bowater's face.

Soon after, the two of them took their leave.

■ ■ ■ ■

"He bleeds very often from his nose and gums, and must rub the latter with a sulfate of soda when they appear swollen and red. He takes mercury and chalk as an emetic — to avoid straining at the bowels. The least thing oversets him, Gunther says — he nearly died from an outbreak of measles last spring, and a sore throat is dreadful; if he coughs, he is likely to cough blood. Sometimes he passes it in his urine, which leads them to believe the internal tissues have frayed. I gather the poor child bumped his arm against a baggage rack when his train carriage lurched unexpectedly before Avignon, and was laid up for weeks upon his arrival here. What should be a bruise for another child, is an incapacitation for Prince Leopold."

Georgie said all this in an urgent undertone, between bouts of coughing, as they walked back to their hotel. She was engrossed, Fitzgerald saw, in the symptoms of the case — many of which she must have heard long before, from the Consort, but which she was cataloguing in her mind now, as she talked to him.

"Gunther says that given the fragility of

the boy's frame, it is a matter of conjecture whether he will reach adulthood; and, as such, he treats him much as he would any other little boy — encouraging him to move freely and gain strength by virtue of exercise out-of-doors, regardless of whether he might sustain an injury."

"Surely he does not take undue risk," Fitzgerald protested, "with the Queen's son in his keeping?"

"Not undue risk," Georgie conceded, "but he certainly grants the child more liberty than his nurse or his mother should do. That is a very *German* view of childhood, is it not? — That all manner of ills might be cured by fresh air and exertion?"

"German, English — what does it matter?" Fitzgerald demanded. "The poor man's not from another planet!"

He was sharply tired, all of a sudden — of the endless travel, the incipient anxiety, and this constant emphasis on race. It was Theo and his social theorists all over again.

"Well," Georgie said mildly, "in a manner of speaking, he *is*. Gunther's twenty-six years old, and up-to-date on all the newest theories. He's not an old woman, like Jenner and the rest of them at Windsor. He'll do Leo good."

Twenty-six. Exactly Georgie's age. Had

she enjoyed talking to Gunther, Fitzgerald wondered — someone equally conversant with science? As opposed to the middle-aged Irishman who understood nothing?

"How long have you known Rokeby?" he demanded. Another fellow with taking manners and an easy competence; his eyes had followed Georgiana throughout the evening, and he had studiously avoided Fitzgerald whenever possible.

"Some years. His brother will be a duke." She shrugged. "One met him everywhere before he joined the diplomatic service. A pleasant enough fellow — and not at all dissipated, which is a relief among his kind. Gunther tells me he has behaved most intelligently toward young Leopold."

"How so?"

"— By leaving him in the Bowaters' charge, of course. There was some concern that the loss of Sir Edward would throw all their plans into disarray, but I gather the entire household is to remain at Château Leader through February, as originally planned."

"Does Gunther know his trade?"

"He did admit that he observed several similar sufferers during his studies at the medical college in Bonn."

"And? Is he likely to save the child?"

Her footsteps slowed. "I hardly know. He talked a good deal of theory. That illnesses are more or less common because certain populations remain isolated — that is to say, they have limited contact with the broader world, and circulate their disorders among themselves, through social intercourse and even intermarriage. In some cases, Gunther says, such populations are less susceptible to disease — they appear to grow accustomed to it, and resist it better than those who are not. In other cases, parochial societies *encourage* disorders to flourish. Entire towns in the Bavarian Alps, he tells me, will manifest certain maladies that cannot be found elsewhere. As though they could be passed among generations, much as the Duke of Wellington's children got his nose — or your Theo got Lady Maude's hair."

"But he might not have done," Fitzgerald countered. "He might have got mine."

"Exactly. Not everyone inherits every aspect of their parents, Patrick. Otherwise, we should all look and act exactly the same — whereas in nature, variety is infinite." She studied him measuringly. "To mention Theo, again — appearances can be deceiving. He *looks* like Lady Maude to an extraordinary degree. But his inner nature —

his intellect, proclivities, even his emotions — may owe just as much to you. It is often the case that conflicts arise between father and son when they are *too much* alike."

Fitzgerald was speechless. He felt raw, exposed — all his vulnerabilities tossed at his feet. She had seen, then, how strained was his bond to Theo; had seen as well how much the boy mattered. How he yearned for an expression of love from his son.

"I confess that I find Gunther's theories quite intriguing," she continued serenely.

"Lord, they seem dead obvious." Her knowledge of him was too shaming. "Families resemble each other. And so?"

"— If the appearance of a nose, or a pair of eyes, or a facility for writing poetry can be inherited," Georgie said patiently, "then, too, can be a *weakness for disease.* This is a point of some *debate,* Patrick. Uncle John was adamant that disease is created by squalour, and infects the water or air, as with cholera and typhoid. In Prince Leopold's case, however, one cannot point to a source of infection. His malady has been present from birth."

"Inherited? From the Queen? Or the Consort?"

Georgie's eyes were suddenly alight; he had hit on the point of the whole conversation at last. "Prince Leopold's malady is exclusively found in males, Gunther says — at least, in Germany."

"So it came from Albert?"

She shook her head. "A man with the disease never has a son with the same disorder."

"So it *isn't* inherited?" Fitzgerald asked, bewildered.

"Please, Patrick — allow me to explain. A man who bleeds will have a healthy son. Males cannot pass it to males. But a bleeder's *daughter* will quite often have a boy with the bleeding malady."

"The illness skips a generation?"

"And is apparently *passed through the mother.*"

"Victoria." Fitzgerald kneaded his temples, trying to comprehend what this might mean. "You're saying the Queen caused the flaw in the boy's blood?"

"As much as anyone can, when the thing is so entirely in God's hands."

"But she's had three other sons! And none of them —"

"None of them got the Duke's nose. That's the way of it, with families."

His footsteps slowed as they neared the hotel. Something she'd said, just now — something she'd said a week ago, in London . . . "Georgiana, have you thought of what you're saying? About the heritability of Leo's disease?"

She looked at him searchingly. "What is it, Patrick?"

"The poor lad got his flaw from his mother. Well and good. But where did *she* get it?"

"Who knows?"

He shook his head. "That won't fadge, love. I've never heard a *whisper* of a British Royal with this kind of malady. We'd have known. You know how people talk — how the gossip sheets speculate. The wild rumours on every front. Princess Sophia's bastard. Prinny's marriage to Maria Fitzherbert. Cumberland's lust for boys. Something as ripe as unchecked bleeding could *never* have been suppressed."

Georgiana frowned. "There's something in what you say. The Hanoverians have always been known for a lurking madness — old King George, for example. But not this frailty in the tissues. The Duke of Kent certainly wasn't troubled by it, at all events. But his wife — Victoria's mother?"

"What did Prince Albert think? He'd have known. The Duchess of Kent was his aunt."

"I have no idea what he thought," she said quietly. "I only know what he *said.* They're

300

often different things."

Fitzgerald waved one hand dismissively.

"He had never encountered Leopold's disorder before," she conceded. "Among his own people, I mean. That's what he *said.* That's why he asked for Uncle John's notes."

"And burned them."

"Yes. Patrick —"

"If Victoria's mother didn't carry it, and her father didn't carry it, then the disease must have come from somewhere else."

"But it's not an illness you just . . . *catch,*" Georgiana protested.

"No. You have to inherit it."

"You're saying —"

"— That perhaps Victoria's father *wasn't really her father.*"

Georgiana drew a rapid breath.

Fitzgerald grasped her shoulders with both hands. "Is that it? Is *that* why she's hunting us? — Because she thinks you know what she's tried to hide from the rest of the world — what has forced her to send her son into exile — *that the Queen of England has no right to be queen at all?*"

"It can't be," Georgie said. She twisted out of Fitzgerald's grasp and began to walk hurriedly into the hotel. "It's too fantastic, Patrick!"

"Does Gunther know what he's told you? — What possible danger he's in?"

"Obviously not."

"But your Albert hired him!"

"At the recommendation of a certain Baron Stockmar, a Coburg doctor who has been the Consort's advisor for years. He's quite old now, Gunther says, but has all the family secrets in his keeping —"

She stopped short, her expression changing.

"*All* of them?" Fitzgerald said softly. "— Then why in God's name hasn't the Queen murdered *him?*"

CHAPTER
THIRTY-FOUR

I tell the world that I made Baron Stock-mar's acquaintance on my eighteenth birth-day, when Uncle Leopold sent him to wish me many happy returns of the day; but the truth is otherwise. It was a morning in June, when I can have been no more than six years old, and was engrossed in fashioning a daisy chain with dear Lehzen in the park at Kensington Palace, where our household then lived. The stems of the daisies were slippery, and the sun was hot upon the back of my neck; I wore white muslin, as was my invariable habit — a strange thing to con-sider of, now, when I shall certainly never in my life wear white again.

And suddenly, there he was: a stranger with an oddly-shaped head who looked at me like a familiar. He had walked up the carriage sweep as though he had a right to be there; and Lehzen actually ran a little toward him, with a glad cry, speaking in

German. This surprised me so much that I crushed the daisies beneath my heels, and rose to stare at the man.

He approached me without the stupid condescension of those who think children know nothing. Because he treated me with respect, I concluded he was safe. When he said, "Let me see your teeth, Princess," I opened my mouth obediently; when he lifted my dress and ran his hands over my shift, I let him feel the strength of my abdomen and bones.

When he had smoothed my skirt to my knees and said in a sober and judicious way, "She will do very well, Baroness. She has childbearing hips," I suddenly felt ashamed. And burst into tears in Lehzen's apron.

Nothing of Albert's life or death would be comprehensible if one were unacquainted with Baron Stockmar. He is above seventy years of age now, but his first steps on these shores lie far back in the mists of time — to the years before I was even thought of. He came to London as advisor to my beloved Uncle Leopold — who at twenty-five was nothing more than a beautiful face and a fine figure of a man; the third son of the old Duke of Coburg, Albert's grandfather, who could give him nothing.

In the year of Waterloo, having fought against the Monster Buonaparte and been much admired among the English for his excellent looks, Uncle Leopold aspired to win the hand of the richest heiress in the world — my cousin Charlotte, Princess of Wales. They married, and were deliriously happy, until Charlotte died in childbed a year later, along with her stillborn son. But it was Baron Stockmar Charlotte cried for, in her last moments; Stockmar who held her cold hand as the life ebbed from her fingers; Stockmar who broke the news of his double loss to my Uncle Leopold in the wee hours of the morning.

Stockmar understood all too well that Charlotte's death meant more than a crisis for his protégé, Leopold; it meant a crisis for the entire British world. For there was no other legitimate heir to the throne of England then in existence. And Charlotte's death is the only reason I was ever born.

It was essential to secure the succession by producing a legitimate Hanoverian heir; and nobody expected Charlotte's father to do it. He was too old and too fat. His brother Edward, the Duke of Kent, was a betting man who rather fancied his chances — provided he could secure the hand of a proper princess. It was *there* that Baron

Stockmar once again proved his worth.

My father was more than fifty, and had kept a French mistress for nearly thirty years. It would be as well, therefore, if his prospective wife were a hardened cynic, quite past her first bloom of youth. Stockmar observed that Uncle Leopold's elder sister, Victoire, the Princess of Leiningen, admirably fitted this bill: She was thirty-one, widowed, and had already produced an heir to the Leiningen principality. There could be no objection to her quitting Germany in pursuit of greater fortune.

My father wrote Victoire a letter; visited her court some once or twice; found her complaisant on the subject of marriages of convenience — as indeed she ought to have been, never having looked for anything else — and the thing was done.

Within a few months of the wedding, Mama was pregnant; within a year, I was born. And though she may have suffered disappointment, as my father's consequence and fortune were far less than his accumulated debts — Mama had in the end no cause to repine. Rivals to the throne died in infancy; and the way to power was clear for *me*.

Having made a Coburg girl Heiress Presumptive of England, Stockmar returned to the Rosenau, where another child had recently been born: *Albert,* the second son of the present duke, whose wife was unhappy and would soon flee Coburg with her lover, never to be seen again.

Like a faery godfather, Stockmar watched over the motherless boy's rearing; reported on Albert's schooling and athletic progress to his uncle, Leopold; and when the hour was ripe, dispatched the Beautiful Teutonic Youth to London, where the most powerful Princess in the world fell in love with him at first sight.

There is something of the Brothers Grimm in the tale, is there not? A little of enchantment, and also of necromancy — of strings pulled and lives crossed, for ends that only the Maker divines. Stockmar has been the canny wizard of such scenes, turning dross to gold with his alchemic wand, his chessman's plotting; and it is Stockmar I must ultimately blame for Albert's death.

It is all there, in his last letter: the collusion between the two. How fortunate for me that the baron showed his hand, in a few lines of shaky script — and that I might with impunity press the letter upon my curious daughter. Confessions may be infinitely useful — when salvaged, carefully, from the fire.

CHAPTER
THIRTY-FIVE

Wolfgang, Graf von Stühlen, stood at the entrance to Wolsey's Chapel on Monday the twenty-third of December, listening to the melodious voice of the organ. "A Mighty Fortress Is Our God." The old Lutheran chorale Albert loved so well. The Prince Consort was being borne into St. George's, Windsor, by the gentlemen who had surrounded him for most of his exile in England — followed respectfully by his son. Von Stühlen had only the barest sufferance for the Prince of Wales, who reminded him strongly of Victoria, but on this occasion Bertie's demeanour was above reproach. There were Lord Torrington, and Sir Charles Phipps, and Biddulph and Grey and of course Disraeli and Palmerston . . . all of them freezing in the chill of that stony place, a welter of black, of shining silk top hats removed in deference; a sea of men.

Ladies did not attend funerals; not even the Queen.

Von Stühlen stared at the sarcophagus in which his childhood friend — his childhood self — lay rigid and cold. *I wish you no peace,* he thought; *no happy repose of the soul.* Albert had gone silently to this grave — he had confided nothing as the most bitter anxiety killed him. That silence told von Stühlen exactly how little, in the end, he had ever mattered to the man he called friend.

Years of following in Albert's wake, as though the role of court-card and careless hanger-on had been fulfillment enough, as though he'd rejoiced in his useless days and desperate cadging for money — had ended in nothing. He still had no idea why *Albert* had been blessed, and not Wolfgang, Graf von Stühlen, when the world abused one as maladroit, and celebrated the other for his charm. Had Fate rewarded Albert's obsession with ideals? His devotion to what he called *Duty?* From time to time von Stühlen thought he glimpsed an answer — in the immensity of Albert's pain. Fate slowly devoured Albert alive; in its boredom, it never even glanced at von Stühlen. His anger and bewilderment were immense. His mouth tasted of ashes.

The champagne flowed freely after the ceremony; that would be Bertie's touch. The same group of men uttered the same tired platitudes, about dignity and nobility and sacrifice, as they drank to the dead man's health and the wretched Queen's sorrow. Von Stühlen stopped only once as he made his way through the crowded reception rooms, still hung in black silk — to answer a question of Disraeli's.

"Von Stühlen! What you've endured, old fellow! A nasty business, that, in Sheerness —"

"Yes," he agreed. "A nasty business."

He reached Paris the day after Christmas.

A rough ferry crossing from Dover, and an interminable rail journey to the capital made tedious by an unexpected fall of snow. He was unruffled by these delays, however; there was no longer any need for haste or stealth in the hunt he pursued. Theo Fitzgerald-Hastings had changed everything.

When the boy lunged for his pistol and attempted to wrest it from his hand, von Stühlen had experienced one of those odd moments that intersect a life, from time to time: an instant of clarity that would hang, persistent as a mirage, before his mind until he died. The duel in which he had lost his eye was one of these. So, too, was the childhood vision of his mother returning from a morning call, with her left stocking laddered — he had seen her depart the house a few hours earlier with the same ladder on her *right* leg, and understood, in a flash of pain, that she had somehow removed her clothes quite carelessly during the interval. In that single image was contained all he need ever know about women: their betrayals, their fundamental whorishness, their stupidity. Theo's death was a crystallised revelation, like all of these.

He had watched the pistol discharge into the boy's collarbone, had seen the mouth open in agony as the young body went down; had known, without hesitation, what must follow. The pool of blood growing on the stones of the ancient forecourt. Jasper Horan seizing the bridle of the plunging horse and the other men hanging back, all of them afraid.

He could have staunched the bleeding. Driven Theo to a doctor in Sheerness in his hired fly. But the boy would have told everyone how he came to have his wound, and von Stühlen saw no point in that. Compassion had never been his failing.

He stood over Theo while his life bled

away, the pistol still leveled. At first the boy thought he was toying with him — that he merely wanted some kind of information — but von Stühlen made no answer to his desperate questions. When Theo finally stopped pleading, von Stühlen had the horse put into the stable and the body laid nearby, in the straw.

Later, at the funeral in Kent — the Earl of Monteith entombing his heir, a collection of somber men walking behind the black horses and carriage — von Stühlen recounted what had happened. How he'd arrived at Shurland intending to pay a call upon Lady Maude — an old acquaintance — and had found the house empty and the boy bleeding to death in the straw, half-conscious. He had done what he could, of course. It had not been enough. But before he died, young Theo had named his killer.

"I would not have thought it of him," Monteith said brokenly, shaking his head. "Even an Irishman ought to cherish his son. Even an Irishman cannot be so entirely a stranger to decency —"

"There was bad feeling between them," interjected the Frenchwoman, Madame duFief, when she met von Stühlen later, at the Earl's seat. "On account of my Lady Maude. Theo could not abide his father, you know. He blamed him. *Poor child.* So much tragedy, so young — it is a family destined for unhappiness, is it not?"

She would, von Stühlen thought, be a useful witness at Fitzgerald's trial.

The afternoon of his arrival, he paid an informal call at the British Embassy.

It was a beautiful old *hôtel particulier* in the Palladian style, just off the Rue du Faubourg St.-Honoré, with a court embraced by two wings and a garden out back. The Queen's envoy to Paris, Henry Richard Charles Wellesley, Earl Cowley, was a stranger to von Stühlen — he had been at his post for the past nine years. But that meant nothing; the Earl was Wellington's nephew and von Stühlen was everywhere recognised as one of the late Consort's intimates. He was accustomed to doors opening without hesitation.

"An Irishman? Wanted for murder?" Cowley sniffed. His own extended family was Irish born and bred, and the scandal must be felt. "I've had no wind of him — *no, sir!* Nor his woman neither. Had all the local community of English into the embassy, of course, for wassail and waits — burning of the Yule log and lighting of the festive tree, don't you know — a few days back; but an

313

Irishman? Not a hair. Should've remembered that. And the lady's beautiful, you say?"

"In her way," von Stühlen agreed. "Highly-cultivated — with an air of intelligence and breeding. Her name is Georgiana Armistead."

"Damme if I don't know what gels get up to these days," Lord Cowley muttered. "Have one or two of my own, and couldn't get them married soon enough. Well! You've escaped parson's mousetrap clear enough, hey? And more power to you. What's the rogue's name, then?"

"Fitzgerald, my lord."

"Fitzgerald! No relation to Leinster's family?"

Henry Wellesley, thirty years before, had married one of the Duke of Leinster's granddaughters — Olivia Fitzgerald. Von Stühlen smiled faintly at the notion of a barrister being related to a duke.

"He's a Papist. No possible connexion of yours."

The Earl blinked owlishly, as though debating whether to resent this German's display of family knowledge — then abruptly slapped his hand on his mahogany desk.

"If the man's a murderer and this Armistead woman is in his keeping, we shall have to do our *all* to apprehend them. I shall speak to the Minister of Police, naturally — but the pair mayn't still be in Paris. You've thought of that, I suppose?"

"Perhaps a telegram, to your consulates," von Stühlen suggested. "Fitzgerald will have submitted his intended route of travel to a *mairie* somewhere, upon landing in this country. There should be a trail we may follow. The consulates will find it — or their local police."

"Damme!" the Earl said again. "A cloak-and-dagger business, enough. Yes, Wentworth — what is it?"

"Lord Rokeby's report from Nice, my lord," said a junior political officer, breezing into Lord Cowley's office. "He appears to have enjoyed an admirable Christmas feast with the ladies at Château Leader."

"Ah! Indeed. Excellent man, Rokeby. Played cricket with his father at Eton, you know. He's standing unofficial guardian to the little Prince sent down to Cannes for his health, now that Sir Edward Bowater has most unfortunately stuck his spoon in the wall. P'raps you're acquainted with the lad?"

"Leopold?" von Stühlen repeated. "Naturally I am acquainted with him. How does

315

the boy fare, in France?"

"Well — hear for yourself!" Lord Cowley settled a pair of spectacles on his ears and commenced to read aloud, to his guest's increasing interest, Lord Rokeby's report of everything — and everyone — who had celebrated Christmas with the Prince in Cannes.

CHAPTER
THIRTY-SIX

Sir Thomas Robinson Woolfield was an immensely wealthy Englishman. He had made his money in the building trade, and used it, during his prime, to bring the seaside village of Cannes into fashion. His great friend, Lord Henry Brougham — who had founded the *Edinburgh Review,* abolished slavery in the English colonies, and sat in Earl Grey's cabinet before his elevation to the House of Lords — liked to say that *he* had discovered Cannes thirty years before, and made it the sanitorium of Europe; and to be fair, it was Brougham's living there when Parliament was out of session that made the village such an object of curiosity to the London *ton.* It was Robinson Woolfield, however, who built the houses the Fashionable Great chose to live in, while they strolled the *promenade des anglais* in Nice.

He had built one such house for himself,

of course — a very grand edifice of limestone he dubbed the Villa Victoria, being nothing if not a loyal subject. Behind and around its classical grey walls he set a botanic garden, filled with exotic specimens impossible to grow in the English climate. It was a perfect place for parties, and for assignations among the palms; for larcenous negotiations and amicable seductions. Lately, he had ordered a croquet lawn to be established there — for the use of Prince Leopold and his circle.

Fitzgerald and Georgiana were standing together, under one of the palm trees, with a gargantuan jardinière of jasmine scenting the air around their heads, watching Leopold as he carefully aligned his square-headed mallet and with considerable finesse, whacked his dark blue ball. It rolled with perfect momentum across the shaved grass of Sir Thomas's perfect lawn, and struck Louisa's yellow ball with a dull thud.

"Huzzah!" he cried, swinging his stick into the air. "Now I must *send* you, Louisa!"

"Of course you must," she sighed, "and we shall all of us be probing among the plumbago for the next quarter-hour while you go merrily around the wickets. I should like to win just *once,* Leo, before I return to London!"

The boy grinned at her, but utterly without mercy; he set his black ball close to hers, put his boot firmly upon it, turned his mallet in the direction of the dense growth of plumbago, and whacked again. His stroke, reverberating through his ball into Louisa's, sent it careening wildly off the shaved grass and into the jungle of Sir Thomas's garden.

"I'm afraid of you now," Georgie declared, as she lifted her mallet. "You're going to dispatch all of us in a similar fashion, aren't you?"

"If you will but give me the opportunity," Leopold said with dutiful politeness. "I always play by the rules, you know. I'm not a poor sport, either. I should like for Louisa to win — *truly* I should — but I do not think she is cut out for it. She doesn't want victory enough. I do. I suppose it's the blood of kings that runs in my veins."

He uttered the words offhandedly enough; but for an instant, as he stood in a blaze of southern sunlight with his head high and his jubilant gaze surveying the company, Leopold looked invincible. The tentative boy of yesterday, too terrified to handle a fretsaw, seemed a chimera of a nursery fable. *What mightn't the lad do,* Fitzgerald mused, *if he could shake this illness off his back?*

Then Louisa uttered a groan of despair from deep within the shrubbery, and the moment dissipated.

It was a tradition, at the Villa Victoria, that Gunther and Leo formed a team. Georgie and Fitzgerald were designated another. Louisa was left to Sir Thomas, who, while not old enough to be her *actual* late father, was certainly old enough to be a father of some kind.

"Good Lord!" he cried, as he set down his whiskey and soda on one of a group of small tables that lined the croquet lawn. "Miss Bowater! How are we to set a fashion for croquet in Cannes, my dear, if the ladies observe you to be perennially on your knees in the flower beds?"

"It *is* unfortunate that Lord Rokeby could not have formed another of the party," Georgie murmured to Fitzgerald. "He's exactly the sort of person Louisa Bowater ought to marry. Well-breeched, no more than thirty, ambitious in his career — none of your Bond Street Beaux — but an intelligent fellow and exceedingly well-bred. I quite like him."

"I never knew you for a matchmaker, Georgie," Fitzgerald chided. "As I recall, you hated the well-meaning busybodies who attempted to order *your* life."

"Am I a *busybody,* Patrick?"

Her chin lifted imperiously. He was pleased to see colour in her sunken cheeks; even her voice was less hoarse than it had been yesterday, at the Château Leader Christmas feast. The sun of Cannes agreed with her, as did the light muslin gown she had unearthed somewhere in a shop, impossible to discover at such a season in England. She had worn black gloves in respect of Leopold's loss, of course. Fitzgerald, like all the men present, sported a crepe armband.

His hand moved involuntarily to cup the nape of her neck, to draw her mouth to his, to kiss away her outrage, and silence the mere suggestion she was matronly — but his fingers clenched in midair.

"Of course not," he said. "You're right about Louisa. Rokeby's a fool. Of what possible use is a diplomatic career if it ties one everlastingly to a desk?"

A cry of triumph emanated from the plumbago; Sir Thomas's debonair moustache and side-whiskers emerged from the foliage, with Louisa's yellow ball held high. Leopold, Fitzgerald noticed, had nearly circled the course in the interval. Sir Thomas's shout, however, put the boy off his stroke; the ball glanced away from the final hoop, and with an exaggerated look of agony, the Prince tossed his mallet over his shoulder and fell to his knees.

"Your turn, I think, Miss Armistead," Dr. Gunther said with a punctilious bow.

"The boy should not engage in dramatics," she murmured. "He'll be bleeding from those knees by bedtime."

In the event, however, Georgie was proved wrong: Leopold was in good enough form that evening to steal away from the Château Leader, and the party of men who unexpectedly called upon Lady Bowater, just after dinnertime.

The eight-year-old understood only part of what was said. He was supposed to be in his nursery, and was forced to hang over the balustrade of the grand limestone staircase in order to catch Lord Rokeby's conversation. His Royal Highness had been in France long enough to recognise the uniforms of the gendarmes. He was worried they'd been sent to carry him back to England — but quickly realised his mistake when the talk turned to murder.

"Louisa," he whispered urgently through her door a few moments later. "You must *help* me. We must *warn* them."

"Who?" she demanded, looking up from

the book she was reading by the nursery night light.

"Dr. Armistead and her friend. Rokeby means to arrest them. Do you think we can saddle the donkeys by ourselves?"

It was Louisa who sent up a note to Georgiana, while she and Leo waited uneasily in the main reception room of the hotel on the Toulon road, trying not to draw attention. As Leo had spent several nights there while Louisa's father died, it was likely the staff would recognise him and fuss. He had very nearly elected to remain outside with Jacques and Catherine, who were tethered to a hitching post; but resolution and courage seemed demanded by the peculiar circumstances. Leopold had endured pain enough in his short life to fully comprehend that such things as discomfort and fear were temporary; on no account should they be allowed to dictate his choices or behaviour. He was, had he known it, singularly like his father Albert in this respect; far more than his brothers, he could subsume the physical to a higher mental purpose. But Leopold, as he grasped Louisa's hand and pulled his soft hat lower on his forehead, thought only that Affie and Bertie would call him poor-spirited if he hung back; and such a thought was insupportable.

"Tell me the tale from the beginning," Fitzgerald said. "Lord Rokeby is come from Nice, with a party of gendarmes, expressly to arrest me?"

"And Dr. Armistead," Louisa said unsteadily. She looked, Fitzgerald thought, as though she had been crying. "There was a telegram from Paris, I gather — with some sort of information — I didn't hear all the talk myself. It was mostly Leo — and we were afraid to linger any longer. It was imperative that we not be discovered overlistening Lord Rokeby's conversation. Else we might have been prevented from warning you."

Fitzgerald glanced at Georgiana. "Very dashing of you, my dear Miss Bowater, but foolish. If we *were* dangerous folk, you'd be regretting our acquaintance by and by. We might carry you and Prince Leo off, as Royal hostages."

"It was Leo who *would* come," she said simply. "He refused to believe you were the sort of man who could shoot his own son in cold blood. Any more than I can believe it. And the idea that Miss Armistead could place all her love and trust in such a monster —"

Fitzgerald stared at her, uncomprehending. His heartbeat had suddenly thickened and slowed, filling his mind with a throbbing roar that demanded all attention. "My *son?* For the love of Christ — what did you say about my son?"

"His name was Theo." Leo reached for Fitzgerald's cold hand, his voice oddly commanding. "Rokeby said so. Did you not know that he was dead, sir?"

CHAPTER
THIRTY-SEVEN

Unlike Windsor, Osborne was a very new house — built some sixteen years previous on the site of an old and miserable Georgian structure overlooking the Solent near Cowes. Prince Albert had designed the house in the Italian style, with warring campaniles — one sporting a clock, and the other, a flag. The central Pavilion was intended entirely for his own family, while guests and members of the Household occupied the wings. Many of those who visited it thought it very ugly, with its marble columns and stucco façades; others found the arrangement of rooms somewhat daring. Most of the principal ones were open to each other — the dining room giving way to the drawing room, and this to the billiards room — around three sides of the central staircase, which made it an airy house in summer and a chilly one in December.

But Papa, Alice thought as she hurriedly descended the Pavilion staircase beneath Dyce's *Neptune Entrusting Command of the Sea to Britannia,* hadn't cared much about the crowds of guests and their accommodation. At Osborne, he'd been trying to find some peace — and found it out-of-doors. With a narrow band of sea between himself and England, he'd tried to recapture the Rosenau of his childhood.

He'd purchased nearly two thousand acres of the Isle of Wight at immense cost, from Mama's private funds. There was a secluded beach where they bathed in machines; a progression of valleys and woods; gardens leveled and drained at Papa's instruction; and of course — their model farm.

We must practice the virtues of life, children, he'd said as the four eldest were given their garden tools, perfectly sized for their hands and engraved with their initials. They'd each planted a tree, which Bertie marked with their names on carefully-painted signs. Later, they'd learned to mould brick and lay stone, the Swiss Cottage rising under their hands, Affie hauling dirt in a barrow like a common labourer. Papa had paid the boys a set wage for the hours they spent with the carpenters. A lieutenant in the Royal Engineers had directed the digging of earthen fortifications. The Cottage had an entire kitchen where she and Vicky learned to cook, scrubbing out the copper pots with their own hands.

They had talked a good deal of the future in those days, while the soups simmered and the bread baked in the wood-fired oven — dreaming of love, and romance, and elaborate weddings. Papa would ultimately determine who they married, of course — and Vicky had spoiled sport by falling in love with the first man she met, at fourteen. Fritz *was* a man, too, Alice thought — ten years older than Vicky — and he'd decided to marry her when she was only ten. His calculations were obviously dynastic; he was Crown Prince of Prussia, she was the Princess Royal of England. He could not have presumed to a better match. But it was dampening, all the same, to think that the snug conversations of the Swiss Cottage had always been pointless. Stupid and unreal. Just dreams.

Alice shuddered slightly as she pushed through the heavy back doors to the terrace, and almost ran down the broad stone steps to the gardens. How often had she fooled herself? Wasted time in hopes and plans, when everything about her life was a foregone conclusion? Had she truly chosen

Louis for herself — kind, charming, good-humoured Louis? Or had she, too, been maneuvered into marriage by Papa?

You cannot marry Louis, Liebchen. The flaw in your blood . . .

Had Vicky even *seen* her own kitchens, in Potsdam and Berlin?

Old Crawford, her favourite of the gardeners, had gone into blacks for Papa. Alice eyed him covertly as she wandered among the winter beds laid out beside the Swiss Cottage; he had probably had his work clothes dyed, she decided, rather than mourning made up fresh. She hoped it had not cost him his Christmas.

"Good day, Crawford," she said as she approached the playhouse door. "How are you keeping?"

"Very well, Your Highness, and kind you are, I'm sure, to ask." He doffed his soft cap and clutched it to his chest, his rheumy eyes filling with tears. "Terrible news about the Consort, if I may presume to say it."

"Yes," Alice replied. She had no desire to talk about Papa, even to Crawford — who had worked under the direction of Toward, the head gardener, on every square inch of Osborne's gardens. The old man's sympathy was immense; it would smother her like a shovel full of earth.

"I can't get it through my head that I won't be seeing him striding down the path from the big house," the gardener persisted, "like always. *Let us cultivate our garden, Crawford,* he used to say — meaning the garden of life, as it were. Very deep thinker, the Consort."

"Yes," Alice said again. "Thank you, Crawford. We shall all feel his absence acutely. What am I to plant this spring? It will be my last garden at Osborne, you know. I am to be married in July."

"Then we must plant lilies, Your Highness, so you've sommat more'n orange blossom to carry to the altar."

She smiled; he read her look as one of dismissal, and touched his hand to his forehead. She began to walk aimlessly among the beds, remembering what had flourished here, what had faltered there. Each of them had a garden, where they were allowed to grow whatever they liked — although vegetables, Papa had said, were an absolute. He liked the idea of them eating what they'd grown — another illusion of self-sufficiency, she thought. But it was true the bits of earth became the only places in the entire Kingdom that any of them thought of as theirs. Even now that Bertie and Affie and Vicky had grown up and gone away, they sent instructions to Crawford each year, about the choice of plants and arrangement of things in their private beds. It was important to know that some part of them remained rooted at Osborne.

And here was Leopold's garden.

Her brother loved roses, and these were carefully set out among a quantity of peonies, whose lush foliage hid the gawky canes even after their flowering was done. In the dark days of December, however, the garden looked like it had been swept by fire — or laid waste by blight. Thorns held aloft on bare sticks, no sign of the petals slumbering beneath the ground. The worked beds looked as raw as a newly-turned grave. She shivered again. What if Leo —

You're reading portents into everything, she chided herself. *It's absurd.*

A bright splash of green on the soil, close to the brick edging, drew her eye; she bent down to examine it closely.

"How is the young master, if I may be so bold?" Crawford asked suddenly at her elbow.

"Very well. You know he is gone to Cannes, for his health?"

"I heard as how he was packed off to France," the old man said darkly. "I don't hold with France for children, myself."

"I'm sure Leo will have the strength to resist its delights." She rose, dusting off her gloves. "What is that green stuff, Crawford?"

He started forward. "You've never touched it, Your Highness? That's a bit of ratsbane I set out for them voles. Ravaging the rootstock, they are. I won't have that, in my gardens."

"But what makes it green?"

"The arsenic," he explained. "Grey in the packet, but green in the earth. Scheele's Green, they call it. Used for all manner of things, I reckon."

Alice crouched down once more, her black silk skirts pooling around her boots, and studied the bright green smear from a distance. It was vivid enough to colour paint, or dye fabric. Or shade the leaves of an artificial flower, for the trimming of hats . . .

"Where do you get your ratsbane, Crawford?" she asked him idly.

"From the chemist's shop, in Cowes."

"Very well. I'll write to Leo about the voles."

That evening, after she had read Bertie's letter from Cambridge a second time — a brief two paragraphs recounting the essentials of Papa's funeral, and a longer passage about Natty Rothschild's latest party, and a prank he and Natty had got up among the regius professors — she sat in contemplation by the fire.

Lacking Violet, Alice had been thrown back on her own resources. She had pled a headache at teatime, and slipped away in the dog cart to Cowes.

It never occurred to Mr. Daggett, the chemist, that a princess might wander into the village entirely by herself. He had talked to her in complete ignorance of her identity — and been most informative.

"Well, naturally, miss, if your flowers were in water the whole vase was tainted," he'd scolded her. "I'm not surprised your kitty died. Wonderful prone to lapping water from vases, cats are . . ."

Alice was explicit about her Snowball's demise: the low fever, the gastric distress, the vomiting and loss of appetite.

Cupric hydrogen arsenite, Mr. Daggett said. A common pigment, known as Scheele's Green, from the Swede who invented it a hundred years ago. Used to colour wallpaper. Paint. Fabric. Even decorative sugars, for use in pastry . . .

She understood, now, what Mama had tried to tell her — with cryptic utterances and frigid contempt. Baron Stockmar's let-

ter — and a quarter-hour with Mr. Daggett
— had made it all quite plain. Papa had
leached the poison quite deliberately from
her bright green leaves, and drunk it down
neat.

Why? she demanded of the blue flames at
her feet. *If you chose to end your life, Papa, I
want to know why.*

But there was no one at Osborne who
could tell her.

CHAPTER
THIRTY-EIGHT

"Dear God," Georgiana said, sinking down on a settee, "you must be mistaken. We all saw Theo leave on horseback, Patrick — he escorted your wife to Sheerness!"

"Tell me everything you heard." Fitzgerald crouched to Leo's height. "Everything you know."

"There's not much." The boy was too pale, but he spoke as firmly as though delivering an oration to an exacting tutor. "Rokeby received a telegram from the embassy in Paris. He'd told them about our Christmas, you see — that we'd all spent the day together; it's Rokeby's job to report my doings in Cannes. And the embassy wired back that you had shot your son, and escaped to France. Rokeby is to fetch you back. But he stopped first to place a guard at Château Leader. You scraped our acquaintance, he said, in order to do us some harm. But that's *nonsense,* isn't it? Because we just stumbled onto you, on the Fréjus road, and you can't have known we'd be there; and anyway, Dr. Armistead is a friend of Papa's. So I told Louisa that Rokeby's got it all muddled and we have to help. Papa would never swerve from his Duty to a Friend."

"I knew there must be some mistake," Louisa added. "Shouldn't you tell Lord Rokeby what happened, Mr. Fitzgerald, and clear matters up — so that we all may be quite comfortable again?"

Fitzgerald stood like a stone in the middle of the room, his expression closed, as though he heard and saw nothing of the scene before him. "Von Stühlen," he muttered. "Or one of his rogues. They crushed my boy when they couldn't find me."

"I'm so sorry," Georgie said brokenly.

"I'll *kill* the man." He glanced wildly around, as though von Stühlen were lurking in the shadows. "That's what I've got to do, Georgie — kill the bloody villain with my own bare hands! Oh, *God* — my boy, my boy . . ."

He turned his back, head buried in his fingers.

From beyond the reception room doorway, there was a sudden bustle of arrival — the sound of men's voices calling, some of them in French.

"Rokeby," Louisa said. "Oughtn't you to *explain?*"

"You'll gain nothing by talking, Patrick," Georgiana warned. "We'll be carried back to London and thrown in Newgate. She'll have us *exactly* where she wants us."

"*Who* shall?" Leo demanded alertly.

Heavy footsteps clattered across the stone floor of the hotel.

Fitzgerald seemed unable to move.

Leopold tugged his hand. "You must take the donkeys, sir. They're tethered out front. We've put the peasant things from the Christmas charades in the panniers. You may wear them, as a disguise."

He had clearly planned this in the haste of stealing from the Château Leader — and Fitzgerald, despite his strange paralysis, recognised the boy's selfless courage. *That blood of kings,* he thought.

"Quickly, through the French window," Louisa urged. "We shall detain Lord Rokeby for a moment. But only a moment."

"Gibbon," Fitzgerald attempted.

"If you will be so good as to ask Mr. Fitzgerald's manservant to settle his bill, and return with our traps to London," Georgie suggested. "And thank you both. We are exceedingly in your debt."

"Sir." Leopold looked beseechingly up into Fitzgerald's wooden face, then dragged him by the hand to the window.

"Lord Rokeby!" Louisa cried from the doorway. "We did not think to meet you here! Leopold and I have been enjoying a bit of a lark!"

They lost themselves among the twisting streets and white houses of Cannes, which glowed faintly in the December darkness as though they had absorbed the phosphorescence of the neighbouring sea. At first Fitzgerald was capable only of giving his donkey its head, and made no effort to guide it, haste being paramount; and Georgiana followed. But at length she thought it wise to say gently, "Patrick — this beast is making straight for its stall at the Château Leader," and Fitzgerald roused himself from the black thoughts in which his soul had sunk, and looked around him.

"We'll make for the Fréjus road," he said, "through the pines. There's a bridle path the donkeys use."

Fréjus lay west, over a mountain pass toward Toulon, while Rokeby and Nice lay east. From Toulon, perhaps, they could find a train north.

They rode in silence for some time. No

one pursued them.

Emerging at the summit of the road where they had encountered Gunther and his party two days before, Georgiana pulled her donkey to a halt and dismounted.

She walked a little way into the trees.

When she reappeared a few moments later, she was dressed as a peasant boy.

"I shall sell these in Toulon," she declared, thrusting her petticoats and gown into one of Catherine's panniers. "We'll need the funds if we're to reach Coburg swiftly."

They stopped that night beneath a farmer's haystack, just past Fréjus. There were thirty miles to travel the next day; they would have to sell the donkeys in Grimaud, Fitzgerald decided, and purchase seats on a public stage. Alone, he would have pressed on through the darkness, forgoing sleep — but the chill night air had settled in Georgiana's lungs. She was coughing again.

He waited until she fell asleep to wrap his arms around her. She needed his warmth. But it was Theo he thought of as she dreamed beside him — another child, vulnerable and beloved, that he'd failed in the dark.

CHAPTER
THIRTY-NINE

"The manservant was taken?"

"Yes," Rokeby said. "He's being held at the gendarmerie here in Nice. We expect to release him, however — it's no crime to be employed by a renegade."

"Unless, of course, one has assisted in his crimes," von Stühlen observed.

"There's not the least evidence this man did so. Or none that would stand up in court."

"And being the servant of a barrister, he presumably knows the rules of evidence?"

"Being an Englishman should be enough," the diplomat retorted.

Von Stühlen repressed a smile. They were so proud of their laws, these English lords, as though an unwritten constitution could erase the barriers of wealth and privilege. They regarded him with something like pity — something like contempt — as the product of a feudal world. And yet, he could learn more from Fitzgerald's valet in half an hour than Rokeby had managed in two days. He understood the fine points of pain.

"I must talk to him," he said with finality. "Particularly if you intend to let him go. And when he leaves his gaol, I will follow him."

"You think he'll go after Fitzgerald, then?"

"Naturally."

Rokeby shrugged. "Suit yourself. It's no affair of mine. I think you've made a mistake, first to last. The fact that Miss Armistead vouches for Fitzgerald ought to be enough. She's above reproach. Didn't you have an interest in that quarter at one time, von Stühlen?"

Had Rokeby witnessed his humiliation at Ascot?

That would account for the determined coldness, the air of tolerating him only for the sake of Lord Cowley's good opinion.

The lines deepened on von Stühlen's face; his teeth bared in a grin. Without warning, he reached across Rokeby's desk and grasped the man by his lapels, pulling him half out of his seat.

"You worthless rabbit," he hissed. "A child could have taken Patrick Fitzgerald. You lost him on a pair of donkeys. He has probably crossed into Spain by now — or taken ship for North Africa. The Queen shall hear *exactly* how you betrayed her trust."

Rokeby stood rigidly; but his eyes held contempt. "Unhand me. Before I'm forced to call you out."

Von Stühlen laughed. "Your career is finished, my friend. Be thankful you've still got your life."

Unlike Cannes, which still retained the air of a seaside fishing village, Nice was a sprawling port, and had been since ancient times. The Greeks had named it for their goddess Nike, and Rome had colonized its streets. Von Stühlen was a student of the classics — like Albert, he had spent hours debating Plato at Bonn — but he rode past the ruins of the Ancients without glancing to either side, until his fly pulled up in the Rue de la Gendarmerie.

Rokeby had spoken with Gibbon before the French police tossed him in a cell and forgot about him. The valet knew nothing of Fitzgerald's plans, however, or even which direction he might have taken from the hotel in Cannes. On the subject of the dead boy he'd proved more forthcoming.

"Mr. Theo was alive when last I saw him, the night of the seventeenth. Escorting his mother to Sheerness, he was; mounted on his hunter, and riding alongside her gig. What happened to him after, I cannot say — my master and I, and Miss Armistead, having took ship across the Channel. But one man has hounded Mr. Fitz from London to Cannes, and that's this German with the eye patch — Count von Stühlen. First Mr. Septimus Taylor was struck down in chambers, and now it's poor young Theo. Mr. Fitz calls the German a killer."

Rokeby was brought to a stand by this account. He knew von Stühlen had been the one to find Fitzgerald's son. It was possible he'd fired the pistol that killed the boy — but it was totally improbable. Von Stühlen traveled with the authority of the Queen. The man had the ambassador's confidence. Why shoot a seventeen-year-old on a remote island?

If after the encounter in his consular office Rokeby revised his opinion of von Stühlen, the outcome remained the same. He wanted von Stühlen out of Nice as soon as possible. He permitted the Count to interrogate Gibbon.

"Strip his shirt and take him out into the courtyard," he ordered Gibbon's turnkey in flawless French.

The valet tore his arm from the gendarme's grasp impatiently. "Leave me be. And get that fellow out of my sight, damn yer eyes."

"He doesn't speak English," von Stühlen said wearily.

A second gendarme hurried forward and grasped Gibbon's free arm. Gibbon was hauled, stumbling, into the courtyard. His shirt was ripped from his body.

Von Stühlen held out his hand for the horse whip. He watched idly as Gibbon was tied by the wrists, hands over his head, to a wooden post in the middle of the courtyard; it was employed, from time to time, for executions by firing squad. The manservant was short, like all of his kind, but sturdy enough; his exposed back made a simple target.

Von Stühlen cracked his whip.

Gibbon let out a yell of shock and pain.

Von Stühlen struck him again.

Deep furrows in the muscle, immediately oozing red.

The whip hissed through the air a third time.

"I don't know anything!" Gibbon screamed wildly. "I don't know where Fitzgerald's gone!"

Von Stühlen strolled toward him, the coils of leather dangling from one hand. The man was breathing heavily, sweat pouring from his face; such a little thing. Three strokes. Von Stühlen had seen men whipped to death in his time.

"I don't care where he's gone," he said. "I want to know why he came."

"What?"

"Why he came to Cannes in the first place. *Tell me.*"

"Miss Georgie's health! She's got an inflammation of the lung!"

Von Stühlen retraced his steps.

He lashed the valet again.

And again.

The man was screaming at every stroke, the whip cutting fresh furrows over old, the skin hanging from his back in raw strips. Von Stühlen considered the choice: aiming for the arms next, and possibly exposing the vertebrae of the neck, or lashing the back repeatedly until the spine was cut.

"Why did he come to Cannes?"

No answer but a scream.

Von Stühlen sighed. This was growing tiresome. He expected the man to die eventually, but he preferred to learn something before he did. He walked toward him again.

"I can order them to dust your back with salt," he said conversationally. "I've seen it done. Agonizing, I assure you. Why did

Fitzgerald come to Cannes?"

Gibbon was sobbing now, his eyes screwed closed. "You killed Master Theo," he gasped. "Didn't you? And said Mr. Fitz done it. You *bastard.*"

"Gendarme — some salt, please."

"No!"

Von Stühlen grasped the man's hair in his fist. "He left you here, didn't he? He ran — and you've had to suffer for it. You don't owe him a thing. Tell me why he came to Cannes."

"To see the Prince," Gibbon slurred. His eyes were barely focusing. "To meet young Leopold. Miss Georgie knows why the lad's ill."

Von Stühlen frowned. He had assumed the Royal Household had drawn Fitzgerald south — there could be no coincidence in that coincidental meeting — but he'd suspected a kidnapping: the boy held hostage against a promise of clemency from Victoria. Von Stühlen still did not know *why* she was hunting Fitzgerald and Georgiana Armistead — the precious letters from Albert he'd used as a bargaining chip had told him nothing. Or at least, nothing he'd understood.

Leopold's illness. There had been one letter from Albert, requesting notes made at

346

the boy's birth; and a second, he recalled now — so insignificant he'd barely read it — informing Dr. Armistead the notes had been burned . . .

Was it possible the Queen was mortally afraid of her own *son?*

Von Stühlen stared at Gibbon. "What about the illness?"

"I don't know. God's my witness, I don't know a thing."

The man was shuddering violently, saliva pouring from his mouth.

"Von Stühlen!"

The voice was Rokeby's. The British consul stood at the edge of the courtyard, a mixture of disgust and outrage on his face.

"Cut him down," von Stühlen ordered, and walked swiftly toward his carriage.

CHAPTER FORTY

Monday, the thirtieth of December, and Lord Palmerston come all the way to Osborne — some three hours' travel by coach and steamer — with his despatch box and papers.

I would not see him at first, my indignation at this violation of my grief knowing no bounds. A note was sent in to my rooms, in the hands of Arthur Helps, the Clerk of the Privy Council — *Lord Palmerston's respects, and would the Queen be so good as to attend the Privy Council meeting, the matter at hand being the successful resolution of the affront to British sovereignty on the part of the United States of America, in seizing two Confederate envoys from Her Majesty's ship* Trent . . .

I tossed the Prime Minister's missive on the fire and said to poor Helps, "Indeed we shall *not.* You may inform Lord Palmerston he is to conduct his business through the agency of Princess Alice."

"Mama!" that serpent's tooth cried in protest — she had led Arthur Helps to my door — "that cannot be proper. I am *not* the person the Government must address, on matters of State —"

"Very well," I told the Clerk. "Pray inform Lord Palmerston he may speak to our private secretary — General Grey."

"General Grey is . . . *was* . . . Papa's secretary, Mama," Alice faltered.

"So he was. And now he is the Queen's. What better person to stamp the Government's papers for them? He will know exactly what Papa should wish. Very well, Helps — you may go."

The unfortunate fellow bundled himself off, and Alice followed — without a word or a look for me. I gather from my daughter's air of disapproval that she regards me as indulging my sorrow — as requiring this fresh expression of melancholy each hour, as a child might demand a sweet. I am quite content to confound her hopes of improvement; to exercise every whim a pitiable widow might dream up; to ignore, in short, all who would urge me to *fortitude*.

Helps very quickly reappeared, with General Grey in tow, to protest the new arrangement — Palmerston delivering himself of a peroration on the nature of monarchy, and the power that resides in my person, which none other may assume. I suppose he is perfectly in the right — although he cannot possibly argue that My Sainted Angel did not often assume the duties of sovereign — that he governed in my place — that he pretended to all the powers of a king, without benefit of coronation. All these, no one would deny. It is Albert's absence — *not mine* — from the Privy Council, that has them in an uproar.

Grey seconded Palmerston's views.

We argued the point by exchange of letter for full half an hour.

It ended with the Council in one room and I in another, the connecting door open between. In this manner, they could record my presence; and I could avoid attending.

Helps carried the papers to and fro across the threshold.

Before I signed, I glanced continually at Albert's portrait — whispering to him in German, all the while. Once or twice I nodded, as though in complete accord with his advice; and only then did I lift my pen.

I am not above appearing *mad,* if it ensures I am left in peace, and left alone.

The questions I might otherwise be forced to answer do not bear thinking of.

■ ■ ■ ■

From one man at least, I may fear nothing.

William Jenner attended our party to Osborne, as is his custom at Christmastime; the man has no family of his own worth speaking of, and his anxiety for my reason is so acute, that he should never have been parted from me in my hour of need. I believe that the doctor dreads the possibility of blame, for having lost so august a patient — he dreads the idea that history will call him incompetent.

"Queries have been raised," he mused last evening when I consented to see him — ostensibly to receive a copy of the death certificate he filed on the twenty-first of December — "theories, conjectures . . . in the *Lancet* and the *British Medical Journal*. It would seem they cannot reconcile my diagnosis with the medical bulletins issued from Windsor."

"How should they?" I demanded reasonably. "We did not authorise a full disclosure of the Prince's condition. We saw no reason to make his agonies public. While there was a hope of his rallying, there was no cause to alarm our subjects with the spectre of his loss."

"You will observe, Your Majesty, that I noted the cause of death as typhoid fever, duration twenty-one days. I marked the onset from the occasion of his fatal walk with the Prince of Wales, at Cambridge."

"Yes," I murmured. "He was struck down. Bertie! That dreadful cross — it was to escape *him* that we fled here to Osborne. But what possible objection should the medical journals make? You were upon the scene, Dr. Jenner — the editors of the *Lancet* were not."

Poor Jenner hesitated. His face is grown puffy and grey; a decade of age has descended in a fortnight. "The Windsor bulletins referred only to a *low fever,* with a generalised depression. We did not say typhoid. And the fact that no one else at Windsor contracted the illness —"

"The *Lancet* is forgetting our nephew the King of Portugal," I said comfortably, "who died of typhoid in November; and our Royal envoys, General Seymour and Lord Methuen, with whom Albert *would* meet, upon their return from Pedro's funeral. No doubt Methuen and Seymour bore traces of contagion."

"But they met with the Consort less than a week before his death," Jenner faltered. "And I cannot deny that the Prince was poorly for nearly a month."

"Nonsense. We repose complete confidence in your diagnosis, Doctor — for why else should the Prince have died? He was a large and healthy man of but forty-two."

When he continued to look troubled, and would have uttered still more devastating truths, I approached within inches of his person and spoke for his ears alone.

"No word of doubt or reproach shall ever pass my lips," I said. "I make you the solemn promise of a Queen. You did for my Beloved what you could, dear Jenner — and I shall be forever grateful for your presence by his bedside, at the last. I believe we may consider the possibility . . . of a knighthood."

Sir William Jenner. How well it sounds.

He went away a trifle cheered, and I, a trifle less so. Medical journals! Pray God that only medical people read them, and not the general run of my subjects! My seclusion, and the sympathy accorded a widow and queen, should end such trouble with time. What is essential, however, is that *nothing more* be found to feed it.

"Don't you wish to know, Mama?" Alice said to me after dinner.

"Know what, my dear child?"

353

"Why Papa killed himself? That is the burden of all your hints, I presume — that Papa was guilty of self-murder?"

"I do not need to ask myself such a question," I returned. "I know how your Papa was destroyed. He was cast into an abysm of despair — by the *horror,* the knowledge of your brother's *misconduct.* I am in full possession of all the disgusting details of Bertie's sordid affair. Your Papa spared me none of them. I can only *shudder* when I look at the Prince of Wales. But your angelic Papa was too good to live with such wickedness."

"Fustian," she said calmly. "Stockmar's letter refers to Papa's accident last autumn, and that was more than a year ago — long before Nelly Clifden."

The baron had said little that was explicit; but what he had said was enough. That is why I saved his letter. I might have quoted it to Alice, from memory.

Your desire for death, revealed to me during our talks at the Rosenau, is one you must fight to your last breath. Whatever the nature of your doubts about your children, my dear Prince, you can do nothing to alter the past. Let us have no more accidents with carriages, no dramatic

354

runaways. Make of each day what you can, by ensuring that it is not your last.

I rose from my chair. "For most of your brother's life, poor dear Papa regarded him as unfit to rule. He strove to improve Bertie's mind and character, throughout his childhood; but to no avail. Bertie's flaws broke Papa's heart. It was the recognition of *failure* — for the Kingdom and the world — that drove your Papa to his grave. And I shall never forgive your brother for it. *Never.*"

"Bertie's flaws," Alice repeated. "The flaw in his blood?"

"If you will," I flashed. "*Yes.* The blood of our Hanover line. You know what the Regent was! And my Uncle William, with his ten bastard children! No amount of whipping could beat the tendency out of Bertie. We tried every method *possible* to break your brother's spirit."

"Thank you, Mama," Alice said. "I see matters quite clearly, now."

And she left me without another word — chastened, I hope and pray, by the evidence all about her of *masculine* frailty.

CHAPTER
FORTY-ONE

They reached Coburg a few minutes past
four o'clock on the last day of the year.

The red-tiled roofs of the stucco houses
tumbling down from the great castle on the
hill were wrapped in shadow, and there was
snow in the cobblestoned streets.

The weather had turned steadily colder as
Fitzgerald and Georgie left the Mediter-
ranean behind them, climbing north from
Toulon, where Fitzgerald — dangerously
low on funds — sold his watch, and Georgie
her dress. They embarked on a train for
Lyon at nightfall, and by dawn had veered
east to Dijon. From there, they went north
through Reims, east again to Namur in
Belgium, and finally crossed the Rhine into
the great city of Cologne — which Protes-
tant Prussia had claimed from the French
after Waterloo. Cologne was several hundred
miles away from Prussia, across a clutch of
autonomous duchies, and its people were

steadfastly Catholic. Constant strife between rulers and ruled was the result — so that Fitzgerald, a scion of another colonized people, felt immediately at home there. The bells of the Angelus tolled and the great cathedral of the archbishopric loomed blackly against the sky. They spent the night in an inn near the river, and pressed on again to Mainz in the morning.

There the direct route ended, and the rails became local affairs, halting endlessly at every Thüringen station between Mainz and Coburg. They were aching and dispirited as they stepped down from the coach at last. Georgiana shivered in her French peasant's clothing, though they had spent precious coins in Namur to purchase a coat for her. She had insisted on posing as Fitzgerald's manservant — and demanded that he call her George.

She had settled into her role and grown more remote with each mile they traveled into central Europe. Perhaps it was her lingering illness, or her sense of urgency. Fitzgerald could not be sure. Once, when they found themselves completely alone in a train car, they had debated what they knew.

"If the Queen fears for her own legitimacy — if she thinks that Leopold's disease betrays her dubious parentage, and threatens her right to rule — I understand why she wants to silence me," Georgiana said. "But any number of people might stumble on the truth. She cannot fight science forever, Patrick."

"Few of us understand your theories, lass," he said gently. "And there's no proof. What we suspect is sheer guess — with the truth sealed by a parcel of tombs. Victoria's devout enough; she'll trust to Providence, and some sort o' Divine Right of Queens, to carry her through."

She looked out through the train window at the rolling landscape of Flanders. "But *you,* Patrick. I don't understand why she's hunting you. That business about Edward Oxford — the assassination attempt in 1840 — how can it matter now?"

"I've given it some thought," he said. "You remember the conspiracy behind the murderous lad? The pistols marked with the Duke of Cumberland's initials?"

"Victoria's uncle — yes."

"Cumberland said he was the right ruler of England. He called Victoria *usurper* in Oxford's letters. Most people dismissed the word, but —"

"You think Cumberland knew something?"

"Or thought he did. Victoria's old dad —
Cumberland's brother — had a girl in keeping for thirty years, a Frenchwoman he
acquired while playing soldier in Gibraltar;
but she never produced a child. Maybe
Kent *couldn't* father one."

Georgie knit her brows. "The world would
know if he had. All the Royal by-blows are
acknowledged. I suppose Kent's mistress
might have been barren —"

"So she might. Cumberland couldn't
prove anything wrong with Victoria's parentage. And he's been dead now at least ten
years. But the Queen still feels unsafe —
there's Cumberland's son to think of, the
present King of Hanover. He might want to
rule Great Britain. And if someone gave him
cause —"

"You're the only person who remembers
that old conspiracy, Patrick."

"I'll lay money Cumberland's son has not
forgot! *Think,* Georgie! To rule the empire
that rules the world! He'd be a fool not to
watch for his chance."

When she still looked doubtful, he persisted. "Why else summon me to Windsor
and make me swear I'd never revive the
story? Albert's dying must have stirred the
poor Queen's fears, all her vulnerability. I'm
Irish, Georgie. She assumes my kind want

her torn from the throne. And if she learned somehow of my friendship for you —"

"— von Stühlen again —"

"She may have believed I'd carry your theory direct to Cumberland. We're both dead dangerous."

They were speaking very low despite the privacy of the carriage, their faces mere inches apart; and regardless of her boyish clothing or perhaps because of it, Fitzgerald was sharply aware of Georgiana's body. His gut constricted; his hand rose to her cheek. Her eyes were dark wells, unblinking; her lips parted; she stunned him then by reaching for him hungrily.

Roaring in his ears, and a wave of heat; the tightness of her arms on his shoulders and the sense of falling into her, like falling into night. Everything in his being — grief, love, the wildness of frustrated touch — came to life and he might have taken her there in the empty compartment without hesitation. But a porter thrust open the passage door, proclaiming the next station in heavy Flemish; Georgiana broke away, gasping.

She was harder than ever to reach after that. Fitzgerald was careful not to touch her again.

■ ■ ■ ■

The river Itz ran through the heart of
Coburg, which was larger than he'd expected. The castle looming on the heights
was uninhabited; Ernest, Duke of Coburg
— Albert's syphilitic brother — preferred
the Rosenau. It lay dreaming beyond the
city's edge, wrapped in its forests above the
river.

"We shall have to ferret out this baron of
yours," he told Georgie.

"That shouldn't be difficult. He's rather
well known."

"But we've got no German, lass. We'll be
marked as foreigners," Fitzgerald muttered.
"That could be dangerous, if von Stühlen is
on our heels."

"I'll use my French," she said brusquely.
"It got us this far."

There had been no hint of pursuit, during
the long hours of relentless travel; and it
was just possible, Fitzgerald thought, that
they had escaped — that von Stühlen was
still in Paris, watching the Channel ports in
the belief that they would double back to
England.

But the suspense — the constant watchful
apprehension — was taking its toll on them

both. Fitzgerald's deepest desire was to turn and face his enemy: make von Stühlen scream his crimes aloud, as he died in pain for Theo's sake. He continued east only by an act of will. The part of his mind still unconsumed by rage recognised that the answers lay in Coburg. If Georgie was ever to be allowed to live her life in peace, the answers must be found.

For his own part, he cared nothing for the future. He could not think past the moment when he confronted von Stühlen in the flesh, and tore his life from his frame.

They stumbled on an inn several streets off the main square. Servants were expected to sleep on the floor of their masters' rooms; hiring a separate one would excite comment. Georgie had accepted this prosaically; Fitzgerald gave her the bed, and took the pallet on the floor. That first afternoon in Coburg she threw herself on the mattress and slept in her clothes like a dead thing.

Fitzgerald studied her inert form, then closed the door gently and made for the taproom. Unlike Georgie, he spoke no French. He thought, however, he could find someone who knew where Stockmar lived.

But would the Baron consent to see them?

CHAPTER
FORTY-TWO

Wolfgang, Graf von Stühlen, was only a day behind Patrick Fitzgerald, and gaining on him every hour.

He knew the roads and towns of the Rhineland and Thuringia, the border lands of Bavaria, as well as he knew his father's estates. He rode hard, on horseback, avoiding the delays of railways and weather; his baggage and his valet followed more slowly behind.

It was a hunch that drove him toward Coburg: a seed in the gut that Gibbon planted unwittingly in the courtyard of a French gendarmerie. It grew during an interlude at the Château Leader in Cannes and would flower, von Stühlen felt certain, in a day or two at most.

He had not tried to wring information from young Leopold — who clearly had helped Fitzgerald escape; the loss of the donkeys was common knowledge in the Bowater ménage. Nor had he approached the girl Louisa, who seemed frightened of him. He assumed he had his eye patch to thank for this — and Lady Bowater, who clearly knew his reputation and treated him with chill civility. Gunther, however, was different. Gunther was German.

Von Stühlen talked to the young medical man of his training in Bonn — recounting his own student days with Prince Albert — and then of the boy in Gunther's charge. He had never really paid attention to Leopold before; Windsor's nursery set held little interest for him.

"This woman doctor," he mused, as though he knew nothing of Georgiana Armistead. "She was acquainted with Prince Leopold?"

"She had examined him — at the Consort's request."

"So she claims."

"Leopold volunteered the fact. I find nothing singular in Prince Albert's confidence; despite her sex, Dr. Armistead is highly regarded in British scientific circles."

"A pity, then, that she should throw herself away on such a disreputable fellow as Fitzgerald."

"Ye-es," Gunther agreed doubtfully. "I must assume we have an imperfect understanding of the facts. I cannot believe a lady of Miss Armistead's — I should say *Dr.* Armistead's — intelligence and character should be capable of duplicity."

They spoke in German, of course, as they walked against the force of the mistral, on the château's terrace: two men shoulder to shoulder, von Stühlen nursing a cigar.

"I see you were susceptible to her charms, my unfortunate Theodore," he said with amusement. He had decided to treat Gunther like a younger brother. "My condolences. But you are not the first to be flummoxed by a pretty face."

"It wasn't like that," the doctor protested. "We talked of theory, always. The heritability of disease."

And as they walked in the weak December sun, waves booming off the Esterelles, Gunther told von Stühlen exactly why Georgie's mind was so stimulating.

By the time von Stühlen made his farewells, the name *Stockmar* had reached Gunther's lips. The Count was intimately acquainted with Albert's old friend.

Three hours later, he was on the road to Coburg.

Christian, Baron Stockmar lived with his wife in the Weber-Gasse, not far from

Fitzgerald's hotel.

It was the baroness who led them to her husband's study. In all the years he had spent in England, he had always traveled without her; and she seemed resigned to this secondary role of messenger, of a life spent in subordination to the demands of the Saxe-Coburgs, barely meeting the baron's eye as she opened the double mahogany doors. She left them to face the dragon: an elderly man with sparse white hair, his neat clothes entirely black.

His hands shook as he took off his spectacles, and he braced them against his knees when he bowed to Georgiana. For this one important call she had abandoned her servant's clothes and donned a bombazine dress and sober bonnet Fitzgerald had purchased for her, second-hand, from a Coburg mourning warehouse.

"I had formed no intention of receiving visitors, and had you been anyone else, I should not have been at home."

"You have our gratitude, sir," Georgie said.

"You may thank your late guardian, Dr. Armistead. Oh, yes — I was acquainted with John Snow. We met in London, during the summer of the Great Exhibition. He was a rising man, then — but already marked by genius. A tragedy, to die as he did!"

Georgiana's lips parted; for an instant, she seemed at a loss for words. "We might say the same of the Consort."

Stockmar smiled thinly. "I have lived too long, when I must bury a man who might have been my son. There are those in Coburg who feel compelled to offer condolences to me — to Stockmar! — who is nothing but an old man with one foot in his own grave. But *you* will hardly be so stupid. Albert spoke of you, some once or twice; and as he rarely spoke of anyone other than himself, in his letters to me, I comprehend what an impression you must have made. Your intelligence." He cocked his head and studied her keenly. "Yes — your intelligence. It is a supreme mark of respect, that he should have admired it."

"I knew how to value his good opinion, sir."

"Of course you did. You are not a fool, like most women. And this gentleman with you — he is your guardian also?"

"At Dr. Snow's request."

"At your age, Dr. Armistead, I should not think you required any. *Fitzgerald.*" Stockmar wrapped his spectacles over his ears — which protruded rather like a monkey's from his bony skull — and consulted a folded bit of notepaper. "You sent me this note from the hotel. *Fitzgerald.* As I recall, it was a barrister of that name who defended the Queen's would-be assassin, some twenty years ago. Are you the same?"

"I am, sir," Fitzgerald said, astonished.

Stockmar frowned at him. "In Coburg, you should never have been allowed to present your case. But that is by the by. Why have you come all this way to talk to me?"

"Because the Prince Consort is dead," Georgiana said. "And because we cannot believe it was typhoid that killed him."

They had agreed, that morning at the hotel, that no word of the Queen's pursuit would pass their lips. It was essential that Stockmar know nothing of their true position; his being Albert's confidant did not necessarily make him theirs.

"Typhoid." The baron began to hunt among the papers on his desk, his palsied hands touching and discarding things with the frustration of age. "I disregarded the bulletins from Windsor — they were pure nonsense — and telegraphed directly to Squires, the Royal apothecary. They told me which medicines the Consort's doctors prescribed. I, too, am a doctor, you realise."

"You diagnosed his illness from their prescriptions," Georgie concluded. "And what was Prince Albert given?"

"Almost nothing but tea and brandy, at the end," Stockmar returned sardonically. "Old women, all of them — Holland. Watson. Sir James Clark. They got him drunk in his final hours, so he wouldn't feel the pain. For years Albert complained of gastric disorders, Dr. Armistead — a perpetual weakness brought on by the cares of his station — but the inclination took a morbid turn as lately as November. The Prince lost the will to fight. Let me read you something."

He settled his spectacles once more, and licked his forefinger to aid in thumbing the pages. "This is from Albert — the very last letter I received of him, dated the fourteenth of November last. *I am fearfully in want of a true friend and counsellor, and that* you *are the friend and counsellor I want, you will readily understand.* You see in what despair he was."

Georgiana glanced at Fitzgerald. "Are you suggesting, sir, that he died of unhappiness?"

"Unhappiness — overwork — disappointment — doubt. A year ago I told his brother, Duke Ernest, that if anything happened to Albert — he would die. His mind was so given over to melancholy, he had not the resources to survive. But surely you cannot have come so far to learn what you already know? Having been acquainted with the Consort, Dr. Armistead, surely you observed his decline over the past twelve-month?"

"To a degree," she replied guardedly. "But what can have occurred in November to make him lose all hope?"

Stockmar shrugged. "I have had a letter from his wife, the Queen. She blames some trifling indiscretion of the Prince of Wales's. As though Albert had not grown up in the Rosenau! Where every kind of vice was encouraged and displayed — Bah! It is nonsense, again."

"You knew him better than anyone alive, I think," Georgiana said gently. "Surely you must have an idea."

"Love is no protection against death, my dear." Stockmar rubbed at his eyes fretfully. "One can see what is best for another soul — one can fear for him — offer counsel . . . and in the end: One is powerless to save him. That is the agony of being human."

Theo, Fitzgerald thought. He rose from his chair and turned restlessly about the room, his agony so physical he could not contain himself. Had he even tried to save his son? Or had he thrown him to the dogs without a second thought? He deserved this Divine retribution. This ripping of his soul in half. He wanted to drown his pain in drink so stupefying he would feel nothing of love or sorrow until he died; but he would not do it with Georgie watching.

She had fallen silent. Stockmar waited without a word, his eyes following Fitzgerald's jerky course about the room. Fitzgerald stuttered, "Sure and I beg your pardon — a brief indisposition only. Pray continue."

Stockmar inclined his head austerely.

"Might the Prince have been anxious about his youngest son, rather than the eldest?" Georgiana suggested. "We understood he sought your opinion regarding Prince Leopold. That you recommended a man of your acquaintance — one Dr. Gunther — to care for the boy in Cannes."

"I did," the baron answered impatiently. "But what of Leopold? He was absent for the whole of his father's final illness. He can have had no effect on Albert whatsoever."

Fitzgerald had the strong impression that the baron was surprised — that the conversation had taken an unexpected turn. Stockmar was unsure how to meet their questions. He stared at them frowningly.

"Leopold's disorder is generally regarded

as a family one," Georgiana observed. "The Prince asked me, more than a year ago, whether any cure was possible — and required me to examine the child. In some wise, I feel responsible for him — my inability to reassure the Consort . . ."

She smiled at Stockmar faintly. "As a medical man, you will no doubt understand. Leopold's condition demonstrated the limits of my science; his fate has haunted me. I suggested that the Consort search for the illness among ancestors of his own line, or the Queen's, to understand the progression of his son's disorder. It appears to be a disease manifested only in males, but passed most often through females."

"Victoria," Stockmar said.

"Yes. Her mother being a Coburg — can you tell us anything at all about the family, sir? Whether Leopold's illness, or something like it, is known among its various branches? Is it possible that the Duchess of Kent, Victoire —"

Stockmar rose. He took off his glasses. His mouth had set in a forbidding line. "There is nothing I can tell you, Dr. Armistead. My service to the august family of Saxe-Coburg was limited to two men — Leopold, King of Belgium, and his nephew Albert. The women interest me not at all.

And now I believe I must bid you both good day — I am an old man, worn down by grief, and I guard my privacy closely."

"We understand, of course," Georgiana murmured, "and are grateful for your time. Perhaps tomorrow —"

"I travel to Erfurt tomorrow, on a matter of business," he said with finality. "It has been the greatest pleasure. Mr. Fitzgerald —"

The baron clicked his heels together, bowed, and reached for the bellpull beside his desk.

The mahogany doors opened so swiftly, Fitzgerald was certain the baroness had been waiting just outside, in readiness for this summons. She stood as still as a statue on the threshold, her aged hands folded over her skirts. Had she listened to their conversation? Did she understand English? She watched impassively as Georgiana curtseyed to Stockmar. Then she turned and swept to the front door.

It was only as they said goodbye that the baroness spoke at last.

"He thinks I see nothing, understand nothing. He thinks I am *only a woman.* Pah!" She spat venomously at their feet. "It is to Amorbach you must go, *natürlich.* Inquire of the equerry's *frau.*"

And the heavy door shut with the softest of thuds behind them.

CHAPTER
FORTY-THREE

Later, Fitzgerald would realise that their decision to push on to Amorbach that same afternoon — it was New Year's Day, 1862 — was one of the odd turns of Fate that kept them from encountering von Stühlen. And blind to the fact that he was on their trail.

"Amorbach," Georgie muttered. "Where in heaven is that?"

"And why should we care?" Fitzgerald added bitterly. He was weary and dispirited; their days of hard travel had ended in a closed door. If either of them was ever to return to England, they needed the truth in their pockets. Nothing else would help them survive.

"Let's find out," Georgiana suggested. "May I buy you a tankard of ale?"

"If you change your dress for trousers, first. Ladies never drink in public taverns."

It was the innkeeper who told them, in

broken French, that Amorbach was the seat of the Princes of Leiningen. The town sat in the northwest corner of Bavaria — an appendage once belonging to Hesse, and tacked on to the region by happenstance. Leiningen's ancient princedom had lain west of the Rhine, where Napoleon seized it for his Empire; after his fall, it had been "mediatized" — absorbed into the Rhineland — though the Prince was allowed to keep his hereditary title. His new home was in the Miltenberg district of Bavaria, southwest of Coburg, not far at all as the crow flew.

"Trains?" Fitzgerald asked.

A local one existed, to be sure. They could change at Würzburg.

They thanked him, paid their bill, and put Coburg to their backs an hour and a half later.

"The present Prince of Leiningen, Charles, is Queen Victoria's half brother," Georgie said as the train chugged slowly south. "Their mother — the Duchess of Kent to us — was married to the old Prince when she was just seventeen. Two children and a decade or so later, he died — and the widow married Edward, Duke of Kent. Poor Kent survived only a year after the wedding. He left his duchess to raise their girl to be queen. But what has all that to do with an *equerry's wife?*"

Fitzgerald frowned. "There were always rumours, I believe, about the Duchess of Kent and her man-of-all-work, Sir John Conroy. He was the Duke's equerry before he became the Duchess's man, after Kent's death. But he was Irish — and had no ties to Amorbach I ever knew."

"The person the Baroness spoke of must be a link to Victoire," Georgie mused. "It is *her* past — or perhaps I should say the Princess of Leiningen's, as she then was — we're seeking in Amorbach. Victoria — or Albert, for that matter — never had anything to do with the place."

"Then we must find out who served as the Prince of Leiningen's equerry in Victoire's time."

"Is anyone likely to remember?" Georgiana threw up her hands in frustration. "She married Kent and left Amorbach in 1818. We're asking the local people to think back more than forty years. Patrick, it's impossible!"

"I know." He ran his fingers through his tangle of hair. "This whole trip has been a fool's errand, hasn't it? We can't exactly drive up to the palace and ask Victoire's son for the name of his mother's lover. He'd be unlikely to know much at all. He must have been a child when she married Kent."

"A servant could tell us something. One of your old retainers, long tied to the Leiningen family."

"Let's hope, then, that they feel no loyalty to Victoire's memory."

They had been expecting something like Coburg: a thriving city, fit for a prince. But Amorbach was a small town lost in the hills and the dense growth of the Odenwald Forest. It was known for its Benedictine abbey, which had been founded in the thirteenth century and converted to a country manor in the last one; for the cathedral that graced its northern heights; and for the schloss that dominated the western edge of town. In between, there wasn't much: pretty half-timbered cottages, a tavern or two, and the railway station where the trains from Würzburg and Mainz arrived each hour.

They were the only passengers getting off. Georgiana glanced about her as they descended to the platform.

"There can't be more than a thousand people in this place," she said to Fitzgerald. "It might be Windsor, but for the trees."

"Let's try a tavern, first."

They chose what seemed to be the principal inn, on a side street not far from the cathedral, with the arms of Leiningen swinging over the door.

Fitzgerald presented himself as an English writer, commissioned to research the life of the late Duchess of Kent — almost a year after her death, he told the credulous, he was preparing a distinguished biography at the direction of the Queen. The work would be serialised in the London papers and published later, in three quarto volumes, by a prestigious British press.

His manservant, George, translated this deferentially into French, which the innkeeper's wife at least understood. She had been educated at the convent school in Mainz. When they had done with the explanations, she conferred in German with her husband, and then called out into the taproom. A hurried confabulation with two men ensued, after which she turned once more to Fitzgerald.

"She says that most of Victoire's household have died, but we must of a certainty talk to the Prince of Leiningen's nursemaid, who is nearly eighty, and pensioned off," Georgiana murmured. "The nurse came from Coburg to Amorbach with Victoire, at her marriage to old Prince Emich, God rest his soul; and now lives with her son, a tenant farmer, near the Schloss Leiningen."

"Eh, that's grand."

"There is also the late prince's old steward, who lodges here in town."

"Ask if the equerry is anywhere to be found."

Georgiana put the question; Fitzgerald saw the woman hesitate, shake her head, and then add a few words.

"Dead years and years ago, she says. And, of course, Captain Schindler — that was the equerry's name — was a military officer, far above the serving class, so she did not even consider of him. But his widow" — Georgiana's voice trembled slightly with excitement — "his *widow* lives with her married daughter, in the Otterbachtal. The innkeeper will draw us a map."

In the end, they put very few questions to the equerry's wife. Not many were necessary.

They found their way to her daughter's house, a handsome and substantial home belonging to an Amorbach burgher, on a morning of uncertain sunshine. The widow Schindler received them in the morning room, which overlooked a snowy garden; a fire burned brightly in the hearth. She was

380

a faded beauty of perhaps sixty, purposeful and calm. To their relief, she spoke French; and again, in the guise of manservant, Georgiana served as translator.

She had married Captain Schindler forty years before, long after the Princess of Leiningen left Amorbach for England. "My husband was in his late twenties, then. When the Princess married Kent, Richard was made head of the schloss's household guard by the Royal Wards — the council that served as Regent for the young Prince Charles, until he came of age. Prince Charles spent a good deal of his youth with his mother in England, you know, when he was not in Amorbach; and the Duchess of Kent — as she became — was exceedingly worried that his throne would be usurped. Old Prince Emich, Charles's father, had a number of bastards — all pretending to the crown. But with my husband at the castle, the Duchess could be easy."

"He was devoted to her interests?"

"Of course," Frau Schindler said simply. "Richard *adored* the Princess. He told me once that he would have died for her. And she rewarded him for it. Even after she went to England and married Kent, she sent him a yearly draft on her bank. *Coutts,* I think it was. I saw the letters come, year after year.

When he died, of course, they stopped."

Georgiana glanced at Fitzgerald.

"Did you ever meet the Duchess of Kent, ma'am?"

Frau Schindler shook her head. "I married Richard four or five years after she left Amorbach. Even Richard did not see her once she removed to England. He did not like her husband, the Duke. He thought the man much too old for Victoire — lacking in vitality. A *mariage de convenance.* The Duke came to Amorbach once after their marriage, before the child was born. *Et voilà!* It was as my Richard said: The Duke was dead before Victoria was a year old. Richard did not see the Duchess again after that. He began a new life. Later, we were married, when I was just sixteen."

A visit to Coburg, before Victoria was born. Yearly payments, from an account at Coutts. Had the Duchess bought her lover's silence?

Fitzgerald calculated rapidly. The Kents were married in London in July 1818. Their child was born at the end of the following May. Victoria must have been conceived in late August or early September.

"Ask her when the Kents visited Coburg," he told Georgiana. "Sometime in the autumn of 1818?"

Frau Schindler shrugged. She could not remember something she had heard about only once or twice, four decades ago.

"How did she lose her husband?"

The door to the morning room was thrust open, and a little boy of about six limped carefully across to his grandmother. He held a tin soldier in one grubby fist; tears stained his cheeks. Frau Schindler went to him, and held him close — then spoke hurriedly in French.

"Her daughter's youngest, and very delicate," Georgiana told Patrick, her brows knitting. "He has just had a bruising fall. It is best that we leave . . ."

Fitzgerald rose and bowed. *"Je vous remercie, madame,"* he said haltingly. "Now ask her, for the love of God, how her husband died."

Georgie hesitated, her eyes on the child. His trousers, wet with blood, were torn above the right knee. She reached into her coat for a handkerchief and began to tear it into strips, then knelt and bound it around the boy's knee. Immediately, red stains soaked through the linen.

Frau Schindler murmured something. Fitzgerald noticed her hands were shaking as they smoothed her grandson's hair.

"It was the same with Richard," Georgiana

translated for him. "The bleeding. One day he fell on the marble steps at Schloss Leiningen — and bled to death."

CHAPTER
FORTY-FOUR

Neither of them spoke as they left the widow Schindler's house. Georgiana had blood on her hands; Fitzgerald stopped in the street and searched for his handkerchief.

"You know, love," he said as he rubbed at her palms, "we can prove nothing. Nothing a'tall."

"But we *know*," Georgiana insisted. "We know what Prince Albert must have discovered. He came back to the Rosenau last September and delved deep into the records, studying his family line. He learned what we learned. *There are no bleeders among his Coburg ancestors.* There are no bleeders in the House of Hanover. The disease must have come from elsewhere."

"D'ye think he met the widow Schindler?"

"Something made him desperate enough to attempt suicide, in that runaway carriage."

"But *why?*" Fitzgerald demanded. "He

never caused this!"

"No," she said quietly. "But neither was he the man to profit from a lie."

They stood for an instant, in silence.

"He probably didn't want to believe it." Fitzgerald balled up his handkerchief. "He talked to yon lady. Thought about her grandson. Read up on the science. Asked for John's notes —"

"And then, in the middle of November, he accepted the truth. To his utter despair. *I am fearfully in want of a true friend and counsellor . . .*"

"The Duchess of Kent had a cuckoo in her nest — and put her right on the throne of England. The Saxe-Coburg fortunes were made forever! Albert went from being the second son of a minor duke, to running the show in England — and his children after him. . . . I wonder if he told his wife what he suspected?" Fitzgerald said thoughtfully.

"She's terrified of something." Georgiana stopped short near the entrance to the inn. "Why hunt for you otherwise? Why attempt to silence me? Why send poor Leopold into exile in France?"

"The boy's hardly pining away," Fitzgerald objected. "He's having a rare adventure, look you. Imagine the scene when he's summoned home."

"That's beside the point. Patrick — what are we going to do?"

"We're going back to England," he said, "and have a talk with the Queen. We must buy our freedom, Georgie — with a promise of silence. In writing."

"You would *do* that? Suppress the truth — swallow the murders of Sep and Lizzie and Theo — to save your own skin?"

She was staring at him accusingly: a pert young boy in shabby clothing, her hands thrust into her pockets for warmth. He yearned to pull her to him and cover her face with kisses; but he simply said, "To save *yours,* my darling, I'd deny the resurrection of the good Lord Himself. Now pack your things. I'll fetch tickets for Mainz. Be ready in an hour."

The Mainz train left Amorbach twelve times a day. From there, the line ran directly to Cologne — and from Cologne, it was possible to reach London in thirty hours. Lacking a watch, Fitzgerald glanced at the station clock: nearly noon on Thursday, the second of January. They could make the two o'clock train and be back in London, barring a major mishap, by Saturday night at the latest.

He spared a thought for Gibbon — not

the first during the long ordeal of German travel — and hoped he'd managed to find his way from Cannes to Dover. A letter to Bedford Square would reach Gibbon only when they did; and if the Metropolitan Police intended to charge Fitzgerald with murder, he must avoid Bedford Square above all else. There would be difficulties re-entering the country — the ports were probably watched. He would have to avoid the usual Channel packets and hire a private boatman, who might put them off discreetly somewhere along the English coast. Was the Queen at Windsor? — Or had she left, as was her custom, to spend January at Osborne House? An English newspaper could tell him. The Isle of Wight was directly accessible by boat, and London could be entirely avoided — if only he still had the *Dauntless.* . . .

Theo.

The thought of Sheppey flared within him, and burned.

He bought two tickets and turned back to the inn. Feverishly calculating expenses. It was possible he would have to sell something else in Mainz. His coat?

Taking the stairs two at a time, he dashed up to his room.

The door stood open, his few belongings

exactly as he'd left them. Georgiana's medical bag. The gown she'd worn to call upon Stockmar. The rumpled pallet where he'd slept, which the maid had yet to tidy. But the single straight-backed chair was overturned, and at the sight of it, Fitzgerald was dizzy with nausea.

"Georgie," he said aloud, knowing she would not answer.

Georgiana was gone.

CHAPTER
FORTY-FIVE

He was waiting for her when she entered the bedchamber: hidden in the shadow between door and wall. She had no time to cry out — he thrust a wad of cotton, dipped in chloroform from her own supplies, against her nose and mouth. In his other hand he held her neck.

She might have kicked him — might have toppled the chair Patrick found on the floor — but the struggle was short and utterly silent. Von Stühlen won.

Later, she understood that they'd been careless: too driven by the scent of their elusive trail to have a thought for their own safety. Von Stühlen had arrived in Amorbach the previous night and learned immediately from the innkeeper — whom he'd known for years — that an Englishman and his manservant were lodged upstairs. He'd watched them leave for the Otterbachtal that morning. He'd watched them return.

When Patrick made for the station and she chatted with the innkeeper's wife as she settled their bill, he'd prepared his strike.

When she regained consciousness, he was slapping her.

She tried to struggle upright, but her hands were bound behind her back. Her mouth was gagged. She was lying prone, on the bench seat of a traveling coach. She stared at von Stühlen, whose head loomed over her, his face expressionless; his hand clenched, and he slapped her again, deliberately. Her gorge rose — chloroform always made her sick — and she knew that she would choke.

She rolled sideways, head hanging over the seat, gagging wretchedly. He tore at the knot he'd made at the base of her skull and she puked all over his boots.

She cleaned them with a shaving towel herself, while von Stühlen held his dueling pistol to her head. When he was satisfied with her work, he handed the boots to his valet — a broad-shouldered prizefighter of a man, who sat beside him in the coach, grinning at her stupidly.

"We'll have to change carriages," von Stühlen observed, rolling down the side windows. "The place stinks like an abattoir. Tell me, Miss Armistead — why did you come all the way to Amorbach in a servant's clothes? You're an insult to womanhood."

Georgiana said nothing. She was bent slightly forward on the seat, her hands tied once more behind her back.

"Heinrich, I can't stand to look at her," von Stühlen said conversationally. "Something must be done. Take off her clothes, there's a good chap."

She definitely kicked him this time — viciously, on the shin — but with a deft movement von Stühlen clasped her knees together and put all his weight on them. The valet started with her coat — dragging it down over her shoulders until it snarled on her bonds — and then ripped her shirt from neck to waist. She had bound her breasts flat with strips of cloth.

The two men stared at her bandaged chest. Then von Stühlen reached for his knife.

It took Fitzgerald a good quarter-hour to decipher what the innkeeper's wife had seen. Her French was heavily accented and he didn't speak the language anyway; it was mostly guesswork, with her husband interjecting a word or two of German unhelpfully along the way. His manservant George had been carried, drunk as a lord, from the inn after settling their bill — and gone off with his new friends in a carriage, rather than a train.

However vague the details, von Stühlen's name was unmistakable.

"Direction?" Fitzgerald demanded.

"*À l'ouest,*" said the innkeeper's wife. "*À Mayence, peut-être.*"

Mainz. He had a railway ticket in his pocket, but von Stühlen was traveling fast, perhaps a half-hour ahead of him; he could not lose time on the agonising local train. Not when Georgiana was in the Count's hands. How had she said he earned his dreadful reputation? — *For raping the unwilling.*

"I need a horse," he told the innkeeper's wife. "*Un cheval. Vite!*"

It was another twenty minutes before he clattered out of the stable on a nag he'd promised to leave in Mainz — and his purse was almost empty.

"Why are you doing this to me?" Georgiana demanded. "Because I laughed in your face at Ascot? Are you so thin-skinned?"

He had chloroformed her again at dusk when they pulled into the yard behind the small woodside tavern. The handkerchief terrified her, because von Stühlen had no medical knowledge at all; he thought of the drug as a means of control, while she recognised it as a source of death.

She did awake, however, in a tavern bed-chamber — her wrists and ankles tied to the bedposts, her legs spread-eagled on the frame. She was completely naked, and the world outside the single narrow window had gone completely dark. The German Count was sitting in a chair in the corner, smoking one of his cigars. She felt the familiar nausea rise and willed herself not to be sick, to steady her whirling head.

Imagine he's a doctor, she told herself. *Imagine this is a medical examination.*

"Thin-skinned?" he repeated. "You exaggerate your individual importance, I'm afraid. Women, you know, will always be interchangeable; like horses, some of you boast better blood or better lines — but you're fundamentally there to be *ridden.* When you, Miss Armistead, chose to ridicule me in the face of the world — the equation changed." He withdrew his cigar and examined it. "A horse that tosses his rider is first broken to bridle — then *sold.*"

Georgiana stared fixedly at the ceiling, her teeth clenched against her fear. It was possible Patrick was following them. It was possible she would be saved.

The door to the room opened a crack, and von Stühlen's valet slipped inside. The Count asked him something in German; the man replied in the negative.

They're watching for him, she thought. *I'm the trap.* And willed Patrick not to come.

"Heinrich has never enjoyed a woman of your quality," von Stühlen observed. "I've told him you're no virgin, of course, but he's pathetically eager to experience your charms."

The valet was already kicking off his boots.

"What do you want to know?" Georgiana asked desperately. Trying to buy time. "Why have you come all the way across Europe, after me? Not because of Ascot. Even I don't believe that."

"It hardly matters." Von Stühlen studied the end of his cigar with his good eye; he was smiling faintly. "You're an abortionist, my dear. And your last patient died at your hands. Lizzie, her name was."

"That's a lie!" she spat. "Lizzie was murdered — but not by me. The poor girl was smothered with a pillow. Did you order it?"

"That's a double murder charge under the Offences Against the Person Act," he continued, as though she hadn't spoken. "— An Act just passed by Parliament this year. Abortion is noted in section fifty-eight. But perhaps you don't follow legislation as closely as you do your prostitutes."

Heinrich clambered into the bed, and straddled her pinioned body.

"What do you want to know?" she gasped.

"Don't worry," von Stühlen said soothingly. "You'll tell me everything you can think of. Heinrich will make sure of that."

CHAPTER
FORTY-SIX

The man shaking out the drugget on the area steps moved with a certain painful hesitation, as though his muscles were sore from overuse. He winced slightly as his hands rose and fell, a cloud of dust billowing from the length of carpet; and then, abruptly, his arms dropped and he turned away from the January morning, the fog that flowed down the steps like a predatory snake. The carpet hung disconsolately at his side; he kept his eyes fixed on the ground. There was a fire in the kitchen hearth, and he was in a hurry to get back to it.

He'd been a cheerful enough fellow before his master turned murderer, the Bobby thought as he strode past Patrick Fitzgerald's doorstep. Bedford Square was the Bobby's route, and often were the times he'd traded gibes with Gibbon. But guilt could do that to a man — rob him of all the joy of living. The valet knew more'n he would say. A prisoner in his own few rooms, he was; a goat tethered for the kill. He knew the police were watching him. Never went out anymore, for all he lived so lonesome, except to buy the odd egg and rashers. Never talked to the neighbours, though some said he'd been sweet on the house-maid four doors down, before everything happened. Waiting, that's what he was — waiting for Fitzgerald to show himself. They were all waiting. Gibbon's return had got the Law's hopes right up. But the man had been back four days now, and no sign of the master.

The Bobby sighed as he went his monotonous way, longing for a sit-down by the fire himself.

The men at the Nice gendarmerie were content to let him die. Rokeby had said that was nonsense, and sent a military surgeon of his acquaintance to salve and bind Gibbon's wounds. The pain, at first, made him faint every time he moved, and a fever set in; but by the second morning, when Rokeby reappeared in his prison cell, he was able to sit up unaided.

"I've told the gendarmes to let you go," the consul said. "Whatever your master may have done, it's clear you had no part in it —

398

if you had, you'd have screamed it to the heavens when von Stühlen whipped you. There's no shame in that," he added hurriedly. "You were served with excessive violence — I may even say, out of all proportion to the cause. Have you enough money for your journey home?"

Perhaps it was guilt that motivated the consul's kindness, or a desire to be rid of an embarrassing episode. Whatever the cause, Gibbon's clothes were returned and his seat purchased on the public stage to Toulon.

He landed at Dover on the first day of the New Year.

The Bobby was right: Gibbon knew the Law was watching him. He'd been met at the packet by a pair of detectives Rokeby had wired from Nice, who escorted him to what they called Scotland Yard — the Metropolitan Police headquarters. There, the same old ground was gone over at the direction of a detective chief inspector. Gibbon told them how his master had found Septimus Taylor attacked in chambers, the day after the Consort's death, and called for a doctor to save him. He explained how he, Gibbon, had watched young Theo escort Lady Maude on the road to Sheerness, as Fitzgerald turned for a boat in the opposite direc-

tion. He told them, moreover, how Wolfgang, Graf von Stühlen — who claimed to
have discovered Theo's body — had pursued
them all the way to Cannes. *A zeal for justice,*
the detective chief inspector murmured. In
answer, Gibbon showed him the wounds on
his back.

The police shrugged, but declined to
throw him into Newgate. They conducted
him instead to Bedford Square. Fitzgerald's
house had been thoroughly searched before
— for what, Gibbon was never sure. They
left the valet in possession of their mess,
with a warning that he was not under any
circumstances to flee London. If his master
returned, he was to inform them immediately — on pain of conspiracy charges.

He settled in, as they expected, to wait.
Fitzgerald would undoubtedly come back;
and it was Gibbon's job to make sure he
ran well clear of the Law. He had identified
three of the men who watched his days by
the end of the first thirty-six hours; loiterers
near a flaming ash can, who took the job in
shifts. They hovered near the gated entrance
to Bedford Square. The mews behind the
house had only one watcher: a gent in a
greatcoat, who lounged aimlessly near the
neighbour's coach house, blowing on his
fingers in the bitter January cold.

■ ■ ■

Gibbon developed a routine to pass the time. Fires in the principal hearths at seven a.m., so the damp did not penetrate the deserted rooms. Tidying of the kitchen and scullery by eight. Slicing and ironing of the newspaper, as though Fitzgerald might require it. General housework and thorough cleaning, such as he rarely found the time to do when Fitzgerald was in residence. An hour with the newspaper over his dinner, which he took at two o'clock when left to his own devices; and the luxury of a pipe to follow. Silver polishing in the afternoon, and assessment of his master's wardrobe — what could be mended, what must be brushed and pressed, what given away to the rag-and-bone men who loitered in the mews. Supper he took in a local pub: a simple affair of bubble and squeak, or bangers and mash, washed down with the publican's porter. A watchful stroll around the square — if Fitzgerald made contact, it would probably be at night — and the throwing of the bolts before an early bed.

He managed the household accounts carefully from the strongbox he stored under his floorboards. They had left London near the end of the previous month, and Fitzgerald's January wages and domestic cash were sorely lacking. Gibbon had a bit put by, however — the steady savings for his old age — and he was not beyond tapping it if Fitzgerald's absence was prolonged. Tradesmen's bills were a nagging worry: If demands proved exorbitant, he would have to consider shutting up the house by the end of the month, and lodging with his sister near the Elephant and Castle. This weighed on Gibbon's mind; how would Fitzgerald find him if he vanished from Bedford Square?

On the morning of January second, however, a new interest appeared to divert his mind.

He had taken to scanning the *Personal* column in the London *Times* while he dined. Quite often the notices were perfunctory, but sometimes they were amusing.

MISS KILDARE'S RESPECTS TO MR. TIMMONS, WITH HER REQUEST THAT HE RETURN, PRIOR TO HIS WEDDING DAY, THE CORRESPONDENCE SHE SO FAITHFULLY CONDUCTED OVER THE COURSE OF THE PAST FIVE YEARS; ALL REPLIES TO BE SENT 25, GRACE-CHURCH STREET, LONDON. . . .

A WALLET OF MONEY, AND THE
DOCUMENTS CONTAINED THEREIN,
SUBSCRIBED MR. A —— PR ——, MIS-
LAID WHILE THE OWNER WAS EN-
GAGED UPSTAIRS AT THE SIGN OF
THE LUCKY PENNY: REPLIES TO MRS.
BARNACLE, PROPRIETRESS. . . .

He could perfectly envision Mrs. Barnacle,
who undoubtedly kept a bawdy house, and
would make the discomfitted Arthur Pro-
theroe pay for the return of his property —
if she did not blackmail him for the remain-
der of his useless existence; and Miss Kildare, who had hoped in vain for an offer
from her young man, only to read the an-
nouncement of his engagement in that
selfsame *Times* . . .

He never expected to read the name of
someone he knew.

PRIVATE COMMUNICATION TO DR.
ARMISTEAD . . .

A brief notice, without the slightest hint
of its author's identity. Replies must be sent
to the postal office, Cowes, to be left until
called for.

It worried Gibbon that this plea — so
oblique, but potentially so important —

403

should go unanswered. Worry nipped at his heels all day, as he shook carpets in the area and ignored the gaze of the local Bobby.

That evening, after his stroll around the square, he sat down at Fitzgerald's desk — and composed his careful letter.

CHAPTER
FORTY-SEVEN

At first she kept her eyes tightly shut, as if she might not feel the rape if she could not see it. But Heinrich's chest was a lead weight on her own and his hands pressed down on her wrists, forcing her arms painfully into the horsehair mattress; he braced one knee against her thigh. She felt the shaming panic rise — the animal instinct for flight, all her muscles contracting away from him — and her eyes flew open.

She looked straight into his face.

He hesitated under the glare of her gaze; his grip eased. Her accusing look had disconcerted him; he was sweating slightly, his colour mounting. To avoid her eyes he buried his face in her shoulder and thrust his pelvis against hers.

Without thinking, she turned her head and sank her teeth into his neck.

He yelled in shock and reared away from her, his skin torn and bleeding: a thickset man, crouched like a wrestler, his hand raised to strike.

Von Stühlen was laughing — a guttural noise entirely without mirth — and Heinrich turned slightly to stare at him, his frame buckling like a whipped dog's. Von Stühlen clapped his gloved hands in a studied way, as though applauding a new star of the comic opera from his private box.

"Highly diverting. A vixen's jaws snap, when she's brought to bay —"

He tore at his cravat, unwinding the linen and running it through his hands; it made a length of rope nearly two yards long. More than enough for a gag.

Georgiana kept her teeth bared and her eyes fixed on his. These were her only weapons.

Fitzgerald might have missed von Stühlen entirely. There were any number of places on the road to Mainz where a traveling coach could halt for the night. At every toll gate that spanned the neatly-tended country roads, he asked for the coach-and-four that had traveled ahead of him. Just past Rodau, on the Darmstadt road, he drew a blank.

He backtracked to the town. There were three principal inns; only two of them provided a change of post-horses. Hand gestures and a few words of German among the ostlers revealed that no coach, and no gentleman of von Stühlen's description, had stopped at either.

He bought a tankard of ale and downed it to steady his nerves. Frustration welled in his fingers, making them twitch on the reins. Though it was barely half-past four, the early winter dark of central Europe was falling. Had the Count pushed on, driving his horses to the limit, and reached a different town — one not on the direct road to Mainz?

Remounting, Fitzgerald urged his tired horse back along the way they'd come. A crossroad bisected the turnpike just before Rodau, running north and south off the main westerly route; the signpost read Bensheim. It was possible von Stühlen had deliberately tried to throw off pursuit. But he would be unwilling to lose much time tomorrow in regaining the main road. Would he dodge north, therefore, or south? Fitzgerald had no idea; he was a stranger in a strange country, without even a rudimentary map.

As his horse pawed the tarmacadam uncertainly in the centre of the crossroad, a train whistle sounded mournfully in the distance. Fitzgerald's head swung north, listening.

The railway ran to Mainz. Von Stühlen would lose the least time the closer he kept to it.

He took the whistle as a sign in the gathering dark, and turned north.

The inn was a small one sitting close to the road: a local affair for farmers and their beer, in a village of a dozen houses. It boasted no stable yard and no ostlers; but von Stühlen did not require a change of horses — he intended to rest his team overnight. Fitzgerald could see the looming bulk of the traveling coach pulled up behind the inn, beside the publican's waggon.

He dismounted, and tied his nag to a post near the tavern door. His pulse quickened in his temples, and his hands trembled slightly; he felt for the repeating pistol he had carried in his coat ever since Shurland. He could not hope to recruit the publican; he could not demand the police. He would have to bluff his way through.

He pulled open the door and stepped inside.

The taproom was full at five o'clock; at least seven men, farmers by the look of them, were clustered in small knots drinking and talking. He stood in the doorway, waiting for the dead silence to fall, for the heads to turn and stare. *"Der Gastwirt?"* he demanded, summoning the German word for *innkeeper* from the sea of words he'd heard that week.

A bearded fellow with iron-grey hair and a withered arm pushed back his chair from one of the tables.

"Ich bin der Gastwirt. Was wünschen Sie?"

"Mein Kamerad," Fitzgerald said with a smile. "Graf von Stühlen."

"Nein," he said stonily. *"Keine Gäste."*

Fitzgerald held up a coin; it was his last gold sovereign. It glinted in the firelight as he tossed it to the innkeeper.

The man caught it in his good hand, and jerked his head toward the stairs.

Fitzgerald left them to their drink.

There were only four rooms giving off the hallway above. One was closed and occupied; a thin line of lamplight seeped over the threshold.

Quickly, he glanced at the open doors lining the passage: old-fashioned affairs that closed with a latch. Possible to lift with a penknife. If no one heard him coming.

He crept silently toward the room where Georgiana must be. And caught the sound of clapping.

A writhing mass of naked flesh. Blood throbbing in his head, clouding his sight.

She saw him standing in the doorway before the two men did. Her eyes widened desperately as she met his gaze and she might have shaken her head in warning; von Stühlen assumed she was fighting the gag, as he brought it down over her mouth.

"If I'd known you were such a fighter," he said in amusement, "I'd have taken you myself."

Fitzgerald's gun butt smashed into the side of Heinrich's head as he crouched on the mattress; the valet fell into von Stühlen with a grunt, knocking him off balance. The Count stumbled to the floor, Heinrich's full weight on top of him. The valet lost consciousness with a sigh.

Fitzgerald thrust his pistol in his coat and seized von Stühlen's neck with both hands. A bullet was too clean a death for such a man; he wanted to feel von Stühlen's pain. He began to pound the Count's head ruthlessly on the floor. For an instant the only sound in the room was the hideous gurgle of a man whose windpipe was rapidly being crushed. Then von Stühlen's fingers locked in his hair and they were grappling together,

Fitzgerald's mind singing with the primal joy of it all. *Revenge.*

"Patrick!" Georgie screamed. "Patrick! Stop it! You'll kill him! *Patrick!*"

"It'd feel grand to kill you," he muttered, as the two of them rolled across the floor, coming up hard against the valet's inert body. "It'd feel grand to cut your bowels from your gut and throttle you with 'em."

"Patrick! Kill him and you kill us all —"

Fitzgerald rolled upright, the miasma clearing. *Georgie.* He pulled out his pistol and laid it coldly against von Stühlen's remaining eye.

"Don't move," he said. "Or I'll blind you, sure as look at you. My bullet might even find that lump you call a brain."

Von Stühlen's jaw clenched; Fitzgerald knew he was reckoning the odds. Could he dislodge the gun, and reach for his own? Could he run the risk of failing — and die because he failed?

Fitzgerald pushed the dead weight of the valet to one side, his gun within inches of von Stühlen's occipital bone. He patted the man's coat in search of a pistol, found it, and tossed it behind him on the bed.

"He has a knife," Georgiana said clearly. "He keeps it in a sheath at his hip."

"On your feet." Fitzgerald grasped the

411

Count's collar and hauled him upright, felt for the knife. "Don't bother shouting for the innkeeper. I paid him to play deaf."

With his foot, he drew forward the room's sole chair and pushed von Stühlen into it, the pistol trained on his head.

The Count smiled up at him. The black canvas patch over his eye was flecked with sweat.

"You shot my boy," Fitzgerald said. "My beautiful Theo, with the life bled out of him. I ought to finish it now, and leave by the window. I'd like your blood on my soul. It might help me sleep of nights."

"But you won't, will you?" Von Stühlen was studying him. "You have it, too. That look of Albert's. You can't do violence to another man, simply because it serves your ends. You're nothing like me — either of you." He leaned toward Fitzgerald, ignoring the angle of the muzzle. "Pull the trigger, Paddy. It's just Fate, having its final laugh at Wolfgang's expense."

"Sure, and I wouldn't give you the joy."

"You think I'm afraid to die?"

"Lord, no." Fitzgerald shifted his pistol deliberately downward, so that it was trained on the Count's crotch. "But I imagine you've the Devil's own dread of maiming. I can think of several ways to make life a burden to you."

He stepped backwards a pace and cut Georgiana's right wrist free. Then he dropped the knife beside her. As Georgiana cut the rest of her bonds, he drew a shuddering breath.

"As you're not afraid to die, von Stühlen," he said brusquely, "I have a confession for you to sign."

The paper was a square Fitzgerald had kept in his wallet; on the reverse was a list of train times and destinations he'd jotted absent-mindedly in pencil. The pen was his; the ink Georgiana found in a drawer in the room. She stripped a sheet from the bed and wrapped it around herself; her own bonds — cut from the bedpost — she used to tie the valet's wrists. He was groaning now, on the verge of consciousness; they did not have much time.

Georgie was dead calm, Fitzgerald thought, but it was the insensibility of shock; it would pass, and the reaction could be frightful. He had not had enough time to look at her. He was terrified of what he might see.

In his lawyer's neat hand, he drew up the words:

I, Wolfgang, Graf von Stühlen, second son of Wilhelm, twelfth Landgrave of Stühlen and Count of Tauberbischafsheim, do hereby declare that I am of sound mind and body, and do confess before the eyes of God and at the mercy of the Queen of Great Britain, Victoria Regina, that I did with malice aforethought and without provocation, kill and murder Theodore Fitzgerald, subject of Great Britain. Also that I did order the assault upon one Septimus Taylor, barrister of the Inner Temple, which assault resulted in said Taylor's death. Also that I did falsely accuse Patrick Fitzgerald, Esquire, of the murder of his son, Theodore Fitzgerald, and of the assault upon his partner at law, Septimus Taylor. Finally, that I did perform these acts at the implied wish of THE QUEEN, Victoria Regina, whose confidence I hold.

Signed by me this second day of January in the year of our Lord 1862.

"Sign it," Fitzgerald ordered, holding out his pen.

"Do you seriously think a confession like this has any value? If you try to use it, I'll deny every word."

"Sign it."

414

"I'd rather you shot me now."

Fitzgerald thrust his pistol against von Stühlen's thigh and pulled the trigger.

The Count gasped and clutched his leg as the bullet ploughed through his flesh; his shin jerked convulsively. "You filthy Irish —" he breathed.

"That's flesh, look you. The next one will hit bone. Or your gut — a particularly nasty way to die. Sign the paper."

"Get me some cloth . . . a towel. The blood —"

"*Sign.*" He shifted the pistol to von Stühlen's left knee.

The Count took the pen; he scrawled his name at the bottom of the page.

Booted feet pounded up the stairs from the taproom; the shot had galvanized the rural drinkers. Fitzgerald seized the Count's cravat from the floor where it had fallen, and knotted his hands together behind his chair.

The innkeeper thrust open the unlatched door.

"Ah. Here are our witnesses, Georgie," Fitzgerald said. "*Gastwirt,* if you would sign your name below the Count's, please —"

Fitzgerald gave Georgie her second-hand black dress and a few minutes to don it, then threw her up behind him in the saddle and kicked his mount forward.

Von Stühlen would pursue them. His leg was bleeding and his horses were tired, but so was Fitzgerald's; he could assume a bare quarter-hour before the Count found a better animal and rode off, regardless of his wounded thigh, to find them.

The railroad cut through the dense Hesse forests a half-mile north of the town, and Fitzgerald made for it, forcing his way through the trees. He followed the rails along the gravel verge in the profound winter silence, snow beginning to fall, hoping against hope that von Stühlen would not find their hoofprints — that he would take the obvious road toward Mainz.

When, perhaps a half-hour later, a train whistled behind them in the darkness, Fitzgerald dismounted and helped Georgie to the ground.

Her hands, where they gripped his waist, were cold as death and her lips were colourless.

He held her close, trying to enfold her in warmth, to tell her of his love without using words, the ache in his throat at the misery she'd endured making all speech impossible.

She clung to him. He felt her body shaking.

"Patrick. I hated being afraid. My fear just gave him more power."

"There, there, lass. You're safe now. Did he hurt you badly?"

"Nothing compared to what it could have been." She reached up with both hands and grasped his head, pulling his mouth to hers, kissing him passionately. "I love you, Patrick. I love you with all my soul. I know it's a sin before God — I know you have a wife —"

"Georgie — I'm not worthy. I'm a crying shame. A drunkard and a care-for-nothing. Georgie, I'm old enough to be your father —"

The train was almost upon them, chugging slowly toward them, the great lantern at its fore catching them in its beam.

"— but I need you more than strong drink or air, more than all else in life together. Georgie — I'll try to do better —"

She put her fingers across his mouth.

Fitzgerald slapped his horse's rump and sent it off into the forest. "Can you jump onto the platform, lass?"

"Lift me," she said.

CHAPTER
FORTY-EIGHT

Gibbon carried the stack of old shoes and worn shirts carefully through the scullery, negotiating the narrow doorway and the three steps to the small back garden. Twenty feet farther was the wrought-iron gate giving onto the mews, and the familiar bearded face of the rag-and-bone man who worked the Bedford Square neighbourhood.

Percy was his name, although Gibbon had formed the habit of addressing him as *Perceval* — this added a fragile dignity to the scavenger's occupation. He was not admitted to the gated central square, but the mews were open to carriage traffic, and thus approachable by all manner of riff-raff; and the riff-raff performed their necessary functions: nightsoil men who cleared the few remaining cesspools (most of the houses had converted to sewer lines, running into the ancient mains), knife-grinders, milk-maids, and coal vendors.

Percy was waiting when Gibbon unlocked the back gate; he placed the clothes carefully in his handcart, and gave Gibbon a pile of coins warm from his wool-mittened palm. They had haggled over prices Saturday, and Percy had returned this Monday morning to collect the goods. Fitzgerald's bespoke castoffs would be sold to a second-hand clothing shop, at a minor profit for Percy; and from there, they would descend through the social scale over the next decade: mended and re-mended and then torn to pieces a dozen times to fit, eventually, the smallest child of the back slums.

The Yard's back-mews man watched the exchange with obvious boredom from his lounging vantage against the carriage house wall.

"Thank you, Perceval — that will be all," Gibbon said formally as he made to close the wrought-iron gate. But Percy was fumbling in his pocket, his look one of leering cunning as he gazed at the valet from under his bushy eyebrows.

"Might be as I've somefink you'll like, Mr. Gibbon," he suggested. "Somefink you've been looking for. Might be as we could agree to a price. If it's worth your time o' day."

He flashed a bit of paper in the soiled

palm of his hand before returning it to his pocket.

"We agreed on the figure," Gibbon said. "I won't give you a penny more."

"Somefink from your master a'zus scarpered," Percy muttered, his eyes shifting to left and right.

"Very well," Gibbon said with studied indifference. "If you insist on the charge — I'll give you sixpence."

"A shilling."

"Ninepence and no more."

"Done."

Gibbon dropped a few of Percy's cooling coins back in his palm; the slip of paper slid into his own.

"Good day," he said distantly, and locked the gate with a clang.

The train they had caught in the woods Thursday night was bound not for Mainz, but Frankfurt. They reached it by midnight, and too tired to go any farther, took a room in a hotel not far from the station.

They registered as Mr. and Mrs. John Smith. Georgiana refused to let Fitzgerald sleep on the floor; she was afraid, she told him, of what might happen — of men bursting through the door, of dreams turning to nightmare. She drew him down into her bed

420

and when he asked if she was sure of what she was doing, she said simply, "I could die at any time, Patrick. So could you. We could be parted forever as soon as we reach England. There's no certainty in the future. I knew that, tonight, when I lay in that man's power — But we're together *now*. I refuse to waste my chance."

"I would marry you tonight if I could," he said.

She blew out the candle.

From Frankfurt they made for Koblenz, and from there, on Saturday morning, reached Ostend.

Fitzgerald had only a pound left in his pocket by that time, not nearly enough to buy their passage across the Channel. He sold his clothes and bought a second-hand set of worker's togs, then spent an hour looking for a steamer that was short a deck-hand.

They had agreed that if he worked his way across to England, Georgie would travel in a respectable second-class berth as though they were strangers. If he could not find work that day, he would try the next. But it was vital, Fitzgerald thought, that she get out of Europe. He wanted her as far from von Stühlen as the sea could put her.

The seventh ship he queried had lost two men to the brothels, and was sailing that afternoon.

It was, Fitzgerald observed with an inner smile, his eternal recurrence: the Irishman who lived by his wits, making his way toward an uncertain future.

By dawn Sunday they'd landed at Dover.

Georgie boarded a train bound for London, and the refuge she hoped to find with John Snow's retired housekeeper is Islington; Fitzgerald made his way to Canterbury, and from there, by gradual degrees and found conveyances, reached London four hours later.

There had been no sign of von Stühlen since they'd left Hesse. But Fitzgerald was not a fool. He knew the Count would discover them, or die trying.

The note had told Gibbon to leave as usual for his supper at the local pub. Tonight, for the benefit of the police, he was to order his food and then seek the lavatory. Fitzgerald would be waiting for him in the alley behind the public house.

A sick thread of excitement was curling in Gibbon's gut, so that for the first time in weeks he forgot the lingering soreness of his healing back. His pulse was uneven and his colour high; if it had not been dark, he'd have given the game entirely away.

He was trailed, as usual, to the Fox & Badger; it had become a habit for the Yard's front-door men to order pigeon pie on these evenings, while Gibbon waited for his bangers and mash. He dawdled until the two of them tucked into their food before making his way to the rear of the establishment.

But his heart sank as he stepped through the publican's scullery, into the cold of the alley. Snow was falling gently on the rutted gravel, and a single man stood with his hands hunched in his pockets, no coat against the cold — a man with a soft slouch hat and several days' growth of beard. A working-class lout where Fitzgerald should be.

"Gibbon," the man whispered softly.

He peered at him through narrowed eyes, stepped down off the rear stoop of the public house. "Lord love you, Mr. Fitz, you're rigged out like a navvy."

"If you don't know me, Gibbon, I've achieved my end."

He offered his hand, and the valet clasped it fervently. "I knew you'd come back to face the music. There's a price on your head — you know that?"

"Yes. But I slipped away when our packet landed at Dover, and I've steered clear of Bedford Square — I'm bedded down for the night at the Inner Temple. The police aren't watching my chambers at night."

"Be out of there by dawn, if I may be so bold as to give advice. And Miss Armistead?"

"— is well enough. Gone to friends in Islington. You found your way back from France — well done, my Gibbon!"

Gibbon swallowed; there was much he might have said, but no time to say it. He reached into his coat.

"Here's some money, and a letter as Miss Georgie should see."

"Good lad," Fitzgerald said with difficulty. "I shouldn't take your bit savings —"

"It's all that's left of the housekeeping. Nobbut two pounds, four shillings, five-pence — I cleared the wardrobe and sold the castoffs." Gibbon found he could not quite meet Fitzgerald's eyes; the world was topsy-turvy, when the valet paid the master.

Fitzgerald turned the envelope in his hands. "And the letter?"

"From HRH Princess Alice," Gibbon said sheepishly.

"What?"

"We've been corresponding, Mr. Fitz.

424

Seems she's mortal desperate to talk to Miss Georgie. It's summat to do with the Consort, I gather. She put a notice in the *Times,* and being curious as to who'd address Dr. Armistead in that manner — and not knowing when you might get a foothold in London again — I undertook to answer it. The Princess thinks I'm Miss Armistead."

"By all that's holy," Fitzgerald said blankly. "What does *she* want?"

"A meeting. Day after tomorrow, in Portsmouth. She's staying at Osborne House with the Queen, I reckon, and means to take the steamer from Cowes."

"I must think." Fitzgerald stuffed the letter in his pocket. "I must consult with Georgie. It could be a trap, Gibbon —"

"Aye. On the other hand —"

"Can you nobble those men who watch our house?"

Gibbon grinned. "Just give me the chance, Mr. Fitz! I've had a deal of time to consider of the problem — and I reckon I can pull the wool over their eyes."

"Good. Meet me tomorrow at Victoria Station. Eight o'clock sharp. We'll take the first train that offers for the south coast. And Gibbon — God bless you. I don't deserve such loyalty."

Gibbon thought of the horsewhip, the sun

of Nice and the gendarmes' courtyard. The man who whispered in his ear the words of Judas: *He ran — and you've had to suffer for it.*

"It's naught to go on about, Mr. Fitz. Mind you don't oversleep yourself in chambers. Wonderful patient the police are, seemingly — and they want to seize you in a powerful way."

He watched as the figure disappeared in the snow, then turned back to his cold supper.

CHAPTER
FORTY-NINE

As it happened, Fitzgerald did not sleep at all that night.

For the past twenty years, the chambers he'd shared with Septimus Taylor had never varied. The two barristers kept separate offices, each boasting a casement window overlooking the precincts of the Inner Temple. The clerks — there were five of them, ranging from Samuel Smalls, age fifty-three, down to a lad they all called Tiffin, who was barely thirteen — sat on stools before their desks, which were tilted to support a variety of ledgers and inkwells. The clerks' room ran the length of the barristers' offices combined, and was windowless, being a reception area for the main chambers; but the clerks had their own fireplace. The room was usually warm and well-lit to accommodate legal writing.

Fitzgerald established himself here, with the outer door barred and an oil lamp burning brightly. He had no desire to attract attention with a midnight glow at his office window, and for the same reason, forbore to light the coal fire. The chambers had a sad, disused, and neglected air; he noticed the stores of tea and lamp oil were running low. But the chaos left by Taylor's attackers had been cleared and tidied, and the folios of clients' papers restored to their shelves. Someone — probably the head clerk, Samuel — had taken care to set the chambers to rights, regardless of the future or whether he might be paid. This small evidence of loyalty cheered Fitzgerald; he stood on the inner threshold of his own office, staring through the darkness, with an ache in his heart. He would not see it again.

Numb in the fireless room and the January cold, he sat himself before Samuel's high desk and filled his pen. In his neat, lawyerly handwriting, with the hard stool boring into his backside, he drew up a fair copy of Wolfgang, Graf von Stühlen's signed confession. It had no legal force whatsoever, but as a salve to his conscience it was immeasurably important.

My dear Maude, he wrote on the covering sheet, *If ever you held any faith in my name, honour that faith now — and read the enclosed. You know how precious the boy was to me. Forgive, if you can, what I cannot change or restore — and all the ways I have failed you. Patrick.*

He sealed the letter and addressed it to Lady Maude in Kent. Then he stole into his shuttered office and by instinct as much as sight, retrieved the strongbox stored in a locked floor compartment beneath his desk. It had always been Fitzgerald's task to manage the chambers' finances; he kept a quantity of cash in the strongbox for the purpose. He left the clerks' monthly salary in an envelope marked with Samuel's name, and took what remained — some seventy pounds — for himself. Then he sat down once more to write out his estimate of the clerks' characters. It was probable no one would hire Samuel or Tiffin or any of the others when they read Fitzgerald's signature on the page; but he owed the boys an honourable dismissal.

It was nearly dawn by the time he finished. He turned down the oil lamp, collected his documents, and gave one last look around his chambers. It seemed, suddenly, as though the life he'd lived there — his marriage, the cases he'd tried and won, Theo and the love for him he'd hidden — was nothing but a dream.

■ ■ ■ ■

Old Mrs. Russell, who had once been John Snow's housekeeper, lived in Albion Grove in the centre of Islington. It was a district of London that had once been prosperous but was now fallen on hard times; the aged Georgian house fronts were dingy with coal smoke. Snow had provided a pension for Mrs. Russell under his will, however, and she kept tidy lodgings; Georgiana had been in the habit of visiting her there one morning each month, to ensure the old lady wanted for nothing. It had been the obvious place for her to turn, after landing from Ostend.

Fitzgerald paid a boy loitering in Hemingford Road to carry a message to Mrs. Russell's door at seven-thirty that morning. The police might be following him, despite his wariness — and he had no wish to incriminate Georgie. But it was Mrs. Russell who answered his summons, her broad pink face suffused with worry. She climbed up into the hansom to give him the news.

"Arrested," she said, "when we'd no sooner sat down to our supper. *An information was laid,* the Bobby told me — though as to *who* laid it, he would not breathe a word! *Abortion!* And her doing her sainted best to see those poor women comfortable, whichever way she can, and never mind the cost to herself. What would the dear doctor say, Mr. Fitzgerald, had he lived to see this day?"

You didn't keep her safe, Patrick, John Snow's voice muttered once more in his ear.

He tried desperately to ignore it. He tried to throttle Snow's ghost, to quell his strident conscience, but the voices kept ringing. Theo's. Maude's. Georgie's. All saying the same thing: *You didn't keep me safe.*

He could not silence them now, but he could push onward through the rising clamour, to Victoria Station where Gibbon was waiting, cautious newspaper raised, in easy view of the Portsmouth train.

"She goes before the magistrate today," he told him, "in Bow Street. I can't appear for her, Gibbon — I'd only get myself thrown into gaol. But I can find Button Nance. I can force that woman to tell the truth. Will you help me?"

Jasper Horan fingered the telegram in his coat pocket. It was the first he'd ever received, and the printed lettering on the stiff yellow paper made him feel important, as though he'd joined the ranks of civil servants and army officers, men too important for mere letters in the post. The telegram had come yesterday, direct from the Dover packet office to the City warehouse where Horan was employed as head watchman. Von Stühlen's name at the end of the brief message.

His instructions were clear: Proceed to Miss Armistead's house in Russell Square and watch the premises for any sign of the lady's arrival. Then report the same to von Stühlen. Horan was not, under any circumstances, to let Miss Armistead slip through his fingers.

He'd told the tea merchant who paid his wage that he was sickening for a fever. He'd hailed a hansom for Russell Square and spent the next four hours and twenty-three minutes watching the premises in question. The house appeared deserted, and Horan had almost given it up as a bad job — when a hired fly rolled to a stop at Miss Armistead's door. The driver had stepped down, and conferred with the personage who answered his ring. After a wait of perhaps ten minutes, the horse stamping and the driver pacing in the cold, a maid appeared with a packed carpet bag, which she handed into the fly. The driver mounted the box —

shook up the reins — and put Russell Square immediately to his back.

Horan, by this time, had engaged a cab and was hot in pursuit. He trailed the fly to Albion Grove, where another maidservant retrieved the carpet bag. It was a simple matter, after that, to report Miss Armistead's whereabouts to von Stühlen.

It was Horan who had the pleasure of summoning the police.

CHAPTER FIFTY

The rookery in St. Giles was colder than it had been three weeks before, but the same smell of cats and unwashed bodies permeated the entryway, and the same cluster of children was draped along the stairs.

A stranger answered the door of Button Nance's rooms: a faded woman with a jaw like a bear trap. She had no interest in Fitzgerald and no time to spare for the dead.

"Fell off Waterloo Bridge," she told them briefly, "couple o' nights back, when she'd took a bit too much; and the little'uns gone to the work'us. No loss, I reckon. She were a vicious ol' bitch and 'ad the pox in 'er."

The workhouse belonged to St. Paul's, the actors' church in Covent Garden, and it was a small matter for Fitzgerald and Gibbon to inquire after the children. Three little girls were pointed out among the welter of grey-clad orphans working the parish mangle; of the boy, Davey, there was no sign.

"Lemme talk up the lads what sweep the crossings," Gibbon suggested. "They'll know summat, I reckon."

It was nearly eleven o'clock, and Georgie would be brought before the magistrate at two. Fitzgerald gave the little girls a shilling each, and left the steaming laundry for the throngs of idle and savage boys who haunted the nearby market.

Davey had never gone back to Button Nance's after Lizzie died.

He took to working the Oxford Street omnibus line from Edgware Road to Bishopsgate: swinging up onto the platform with the crowd of working-class men each morning, and pinching a pocket or two before leaping off into the darker byways. When another 'bus came by, he repeated his performance, the wallets and purses tossed each time to the guv'nor what kept him fed, in an attic room full of similar boys, deep in the heart of his old rookery. Davey had quick, delicate fingers and agile legs; the work came easily and paid better than sweeping crossings. He lived now only four streets away from St. Giles, in a warren of windowless and airless rooms lined with pallets, where he slept most nights; days he spent on the street. Twice, he had glimpsed his little sisters in the St. Paul's workhouse yard; but it did not do to stare at them too long. They might notice Davey, and call out — and Davey had vowed never to be taken alive into the parish workhouse.

He was standing on the corner of Oxford Street and Tottenham Court Road, eyeing an approaching 'bus that looked sadly empty so close to the noon hour, the wet straw of the inner compartment sifting dirtily down the platform steps, when a hand clapped him on the shoulder. Instinctively, he twisted free and darted to one side — straight into Fitzgerald's arms.

"Wotcher," he snarled. "I ain't done anyfink. Lemme go!"

It took both of them to carry the struggling boy into a nearby public house, and it was only when Fitzgerald threatened to turn him over immediately to the police that he stopped calling loudly for help and grudgingly agreed to accept their offer of small beer and a pasty.

They sat with Davey firmly between them, Gibbon holding the boy's left wrist. Fitzgerald waited until he had devoured most of his meal before he even attempted to get the boy's attention; he had known that look of starvation intimately before.

"Would you like another?" he asked, and when Davey nodded, his mouth too full to speak, Fitzgerald jerked his head at Gibbon. "You order. I'll be all right. The lad won't run while we feed him."

When the valet stepped cautiously away from the table, a look of misgiving on his face, Fitzgerald told the boy, "I'll give ye a pound for an afternoon's work. That's money you won't have to share with anyone else — provided you keep it hidden."

Davey raised his eyes from his empty plate and studied Fitzgerald narrowly. "You're the toff what came with the lady," he said. "When Lizzie was sick. Afore she died. But you're not a swell no more. I reckon you ain't got a pound between you, you and the other cove what calls you *mister.*"

Fitzgerald drew the note from his pocket and held it in front of Davey's face. "I don't keep my wallet in my coat, so don't get any ideas. This is yours — provided you earn it."

"Wot's yer lay?" Davey demanded.

"Justice," Fitzgerald said softly. "For your sister Lizzie. And the lady who tried to save her."

A shadow passed over the boy's face and his eyes slid away. For perhaps thirty seconds, he weighed Fitzgerald's words. Then, without warning, he darted out of his seat and shot like lightning for the public-house door.

St. Giles Street, where Lizzie had died, fell under the Bow Street magistrate's jurisdiction. Georgiana had spent a restless night in one of the old magistracy's cells, attempting to learn what she could of the charges against her. She gathered that Button Nance had informed Bow Street of her daughter's death at the hands of an abortionist, and had named Georgiana as the party responsible. But Button Nance had disappeared. The man who had caused Georgie's arrest was a complete stranger to her.

A half-hour before she was to appear in front of the magistrate, an ancient with a face like a sun-dried orange materialised at the door of her cell. His fingers were stained yellow with tobacco and a trail of snuff dusted his waistcoat; he wore a grey peruke on his bald scalp. He peered at her distastefully through the bars.

"You are Georgiana Armistead?"

"I am. But I have not the pleasure —"

"I am your solicitor, madam." The old man's voice was dry as paper. "Unless there is another you would prefer to act for you?"

Georgie stared at him.

438

"You are accused of committing abortion. That is a crime under section fifty-eight of the Offences Against the Person Act, 1861, passed into law by act of Parliament, 24 & 25 Victoria. It is punishable by death. Or possibly transportation, should you wring the hearts of the jury. Our purpose today is merely to hear the charges read against you. Your trial, should you be committed to trial, will occur at the next Assizes, by which time you will, of course, have retained a barrister. Have you any money?"

"I beg your pardon?"

"*Money?* To meet your legal obligations?"

"Of course," Georgiana stammered. "I can give you a draft on my bank."

"My fee is five pounds. Have you anything you wish to say?"

"I should like to know your name, sir."

He closed his eyes in a gesture of long suffering. "I hardly think that is necessary. Until, of course, we come to the matter of payment. You will protest your innocence, Miss Armistead. It is the only possible defence available to you."

She had hoped, in her heart of hearts, to see Fitzgerald in the room that served as Bow Street's court. But there was no one present except a small knot of the Accused, awaiting their fate before the magistrate, and the solicitors who had agreed to act for them. Such men were the scavengers of the legal world — they hung about the magistracy in search of clients, hoping to collect a fee for their casual representation.

At the rear of the room stood a barrel-chested man with overlong arms and a simian aspect; Georgie felt his gaze follow her as she was led forward by a constable. She was trembling, the exhaustion of recent days overwhelming her, the words *punishable by death or transportation* screaming insistently through her brain. *Punishable by death or transportation.*

"You are one Georgiana Armistead, spinster, of Number 113, Russell Square . . . that you did willfully and knowingly commit the dreadful act of abortion on the night of fifteenth December last, on the person of Elizabeth Tyler, age fourteen, of this parish, who subsequently died of injuries of your infliction . . . Who brings these charges?"

"I do, Yer Honour."

Georgiana glanced over her shoulder; the simian man at the back of the room, leering at her. *Punishable by death or transportation.* She had never seen him before in her life, yet there was something familiar . . . a knot of figures on the roof of a tenement building, her booted feet sliding on the ice . . .

"Miss Armistead," the magistrate repeated, "I asked whether you have anything to say in answer to these claims."

She looked at him: a lined face, bleak eyes, no expectation of innocence. "Your Honour, I am a doctor certified by the Medical College of Edinburgh. The child's mother called me to Lizzie's bedside on the fifteenth of December, when fever and generalised infection had already weakened the girl's frame. I examined her and found that an abortion had been done some days previous, by a hand unknown to me. I administered chloroform and removed the child's uterus, which was gangrenous. I learned later that evening that the child had died. I deeply regret the fact of her death — but regard myself as in no way responsible for it. I am innocent of these charges."

The magistrate regarded her steadily. "I am astonished, Miss Armistead, that you would add insult to the injuries already committed, by claiming to be a *doctor.* Mr. Troy, you are acting as solicitor for this woman?"

"I am, Your Honour," replied the ancient wearily. "Perhaps we shall discover that she is mad."

From the rear of the room came a stifled

guffaw.

It was over, and Patrick had not come.

Dazed, Georgiana allowed herself to be led from the front of the room once more, the hand of the same constable beneath her elbow, the simian face leering from the shadows. *Punishable by death or transportation. If she managed to wring the hearts of the jury.* If she suggested that she was mad. If she denied the truth of her own science and threw herself on the mercy of the ignorant —

"Gibbon," she said aloud, as her eyes met those of the valet standing in the doorway.

His gaze flicked over her; he gave a barely perceptible shake of the head. With both hands he held the upper arms of a young boy, his head hanging, who appeared to have been dragged through the doorway. With a quickening of her heart she recognised Davey.

"Mr. Troy? Where is Mr. Troy?" Gibbon called clearly. "I've evidence as he'll wish to hear."

"I am Mr. Troy." Georgie's ancient sighed. "If you must needs speak, perhaps we might adjourn to the Bear — ?"

"No," Davey burst out. "I've come to see justice done. Mr. Magistrate, sir —" he

442

raised his hand and pointed at the barrel-
chested man with the leer — "the lady
didn't hurt my sister Lizzie. *That* cove did.
He put a pillow over her head and stifled
the life out of her. His name is Jasper Horan."

CHAPTER
FIFTY-ONE

When he received Odaline Dufief's card that Wednesday, the eighth of January, von Stühlen held it in his palm for several seconds, debating whether to deny his presence.

He had returned to London only hours before, well aware of the risk he ran. But his signature at the base of a damning confession meant he had only two choices: to live out his days in poverty in Hesse — where the family's mortgaged estates held nothing for him — or to hunt Patrick Fitzgerald down, and kill him. So much was within his grasp: a comfortable income. An English title. His hand in Victoria's purse as a condition of his lifelong silence. He would not give up any of these; he did not accept the inevitability of death.

He was hampered in travel by the wound in his leg and the disappearance of his valet, Heinrich — who had vanished into the night somewhere around Rodau. Solitude and pain honed his taste for violence; honed his calculations as well. Georgiana Armistead was the lynchpin of all his plans. She alone could bring Fitzgerald to bay: If von Stühlen found her, threatened her life and security, the Irishman would walk freely into his trap.

Luck favoured him. Jasper Horan did his work well. The girl was stupid enough to send for her clothes in Russell Square.

He was waiting, now, for Horan's report from Bow Street — he would not go near the magistrate himself, out of fear of that signed confession. When he took Fitzgerald, it would be in isolation and darkness, far from the aid of the Law.

He weighed the stiff card in his hand. *Odaline duFief.* He had no time to spare for a social call, but the woman might prove useful — she might know where Fitzgerald would hide. She obviously wanted his blood as badly as von Stühlen did.

"Show her up," he ordered the porter. "She's alone, I expect?"

"Quite alone, sir."

"How daring of her." Von Stühlen smiled.

There was one benefit of maintaining the fiction that Papa had died of typhoid, Alice thought; it allowed her to plead a vague and potentially dangerous set of symptoms throughout those first few weeks of January, and no one — not even Mama, for obvious reasons — would attempt to argue with her. Uneasy headaches. Loss of appetite. Restless sleeping. All the members of the Household, even the servants, were worried she was sickening for the dread disease — she who had nursed Papa to the last.

She cultivated the habit of retiring to her room at midday, reclining on a sofa with her books or her writing paper. Her old nurse ordered everyone at Osborne to leave her in peace. From time to time she felt Mama's eyes follow her in speculation — from the Queen at least she had no secrets; but Mama's hand was stayed. She could not proclaim to the world that her daughter was promulgating nonsense.

So when Alice left her rooms that Wednesday morning, no one was available to watch her hurried flight down the broad backterrace steps. She avoided the stables. It was more than a mile's walk into Cowes, but she had allowed herself plenty of time. She knew the Portsmouth steamer's schedule by heart. It was only as she attempted to board, heart pounding and mind singing at her escape, that someone had the courage to speak to her.

"Bonjour, madame."

Von Stühlen bowed with his usual grace, but Odaline duFief seemed unimpressed. She was heavily veiled against the January streets and carried an enormous fur muff; her clothing was black and severe. *Mourning,* he thought. *How she embraces the old bitch's cause! Or is this for Albert? More of the national hypocrisy?*

"You are very good to receive me," she murmured; he caught the trace of an accent, the glint of unblinking eyes behind the veil.

"Not at all. I imagine we both work toward the same end — justice for that unfortunate boy. Pray sit down, and tell me how I may serve you."

She did not accept the invitation, but crossed the carpet deliberately, as though drawn by the sound of his voice.

He hesitated, aware of something unanticipated in her manner. She was too much in command of herself — she had no desire for complicity, though she halted barely a yard from his face.

"My husband, you see, has told me all about you." She withdrew one black-gloved hand from her muff and reached dreamily

447

for her veil. As he watched her unwind its smoky length, the face emerging like an apparition, the muff dropped carelessly to the floor. In her free hand was a gun.

"Lady Maude," he stammered, stepping backwards. "I thought —"

"You thought I was a fool," she said.

And fired at his heart from point-blank range.

"Good morning, Your Highness," Georgiana said quietly in the girl's ear.

Princess Alice turned, an expression of fright flitting across her features.

"I am Dr. Armistead. You wished to speak with me, I believe? I thought it best to come to *you,* rather than demanding the exertion of a Solent crossing."

"Dr. Armistead?" The Princess's gaze flicked past Georgie to the pair of men standing several paces behind her. "But . . . you are a *lady* —"

"I am also qualified in medicine. Your late father the Prince Consort was a valued acquaintance. It was to speak of him, I believe, that you placed that notice in the *Times*? Although, to be frank, he was never my patient, Your Highness. He consulted me on behalf of your brother."

Alice said nothing for an instant, glancing

about with a hunted look.

"We have engaged a fly," Georgiana attempted. "If you will consent to enter it, we may speak in complete privacy. For my part, I promise no harm shall come to your person or reputation."

"Of course. It is only that — If only I could be certain —"

"That I am who I claim?" Georgiana smiled. "Would it help you to know that I am recently returned from Cannes? That I met your brother Leopold there? And that he was so kind as to lend me his donkey, Catherine?"

"Leo!"

"The Prince and I are old friends. It was he your Papa required me to examine."

Alice's expression clouded. "Then I was wrong. I thought perhaps you knew something of my father that I did not — that you might be capable of dispelling some grave fears that have attended me since his tragic death — but if you were *Leo's* physician —"

"There is much that we might discuss," Georgiana said carefully. "But not in such an exposed place. May I beg to introduce another who is closely concerned in these affairs? Your Highness, may I present Mr. Patrick Fitzgerald to your acquaintance?"

■ ■ ■ ■

She stared down at his body where it lay on the carpet, blood spreading across the elegant white shirtfront, a darker stain on the black cloth of his waistcoat. His sensual lips were parted, exposing the teeth; his one good eye stared coldly at the brass fender.

She had an idle fancy to remove the eye patch and probe the empty socket with her finger; or to kneel down and kiss those parted lips — either would have been a sensation she might have enjoyed, in the past. But she was so very tired now. To kill him had required all the attention and energy she could summon from her dying frame, all the mental force she could muster. She wanted, now, to sleep.

Maude did not intend to hang for von Stühlen's murder. She would not appear at the Bar to offer her confused testimony. She simply placed the copy of the Count's confession in his dead right hand, and composed herself in a convenient chair. When the porter's running feet had reached the door of the third-floor flat, she fired the gun a second time.

CHAPTER
FIFTY-TWO

I was pretending to read one of Palmerston's dispatches, which the excellent Mr. Helps had conveyed across the threshold — although in truth I was composing a letter to my daughter Vicky, full of sad reflections upon Those Who Are Gone — when Alice appeared at the door of my private sitting room.

I barely glanced at her, having lost all patience with her melancholy airs and her wicked attempts to cultivate illness. It is a very good thing that she is to be thrown away upon Louis of Hesse — who is nothing but a Ludwig, after all, dressed up in a French name. Kind but dull, and his teeth so very bad that even our dentist could do nothing with him.

"I am not at leisure, Alice," I said firmly, my eyes upon Vicky's letter. "I have not the quantity of hours you seem to spend in reading your books. I must guard my moments jealously."

She ignored my words and walked without hesitation into the room. To my surprise, a small cavalcade followed: William Jenner, with an expression of marked ill-ease upon his countenance; the despicable Patrick Fitzgerald; and a lady . . . a lady whose name I fancied I could summon. It was she who closed the double doors behind her, and remained, like a sentinel, before them. She was far too beautiful to bear looking at. I remembered her handwriting on the page — the satisfaction of the flames . . .

I rose from my desk in cold fury.

"We must and shall speak with you, Mama."

Alice's face was quite pale and her features haggard; I might almost have believed in her spurious illness as she stood before me so straightly, all her father's stubbornness in her upright frame.

"Mr. Fitzgerald you know. But Dr. Armistead is a stranger, I believe — in person, if not in name."

"Not in name," I agreed. "But I have no wish to make *Miss* Armistead's acquaintance. She is guilty of abortion and her paramour of murder. Jenner — Summon the footmen and we shall have these two bound over to the Law at once! I must thank you, Alice, for doing what others less worthy of trust could not!"

My physician extracted a handkerchief from his coat and mopped at his brow. "Forgive me, Your Majesty. Forgive me."

"Dr. Jenner is here at my request," Alice said. "I intend that he shall bear witness to all that is said. I applied to Georgiana Armistead from the depths of my misery — in my effort to understand the despair that drove Papa to take his own life —"

"Silence!" I hissed, appalled at this frankness, this exposure of our veiled intimacy — and before such a figure as William Jenner, whose unwitting complicity in Albert's death has been the foundation of all my security. "You shall not speak of it. I shall *not* listen."

"Dr. Armistead told me what I believe you must already know: that Papa was aware our Leopold's illness is a hereditary malady. That all of us may bear a similar flaw, and pass it, indeed, to our children. That there is no possibility of cure. It was for this reason he urged me, on his deathbed, to break off my engagement —"

"Nonsense," I said. "Leopold's frailty is nowhere evident in the family — neither in the Hanoverian line, nor in Albert's. It is an act of Providence. A tragedy of Fate. That your Papa could not accept God's Will is a measure of how much his science failed him, Alice."

"It was to suppress all rumour of this . . . flaw," Alice continued implacably, "that you pursued Dr. Armistead and Mr. Fitzgerald across England and Europe, with every kind of calumny and crime thrown at their heads. You should rather have seen them hanged, Mama, than admitted to the world Papa's weakness."

"That is a lie," I said flatly. "I allowed the Law to take its course. You have been *imposed* upon, Alice; your new friends are criminals, unworthy of your trust. Jenner, how long must I listen to this? My nerves —"

"Wolfgang, Graf von Stühlen, is dead, Your Majesty," Jenner murmured. "I received a telegram to that effect from London, but a quarter-hour ago."

I stared at him and felt my legs buckle, my bulk slide downward, back into my chair. My arms rested heavily on the desk frame; but for its support, I fear I should have fainted.

"You killed him?" I inquired blankly of the scoundrel Fitzgerald.

He shook his head. "The honour, I fear, goes to my late wife. But von Stühlen gave

454

me this before he died."

He held out a sheet of paper, and mesmerised — still unable to move — I listened while he read the bitter words.

. . . *"Finally, that I did perform these acts at the implied wish of THE QUEEN, Victoria Regina, whose confidence I hold. . . ."*

"Impossible," I murmured, my eyes upon Alice.

"Von Stühlen signed it," the Irishman said. "But I will undertake never to reveal its existence, Your Majesty, on one condition."

I stared at him, awaiting the inevitable words.

Fitzgerald held my gaze. "That you swear, before Her Royal Highness the Princess Alice and Dr. William Jenner, that you will never again pursue me or Georgiana Armistead at the peril of our lives and reputations."

I let out an unsteady sigh. It seemed a small enough thing, in exchange for the world.

They have formed the intention, I gather, of emigrating to Canada; and indeed, do not even return to London, but rather will embark with their manservant upon a transatlantic steamer out of Southampton, bound for Halifax.

I signed the trifling paper Fitzgerald presented for my perusal; saw Alice and Jenner witness its execution; and reflected that the Irishman had achieved what even Palmerston could not — he had compelled my attention to a grave matter while breathing the air of the same room.

It was unclear to me what, exactly, they knew or suspected — whether they understood the dreadful uncertainty that hangs over my parentage. Whether they guessed that Albert had recognised it, through the enormity of Leopold's illness — and being a noble soul, incapable of deceit, or of profiting by the indiscretions of others, had insisted that I must abdicate in favour of my cousin, Ernest of Hanover, the unequivocally legitimate heir to the throne of England.

That a prince who possessed the freedom of the world — an unlimited power to act in the name of good — the adoration of his wife and the blessings of his children — should seek to lay down that gift, and to rob his heirs of the greatest Empire on earth — is a kind of insanity for which there is no possible forgiveness. It was the final act of usurpation Albert could commit: to take from me my only purpose in life, the purpose for which I was born.

He was an Angelic Being, far too good to live.

I had to put him down like a sick dog.

I ought to thank Fitzgerald and his doxy, I suppose — they have rid me of a tedious burden in von Stühlen. The Count thought to slip his noose around my neck, like so many gentlemen before him. I should not long have endured the knot; but to free myself, indeed, I might have been forced to an unpleasant exertion.

Once Alice is married and Jenner rewarded with his knighthood, I may reasonably expect to live out my sad years in untroubled solitude. I shall be a walking monument to my Beloved Albert, and exhibit to an admiring public the *fortitude* with which Majesty endures an irreparable Loss. I may live to see all of Albert's children take their rightful places among the kingdoms of the world, and know that my descendants shall hold sway in England for centuries to come.

But I confess I hate the very name of Patrick Fitzgerald.

AFTERWORD

This book is entirely a work of fiction. It derives, however, from the peculiar childhood and destiny of Queen Victoria, the genetic flaw of hemophilia she passed to three of her children, and the sudden death of her husband at age forty-two from a poorly diagnosed gastric complaint — which may have been stomach cancer or a perforated ulcer, but which almost certainly was *not* typhoid.

Victoria's life has been chronicled and assessed in more volumes than one can enumerate. Those I found chiefly useful in writing this novel were: *Victoria: The Young Queen,* by Monica Charlot (Basil Blackwell Ltd., 1991); *A Royal Conflict: Sir John Conroy and the Young Victoria,* by Katherine Hudson (Hodder and Stoughton, 1994); *Queen Victoria: From Her Birth to the Death of the Prince Consort,* by Cecil Woodham-Smith (Knopf, 1972); *Victoria: An Intimate*

459

Biography, by Stanley Weintraub (E. P. Dutton, 1988); *Victoria R.I.,* by Elizabeth Longford (Harper & Row, 1964); *Queen Victoria,* by Lytton Strachey (Harcourt Brace Jovanovich, 1921); *Queen Victoria in Her Letters and Journals,* selected by Christopher Hibbert (John Murray, 1984); and *Queen Victoria: A Personal History,* by Christopher Hibbert (HarperCollins UK, 1999). The matter of Victoria's hemophilia is taken up in *Queen Victoria's Gene: Haemophilia and the Royal Family,* by D. M. Potts and W. T. W. Potts (Alan Sutton Publishing Ltd., 1995).

Almost as many works address the life and legacy of Prince Albert. Chief among these are Stanley Weintraub's *Uncrowned King: The Life of Prince Albert* (The Free Press, 1997), *Prince Albert: A Biography,* by Robert Rhodes James (Knopf, 1984), and *King Without a Crown,* by Daphne Bennett (J. B. Lippincott & Co., 1977).

The first woman to qualify as a medical doctor in Great Britain did so in 1867. Unlike Dr. John Snow, whose work is now part of history, Georgiana Armistead is a fabrication; but her character is drawn from such figures as Elizabeth Blackwell, whose *Pioneer Work in Opening the Medical Profession to Women,* first published in 1895, recounts the enormous difficulties and challenges such women faced. The state of medicine in 1861 may be traced in Roy Porter's *The Greatest Benefit to Mankind* (HarperCollins Publishers Ltd., 1997), *The Scientific Revolution in Victorian Medicine,* by A. J. Youngson (Holmes and Meier Publishers, Inc., 1979), *Cholera, Chloroform, and the Science of Medicine: A Life of John Snow,* by Peter Vinten-Johansen et al. (Oxford University Press, 2003), and Steven Johnson's excellent *The Ghost Map* (Riverhead Books, 2006).

The state of the Irish in London in 1861 is taken up in such works as *Exiles of Erin: Irish Immigrants in Victorian London,* by Lynn Hollen Lees (Cornell University Press, 1979), *A Survey of the Irish in England, 1872,* edited by Alan O'Day (The Hambledon Press, 1990), and *Men of Blood: Violence, Manliness, and Criminal Justice in Victorian England,* by Martin J. Weiner (Cambridge University Press, 2004). As always Leon Radzinowicz's multivolume *History of English Criminal Law* also proved invaluable (Stevens & Sons Ltd., 1948).

Prince Leopold grew up under the obsessive shadow of his mother, who attempted throughout his short life to prevent him from entering society or the world for which his intelligence and charm clearly fitted him. Her most telling comment about the boy was expressed in a letter to his sister Vicky — that even the death of a *good* child who suffered illness was preferable to the healthy life of a son (like Bertie, the Prince of Wales), whose morals and character must always disappoint. Leopold died at age twenty-eight in the town of Cannes he loved so well, of a cerebral hemorrhage caused by falling on a flight of stone stairs. Something of his life and personality may be gleaned from Louisa Bowater's account of her time with the young prince, *The Journals of Lady Knightley of Fawsley,* edited by Julia Cartwright (John Murray, 1915), and in *Prince Leopold: The Untold Story of Queen Victoria's Youngest Son,* by Charlotte Zeepvat (Sutton Publishing Ltd., 1998).

Princess Alice did indeed marry Louis of Hesse, in a July, 1862, ceremony at Osborne House — and died at the age of thirty-five from diphtheria. Her son Fritzie — godson to her brother Leopold — died of hemophilia as a toddler in 1873. Her daughter, Alicky, married Tsar Nicholas II of Russia — and passed hemophilia to her son, the tsarevitch Alexis. The Tsar and his entire

family were executed by firing squad at Eka-
terinburg in 1918.

Hemophilia is carried in a recessive gene,
and it appears to have passed out of the
British royal family as of the twenty-first
century. The questions and mysteries of the
past — including the source of Victoria's
untraceable disease — remain.

Stephanie Barron
DENVER, COLORADO, 2007

ABOUT THE AUTHOR

Stephanie Barron is the author of nine bestselling Jane Austen mysteries. She lives in Colorado, where she is at work on her next novel of historical suspense, *The White Garden,* which Bantam will publish in 2009.